Blood of the

Winter Solstice

Blood of the Winter Solstice

The Night Witch Series
A Widow's Watch Novel
~Book 2~

Continuation of Gaea & The Night Witch

Mark E. Welch

The Book of Belphegor

Bound in human skin, from a man condemned to eternal damnation, the Grimoire is an ancient magical book that contains powerful spells, incantations, and hexes. Its origin is unknown to most, but it is believed to predate the Egyptian Empire. Some claim it is not of this world or the living.

One thing is certain: the Grimoire is coveted by witches and warlocks who seek to harness its power for good or evil purposes. Those who know understand that many books have been bound in a similar manner. Still, the Grimoire remains the first and only one infused with dark magic from the underworld, where it was written and eventually unleashed upon the world with one intention: to destroy humanity.

~ Unknown Coven Scribe

CONTENTS

CHAPTER 1
Planning for a Black Sabbath

In the icy grasp of Northern Russia, where howling winds echoed the screams of the damned, winter reigned with a merciless chill. The sun rarely showed itself during the winter in this cursed land of ice and snow, and people seldom visited it. Those who dared to venture into the northern wastelands did so at their peril. Yet, one individual dared to enter and covet this desolate domain.

The High Priest walked through the halls of his residence; his mind focused on the upcoming gathering of witches and warlocks. His black robes matched his hair and eyes, darkened from decades of practicing black magic. He chose not to adorn himself with excessive jewelry, wearing only the Ring of Narcus and the Pendant of Goron, both symbols of his identity as the High Priest of the Obsidian Circle.

The gathering was scheduled to take place in a remote part of northern Maine. The location for this dark assembly was not his choice. He would have to travel to the Winter Solstice gathering in the nearby village of Van Buren to gather information needed to complete a crucial task. The purpose of this sinister gathering was of utmost importance: the Grimoire had vanished. This book pulsed with dark energy and contained powerful spells capable of killing. Even he, a Master Archmagus, could barely comprehend the malevolence contained within its pages.

The incantations within the Grimoire promised unimaginable power, but they came at a terrible price, capable of bringing even the strongest individuals to their knees. His coven was weak and naive—a liability of foolish souls unworthy of wielding such dark magic. He dedicated himself to reclaiming the Grimoire to protect the world from chaos and to prevent others from misusing its power. The High Priest of a dark coven, always cautious, whispered warnings about the dangers the Book of Belphegor posed. Once he had coveted the dark magic and studied it, using it for himself, power to control and conquer. But the price was too steep to pay, and when the Grimoire was lost, he did not try to find it. Deep down, he still struggled to keep his desire for that power in check.

Every Winter Solstice, as far back as he could remember, had culminated in some form of trouble, whether caused by those with differing opinions on various matters or by a long-standing feud that dated back decades. It wasn't between the common revelers who attended the numerous festivals or even the Wiccan communities that existed in mass throughout the world. It was covens, such as his own, that knew magic and practiced it for either good or evil purposes. Such disputes commonly resulted in bloodshed. Boris Sergev had been the High Priest among his ranks for as long as he could recall, and he would not tolerate any disruptions to this year's Black Sabbath. There was too much at stake, and he was already aware of a few who sought the Grimoire, believing he knew who might possess it. The young witch in question was not qualified to hold it. So far, he believed she had not attempted to use the powerful spells contained within its bindings, and if Count Boris Sergev had any say in the matter, she would not have the opportunity. If his intel was correct, she had the Book of Belphegor, and if she didn't, then she was close to acquiring it.

The chief enforcer of the High Priest was Isobel Argante, a powerful witch from the Baltic region of Latvia, though she was of half-Scandinavian descent. Her lineage was rich, spanning centuries of ancestors who practiced dark magic. Isobel was not only a formidable witch but also incredibly loyal. She had risked her life numerous times for him during battles. All but one occurred before her time: a battle against a rival necromancer from Asia who desired the Grimoire for himself. The two wizards had clashed, but no winner emerged from their struggle. They had no reason to duel again once they learned the book had disappeared without a trace.

The Count entered a tower and climbed the spiral stairs that led to his study and altar room. He performed his rituals and magic in this place, and what was needed to run and maintain the coven in order. Without order, chaos reigned, and with it came turmoil, destruction, and death.

The room was spacious and elaborately adorned with tapestries and artwork created by some of the world's finest artisans. His collection was large and impressive, featuring works by artists such as Monet, as well as a piano that once belonged to Beethoven. The tapestries dated back to the Roman Empire, and a few predated the birth of Christ, originating from China. None of these held the importance of the Grimoire.

He walked to the window and gazed across the Chukotka Mountains stretching northward. The landscape was shrouded in darkness due to the polar nights that envelop the region each year, with only the moon and stars providing light. Most people living near the Count did not have electricity, unlike him, and the population was small, primarily composed of ethnic Russians who tended to keep to themselves. They were deeply rooted in superstition and wary of anything unusual, so he made it a point to remain reserved, avoiding any undue attention. The Count's residence was far enough from the nearest settlement that it rarely attracted local interest. Sergeev smiled; he had chosen the perfect location to practice his dark arts.

Most of his coven was unaware of the High Priest's chosen dwelling, as he preferred to live in the shadows, much like many of his coven members, who valued their solitude. The practices of a dark witch or warlock were deeply personal, and they did not share lessons learned or new spells, hexes, or concoctions. Except for Isobel, no one had been invited to have an audience with his eminence, and the warlock preferred it that way. He ruled the members of his coven from a distance, appearing only when necessary. He entrusted communication with them to Isobel, managed through the mail. This Black Sabbath was an exception and was desperately needed.

"You are stealthy, but not so much that I did not hear you approaching." The Count smiled and turned to greet his visitor. "Isobel."

The woman was half the Count's age and strikingly beautiful. Standing at 6'2", she was six inches taller than her leader. Her platinum blonde hair fell to her mid-back and did not hold a curl. Her eyes were sharp, keen, and blue, reflecting intellect that surpassed that of most humans. Furthermore, her magical prowess was extensive and powerful.

"My Lord." She said, walking over to him. "You called for me."

"Yes. Are the preparations made for our journey to the United States?" he asked, his English thick with the overtones of his native Russian language. English was not his favorite; it was full of dialects, some of which were nearly impossible to understand. A heavy dialect from the northeastern part of the country populated their destination. He had visited Maine many years ago on a sightseeing trip across the country, a luxury he now considered a waste of valuable time.

Isobel watched closely as he gazed out the window. She understood when to respond and when to pause. A second question typically followed his inquiries.

"Was the aircraft chartered?" He added.

"Yes. We will fly out of Sabetta." She answered in perfect English.

Sabetta International Airport, located in Sabetta, Yamalo-Nenets Autonomous Okrug, Russia, was the world's northernmost international airport chosen by Sergev for its remoteness.

"We will travel the day before departure and stay in Sabetta overnight. I've arranged for lodging at a house near the airport."

Sergev admired her mastery of languages. So far, he knew of eight that she spoke fluently, and he expected to hear more than he had already encountered.

"And the aircraft itself?"

"It is a Lear Jet. I made the arrangements from our firm in Sweden." She answered."

"And the pilot?"

"Trusted. We have used him before." She reassured.

Sergev nodded. "Wise choices. I prefer to keep Moscow, how do they say in America? In the dark about our trip. The KGB need not know of us or our coven, let alone of our business dealings."

Isobel wandered to a desk in front of a bank of windows that overlooked the mountains. She opened a small wooden box, took out a cigarette, and lit it, inhaling deeply. "Are we certain the Grimoire is in this State of Maine?"

"Everything that I have learned says yes." Count Sergev walked to the desk and turned on the computer. "The question is whether it will be at the winter solstice gathering. If not, we will need to make inquiries about its whereabouts. I intend to return to Russia with it at any cost."

She looked at the seriousness in his face.

"At any cost." He reiterated.

"If it is there, we will find and retrieve it," Isobel said with icy confidence. "Any that stand in our way will pay a price."

Count Sergev knew all too well how deadly Isobel could be when the situation demanded it. He hoped it wouldn't come to that and that the book would be surrendered willingly. Bloodshed attracted unnecessary attention that he neither needed nor wanted.

"I hope to retrieve the Grimoire without incident, Isobel. Let us hope this is feasible," he said, picking up a ceremonial dagger and running his finger over the blade's edge. Its sharpness cut into his skin, drawing a thin line of blood.

"Let us hope." She replied somewhat sarcastically. "I do not share your belief in a peaceful exchange. There might be rival covens on their quest to find the Grimoire as well. Some will not show the restraint you propose and hope for. Some will simply kill, take, and return to the shadows. The Black Dragon could very well have the same information that you have."

Sergev nodded at the name and was well acquainted with its High Priest. The same man he had battled over the Grimoire long ago. He ignored her comment and continued his train of thought. "Which could leave us with one hell of a mess to cope with." He replied, returning the dagger to its place on the altar. "To this, I have laid a plan, if you will. I have a contact who is already in Maine; he is American and lives in the States."

"Oh?" Isobel was intrigued.

He smiled and faced her. "I do not tell you everything as some things need not be told until warranted." The Count thought for a moment. "He is a necromancer and has an interest in the Grimoire. To what extent, I cannot be sure. But he has proven himself to be useful and loyal. He gives me no reason to distrust what he tells me."

"But the Grimoire has ways of bewitching. He could be easily swayed." Isobel warned.

"This is true. I could feel its power and its calling, even from a great distance. Now, the Grimoire has gone silent."

"Perhaps a witch has the book and laid a spell upon it? Isobel suggested.

"That is possible. Or it is cloaked in some manner unknown to me. Either way, it remains hidden," Sergev admitted.

"And this man?" Isobel asked.

"He is a younger man, perhaps in his early forties. He goes by the name Gunther and has been part of our coven his entire life. His grandfather brought him in. I don't know much about the man, and I met him only once when I was in the United States; however, I did know his grandfather, a powerful archmagi. Gunther, I have kept in touch with him as he has been a reliable contact for the coven, especially now that the Grimoire has resurfaced after all of this time."

"He is assisting in the search for the book?"

"Yes. He has been doing just that. His last communication was that the book had been stolen from a museum, and the thief had been caught, but the Grimoire was lost." Sergev paced the room as he thought and spoke.

"Where do you believe the Grimoire is?"

Sergev sat down at the computer, which displayed a map of Maine. He zoomed in on the northern part of the state. "Van Buren," he said, pointing to the small town. "That's where we are going. It is the location of the region's Winter Solstice festival, and I believe that it will attract the possessor of the Grimoire. For what reason I do not know, but I am confident that Van Buren is a key to finding the book. The last known location was farther south, possibly near Mount Desert Island."

"A desolate place?" Isobel asked.

"On the contrary. The island is a natural refuge for wildlife and is surrounded by water, including the Atlantic Ocean. It is a very beautiful place. Once again, I have only been to it once, and it was years ago."

Isobel leaned forward and examined the map.

"The population in Van Buren is currently about two thousand, but during this year's Winter Solstice, it is expected to swell to thousands as there will be some musical demonstration coinciding with Winter Solstice. Only about fifteen percent of those attending will be practicing witches and warlocks; the rest are tourists and locals for the celebration. Just one percent will be able to wield and use magic. Practitioners of dark magic will comprise less than that. As you can see, we will be among the few who possess these abilities, and not all members of our coven will attend. How many did you say?" he asked Isobel.

"Twenty confirmed." She answered. "Many did not respond to the invitation that was sent to them. Some declined to attend."

"As it is with our coven these days. Weak." Sergev sighed and shut down the computer. "Once we numbered in the thousands, and many were powerful in their craft. Now we number only a few hundred, and of those, most keep to themselves and hide in the shadows."

"I know this. My family has been members of the Obsidian Circle for centuries. I have heard the tales of the coven and its influence upon the world. We were indeed powerful."

"Indeed." Sergev said, standing. "Now, when do we leave?"

"First thing tomorrow. I will inform the driver to be ready."

"Sometimes it is confusing with this endless night. Very well. In the meantime, please make yourself comfortable and join me for dinner. Say around seven?"

Isobel nodded. "I will be happy to join you."

Deep within the shadowy depths of a root cellar in Maine, shrouded in a suffocating lead blanket and imprisoned within an unyielding iron box, a sinister relic lay in wait. Enshrouded in dark magic, the Grimoire, Book of Belphegor, remained hidden, its malevolent spells, cursed incantations, and wicked hexes concealed from the naive world above. This vile creation was ageless, a testament to the twisted genius of its maker, mocking the fleeting lives of those who sought to wield its power. For millennia, it had endured, feeding on the despair and ambition of men, biding its time as the forces of darkness conspired to revive it. The hour of reckoning drew ever closer, and the Grimoire hungered for freedom, eager to unleash chaos upon the unsuspecting world once more.

CHAPTER 2
A New Year's Resolve

Christmas was celebrated at the Pepper Mansion, where the Pepper and Pender families gathered. A world-renowned author, Bill Pender, formed a close friendship with Robert Pepper after the editor discovered Bill years ago, upon retirement. Bill's novel, The Emissary, catapulted him to fame, becoming a number one bestseller and later adapted into a blockbuster movie, making Bill wealthy.

After Bob Pepper retired and moved from New York City to Maine, he and his former secretary, who became his wife, developed a close bond with the Pender family. Even the Pender children affectionately called Bob and Dottie "Grandpa" and "Grandma," much to their delight.

As the new year approached, addressing the Grimoire once and for all had become imperative. Both families were well-informed about the book and did everything they could to assist with it. Ultimately, it was up to those who understood it best.

Gaea Pender sat in her grandfather's office with her boyfriend, Marc Broussard, and her roommate, Himiko Aoki. All three were students at the University of Maine, Orono: Gaea and Himiko were psychology majors, while Marc was majoring in meteorology. Although they were the same age, Gaea and Himiko were not your typical students. Gaea was a powerful psychic medium with abilities that extended beyond simply sensing and communicating with the dead. She could also perceive the existence of demons and other entities, whether they were benevolent or malevolent. A recent encounter with the demon Belphegor had been both frightening and enlightening. Neither of her companions had attended the exorcism at Shaw Manor, and she hoped that her dealings with demons were finally at an end.

Marc had met Gaea at UMO a year earlier and was immediately captivated by her charm and natural beauty. His passion for the weather sometimes bordered on annoying, but Gaea was drawn to him for his French accent, comedic personality, and good looks.

Himiko, an exchange student from Japan, was a practicing witch. Although her knowledge of the craft was limited to herbs, meditation, elemental spells, and incantations, she studied it diligently. Her insatiable appetite for learning proved invaluable in their latest predicament.

The trio had come into possession of an evil book called the Grimoire, which was discovered in Gaea's sister Vicky's restaurant, Cinnamon Woodfire, located in downtown Bar Harbor. Vicky found the book hidden in a closet when she took over the establishment. Gaea had made contact with a deceased piano player who seemed to have a connection to the book and insisted it be returned to the closet, claiming it was not theirs to keep. Gaea disagreed and removed the book from the restaurant, temporarily placing it in the old family chapel on the Pepper Mansion estate on the outskirts of Bar Harbor.

As they delved deeper into the secrets of the human skin-bound tome, they realized that possessing the Grimoire was becoming more dangerous than merely a nuisance. Someone was determined to obtain the book and would stop at nothing. A Night Witch had been stalking the university campus. Through some basic detective work, they uncovered her connection to black magic and the occult, as well as the location where she practiced her craft on the now-deserted Upper Campus of the university. It didn't take much to suspect the Night Witch's motives and intentions. Recently, it appeared that another individual was also intent on finding the Grimoire, in addition to the Night Witch.

Feeling the urgency of their situation, the trio knew they needed to dispose of the book while ensuring it didn't fall into the wrong hands. Their options were limited, but they devised a plan to seek help during the upcoming Winter Solstice festival in northern Maine. Although the actual Solstice had passed on December 22nd, a series of back-to-back nor'easters had forced a postponement of the festival until early January. The date of the Winter Solstice was the first day of winter, and its delay was frustrating for the practicing witches and warlocks attending the event, as it held immense spiritual significance for them. Tourists, however, didn't mind the change; to them, a festival was a festival, and at least it hadn't been canceled altogether. Those who practiced dark magic considered the shift in date irrelevant, as they would set their Black Sabbath celebrations according to their own needs.

The trio sat in Robert Pepper's office, Gaea's dad's former publicist, located within the Pepper Mansion, planning their next move when Aerin Pender abruptly interrupted them.

"I was thinking," Aerin said as he barged in, "why not just go ahead with the old plan of tossing it into the Atlantic Ocean?"

Aerin, still in his preteen years, was an exceptionally gifted psychic medium with ties to the occult. He confronted Belphegor directly during the exorcism at Shaw Manor, with the Archangel Michael intervening to assist him. Aerin took pride in his accomplishments, angelic intervention or not, and was eager to contribute, even if his help was occasionally unwelcome.

"It's too risky, Aerin," Himiko answered. "We don't know where the two are searching for it. They could be close and just waiting for an opportunity."

"You're right, Himiko," Gaea said, taking a potato chip from a bag on Bob's desk and tossing it into her mouth. "So far, the book is safe where it is hidden. The protection we gave it seems to be blinding whoever is searching for it, including the Night Witch. By the way, I believe she is a psychic medium, Himiko."

"That's all we need," she said, reaching for a chip. Himiko had warned about the dangers of a witch who was a psychic medium and the threats it posed, especially since her own mother was one. Seeing Gaea's abilities firsthand terrified her because she feared that someone who could communicate with the dead and potentially control them through dark magic would be extremely dangerous. It was a necromancer's dream come true and a nightmare for the living. "A necromancer could control the dead with that book. Imagine if she could raise the dead and control them!"

"I don't want to imagine," Marc said, taking a drink of his Diet Coke. "All of this is scary as it is. I just want it to end."

"You don't have to deal with it, Marc," Gaea said quietly. This problem is ours, Himiko and I. You can go back to campus."

"Like hell!" He retorted. "I'll be damned if I leave you to face this alone, Gaea. Or you, too, Himiko. We are in this together. I've invested too much to quit now. And I would never desert either of you."

Gaea smiled, bent forward, and kissed her boyfriend. "I know."

"Well, it was just a thought," Aerin said. "See ya!" He turned and left.

"So, here we are," Gaea began. "New Year's Eve is tomorrow, and the festival is a week away. Why is the celebration next month? I have no idea. The Solstice was on the twenty-second."

"The weather," Marc said. "These blizzards have been bad enough to postpone just about anything. Even the start of winter."

"True." Himiko laughed, "And we better be glad it is next week. It gives us time to plan."

Gaea took Marc's Coke and took a sip. "If the celebration had come and gone, I don't know what we would do."

"Plan A?" Marc suggested. "I guess we would be trying to dump it into the ocean."

"Well, it's not passed, so how will we do this?" Himiko was eager to begin the actual planning.

"Thanks to Grandpa, we at least have lodging," Gaea said, standing and stretching. It's only one room, and I'm not sure if there are even two beds. If not, we will all have to share one."

Marc grinned and looked at the ceiling.

"You perv!" Gaea laughed and lightly slapped him.

"What did I do?"

"We know what you were thinking!" Himiko added.

"I was thinking about next week's weather. I don't know what you two are getting at." He lied.

Gaea shook her head. "So, as I was saying, a place to stay is taken care of, and Marc, I am sure you will find the floor comfortable."

He stuck his tongue out at his girlfriend.

"Food shouldn't be a problem either. It's a festival after all." Gaea added. "Plus, even a small town like Van Buren will have a restaurant or two along with fast-food places."

A light knock on the door made their heads turn. The door opened, and Bill's head peeked in. "Making headway?"

"Just getting started." His daughter said.

"Great. Let us know the plan when you have one, ok?"

"Sure, Dad. We will."

The three talked late into the evening, trying to develop their plan once they arrived in Van Buren.

Gunther wasted no time taking his daughter, Seraphina, off Mt. Desert Island after losing the Grimoire. He had no idea who had taken it, and as far as he was concerned, it could have been another warlock. It was wise to contact the leader of his coven about the recent events regarding the book's whereabouts.

His daughter had been ineffective, even with her abilities as a psychic medium. She also had no idea of its location. Compared to others in the coven, she was a weak witch. With no leads, it was time to regroup, head to Van Buren, and join their coven for the Black Sabbath and further the search.

First, they would go to the university to collect her belongings. It was unsafe to leave her tools of the trade where they might be discovered during her absence.

For now, she could leave the pickup truck in the school parking lot. It would raise no suspicion and would be a safe place to store it for the time being. He also needed to assess her strengths and weaknesses in preparation for a potential confrontation should they encounter the Grimoire's possessor. A fight would ensue over the book and who would ultimately obtain it. He was sure of it.

Then there was this issue of her making a pact with Belphegor the Defiler. He had never dealt with a demon, but he knew that no profit could come from it. He did not know how to save her if the Defiler chose to take her. Gunther understood his magic, but it was no match for a demon from the depths of Hell. He hoped that the leader of his coven, the High Priest of the Obsidian Circle, could provide an answer that might save her. She was a foolish child who did not think things through, which could cost her life.

"How long will it take you to gather your belongings?" he asked, opening the trunk of the older model Mercedes-Benz as she walked back to the car after parking her pickup. He had always wanted a prestigious vehicle but had to settle for a fifteen-year-old diesel with relatively low mileage. The sedan was older, but it served its purpose. Light snow had begun to fall, and Gunther cursed himself for not checking the weather report. He hoped the storm had blown itself out and was not worsening. He intended to return to his condo in Biddeford, Maine, before sunrise.

"Just a few minutes," She replied, placing the items she had brought to Mt. Desert Island into the car. "I don't have much to pack up."

"Good to hear. We need to get on the road. Do you need help?"

She shook her head no and ran off towards the chapel.

Gunter shook his head as he realized what she was getting into. "A freakin' church." He muttered, shaking his head.

The library fell silent as one of the household servants entered with a bottle of wine and some glasses. She set them down on the coffee table and quickly left the room.

"So that is pretty much the plan." Gaea finished explaining to her parents and the Peppers. "Where is Vicky?"

"At work. You can fill her in later." Bill said, pacing the library floor. "So, let me get this straight. You three drive up to Van Buren, check into that hotel, and start asking around at the festival? That's it?"

"That's pretty much the plan," Himiko confirmed.

Gaea's mother, Cathy, looked confused. She was an educated and talented historian who specialized in antiquities and had identified the cover of the Grimoire as being made of human skin. "Is it just me, or does that sound like you are asking for trouble? The book is valued highly in occult circles, correct?"

Himiko nodded.

"And some would do anything to possess it?" She continued.

Another nod.

"One might even say kill for it?" Cathy finished and looked at her husband in disbelief at what she had just heard.

"Not necessarily just ask around about the book," Marc said, trying to clarify Gaea's remarks. "We would beat around the bush, so to speak. Ask about books of a magical nature to see if we could pique an interest. Gaea can use her abilities to sense whether the person we are talking to might know more or how he or she might feel about our inquiries."

"So, Mom, we wouldn't be inquiring about the Grimoire directly. Hopefully, I can figure out who might know something and if their intentions are good before we disclose any information about the book. After all, we're not looking for it but for someone to take it from us."

"The plan seems sound enough if you are very careful," Bob said. "Some individuals you will be dealing with could be shady and dangerous."

"Very careful," Cathy warned. "I don't need my child returning home in a box.

"I agree!" Dottie said. "You three are my family, and I don't know what I would do if anything happened to any of you." She hugged Marc tightly, causing him to blush.

Gaea giggled at his embarrassment, then turned her attention back to her parents. "So, we will be extremely cautious when dealing with people at the festival."

"Most will be tourists," Himiko added. "But there will be witches and warlocks mingling in the crowds. It will be up to us to determine where they are, who they are, and what they are."

"I don't understand *what* they are?" Bill asked.

"Yes, Mr. Pender," Himiko explained. "Some will be warlocks, either dark, neutral, or good. Same with the witches. There are also different types, as practicing magic is a diverse activity. We think that one of the two after us was a necromancer."

"One that seeks to speak with the dead and possibly raise a dead person from the grave," Gaea clarified. "And that's not the worst of it. The Night Witch is also a psychic medium like me, which makes it easier for her to contact and converse with dead people."

"This Night Witch is a necromancer?" Cathy asked, pouring herself a glass of wine.

"We believe so," Himiko said. "You see, the term Night Witch is more of a description of a witch who practices dark magic and may dabble in the occult. A necromancer, well, is what Gaea explained."

"I see," Cathy thought for a moment. "This sounds like such a person could be very dangerous to anyone or everyone around them."

"A person with knowledge of magic and possessing the Grimoire could be a devastating individual, yes."

"Thus, the need to keep the book out of her hands or any such person of the same ilk, for that matter," Bob interjected.

"I agree, Bob," Bill said, sitting on the couch beside his wife.

Dottie had been staring out the window, watching light snow dance across the estate front lawn. "Strange." She said to no one.

"What is it, dear?" Her husband asked. "What's strange?"

"Oh?" She seemed caught off guard, as if awakening from a momentary daydream. "Nothing really. It's just that all of these occurrences with our family revolve around Gaea's abilities. I'm not laying blame, mind you. She has no choice in this matter, so it seems. Are you a magnet of some kind, honey?"

It was Gaea's turn to be caught off guard, and she couldn't help but feel responsible for everyone's fear and uneasiness. "I don't think I am." She answered, pondering the comment for a moment. "I didn't have anything to do with the haunting at Shaw Manor. And I didn't bring that statue into the house, although I recall hating it. And the demon was more after Aerin than me. No, I don't think I am a magnet. I seem to be in the wrong places at the wrong times."

"Of course you are not to blame for any of it, Gaea," Cathy said, putting her arm around her daughter. "I was responsible for that statue, and your father and I bought Shaw Manor, not you. You weren't even born yet."

"And this book came to us through the restaurant I bought and convinced your father to invest in," Bob added. "You were off at school studying."

"But I was involved unknowingly because of the Night Witch. We stumbled upon her at the Bear's Claw on campus when Marc and I met there for lunch. "Himiko, I suspect that the ghost of a deceased girl gave me a reason to be concerned about the Night Witch. You brought the potential threat to our attention. In any case, everything has come full circle, and now we have that dreaded book. I wish I didn't know about the Night Witch or the Grimoire."

"But we do know, and we have the book," Himiko reminded her friend. "I don't want to deal with this either, but it seems that somehow we've been chosen to confront it."

"I for one am resolved to see this to the end," Gaea stated.

"Your New Year's resolution?" Marc asked half-jokingly.

Gaea looked at him.

He looked down into his glass of wine.

No one had noticed Aerin had quietly entered the room and taken a seat near the door of the library until he suddenly spoke up, "Gabriel chose all of you."

They all looked at the boy. Cathy dropped her glass of wine on the floor.

CHAPTER 3
A Lesson in Hand-Casting

Gunther and his daughter didn't speak during the drive south to the Biddeford Pool community on the coast of Maine, just south of Portland. Unlike most of his fellow witches and warlocks in the coven, he did not hide in the shadows. He was not wealthy and had to work for a living to make ends meet. He held a position as a history professor at the University of New England in Biddeford. The unassuming role of a mild-mannered teacher at the small school suited his lifestyle perfectly. He had plenty of free time to utilize the university library, not for his job, but to study subjects related to his craft: dark magic. He conversed with only a few people, one of whom was Dr. Bastien, the curator of the Wells Museum, and that was rare. Being next-door neighbors, they would occasionally run into each other.

He had only a few days to teach Seraphina some spells she might need for the Black Sabbath. He had previously tried to instill some skills in hand casting when she was younger, but she never really embraced it. She preferred incantations and hexes for performing her magic. Hand casting is the technique of using a spell along with an incantation, combined with the earth's surrounding energy, to cast it at an object or opponent. The more powerful the spell, the more significant the result. Some practitioners can cast spells by hand with deadly effects. Other methods are less practical for hand-to-hand combat and may take time for the spell to affect its intended destination or target, although they can help place a hex over long distances. Gunther hoped his daughter had maintained some skill in hand casting. If not, they might be in trouble.

There was one spell in particular that he had mastered and wanted his daughter to master as well. It involved both the actual spell and the verbal incantation for it to work and was somewhat tricky to learn. Once mastered, it could render a person unconscious, which was a preferred outcome that did not involve death since murder is frowned upon in today's world. That spell would be the one they would work on, as time was limited. If she was a quick learner, so be it; they would move on to another.

Gunther pulled his Mercedes-Benz into the garage, pressed the remote on the visor, and watched the door close in the rearview mirror. Reaching over, he nudged Seraphina awake.

"We're here." He said as he opened the car door.

She stretched and climbed out of the car.

"You'll find your room just as you left it. You'd better bring in your belongings right away. I don't want it in the Benz if I have to go to the university, okay?"

"Okay," She answered sleepily. "Can you open the trunk?"

Gunther pulled a lever inside the vehicle, and the trunk opened. "I need to make a phone call. We will talk later. You. Better try and get some more sleep."

Sleep felt like a fantastic idea to Seraphina. She hadn't been getting much rest for weeks, and her waking hours were spent searching for the Grimoire and avoiding the Medium and the weak witch. Now, it seemed both were out of her control for the moment. A warm bed and a hot shower in a safe place were incredibly inviting.

"Thanks." She replied and shouldered her backpack.

Gunther vanished into the house, leaving his daughter to manage her belongings. He had to call Sergev, which he rarely did unless it was absolutely essential. The Grimoire was.

Aerin Pender spent his Christmas vacation trying to avoid trouble, but that seemed difficult. No matter what he did, he attracted the ire of one adult or another in Pepper Mansion. His latest mishap involved attempting a balancing act on the banister two stories above the great room. Grandpa Pepper caught him in the act and delivered a twenty-minute lecture in the kitchen about the dangers of falling and breaking his neck. Fortunately, the old man didn't have the sternness he once possessed, and Aerin got off relatively lightly, leaving, satisfied with a promise not to attempt it again and a cookie.

Once a harsh and unyielding businessman, Robert Pepper didn't have it in him to be too hard on anyone anymore. He attributed this change to the passage of time and the fact that he now had a family who truly cared for him. His wife joked that he was trying to earn his way into heaven, and he thought she might be right.

When the family gathered in the library to discuss their plans for Van Buren, the last thing they expected to hear was Aerin's revelation. They were already aware of angels' existence, especially after the appearance of Michael at Shaw Manor, when he cast the Demon Belphegor back into the underworld before Bill and Gaea's eyes with Aerin's help. So, when Aerin claimed that Michael had chosen them to tend to the Grimoire, it shouldn't have shocked them. But shock them it did.

"Aerin, are you saying Michael the Archangel is part of this, too?" Cathy asked her son.

"I think so," he replied meekly. "I had a dream that he wanted Gaea to do something with it. I guess he meant all three of you or the whole family."

"How can you be sure?" Bill asked, moving closer to his son. "It was just a dream, wasn't it?"

Aerin shrugged. "I'm not sure."

Bill turned to face the group. "If it's just a dream, it doesn't mean anything, right?"

"You're the one who saw Michael," Cathy pointed out. "You, Gaea, and the priest, so you tell us."

"Yeah, but Doug didn't remember a thing," Bill added.

"He was possessed, Dad," Gaea said.

"If Michael is involved, that could mean the demon Belphegor is also." Bob looked visibly worried. When things turned to evil demons, he became very concerned. "Maybe I should talk to the Catholic Diocese in Boston, as I did last time."

"Hold on, Bob," Cathy said, pouring another glass of wine. "We don't know that any of this is factual. Aerin did say it was a dream."

"He thinks it was a dream," Dottie added. "But what if it wasn't?"

"I don't think we should get ahead of ourselves on this," Bill said, opening a beer. He felt as if he were coming unhinged with everything. He needed to calm down. "Last time, Michael intervened when needed. What's to say that if— and I do mean if —he is involved, he won't do the same this time?"

"We don't know," Gaea said. "We can't assume that he will. We need to move forward with our plan and evaluate as things unfold."

"I agree with Gaea," Himiko said adamantly. "After all, we have an edge with Gaea being a sensitive."

"There may also be sensitives at the festival," Gaea warned. "But we will have to deal with that if it arises. I wouldn't put it past a magic user to enlist one to gain an edge of their own."

"Alright, so we proceed as if Aerin's dream was nothing more than a dream," Marc suggested. "But it would be wise to keep our wits about us for any signs of divine intervention."

"Of course," Gaea agreed. "Marc, Himiko, let's go check on our box."

They all stood to adjourn the meeting when Aerin spoke again. "Michael said the Grimoire will be safe in the root cellar."

Gaea, Himiko, and Marc exchanged worried glances.

"Have you been snooping?" Gaea demanded.

"No. Michael told me in the dream." Aerin replied.

"This is getting weird," Marc said. "Let's go."

The ride to the appointed lodging was uneventful, and Sergev and Isobel mostly discussed coven business, the what-ifs, and the possibility of various outcomes. The trip took a little over four hours, and they arrived at their destination shortly after 11 am, although it might as well have been 11 pm, as it was dark. However, the small town was well lit, and the driver navigated his way skillfully.

Their destination was a house owned by another coven member, although the witch was not there. It was her childhood home, and she now resided in Cyprus. She held onto the property in case she needed a place to escape or for situations like the one that was presenting itself.

The house was large, one of the biggest in Sabetta, with six bedrooms and three bathrooms. The family that once lived in the home had been prominent in the area. Isobel explained that the patriarch had once been a high-ranking member of the KGB before being arrested and tried for treason. He managed to get his wife and daughter out of Russia before they could face charges as well. The agent was executed, his wife eventually caught in Ukraine, flown back to Russia, and imprisoned in a gulag not far from Sabetta. The daughter, Cristiana, successfully evaded capture and was able to slip into the shadows with the coven's help. As an avid practitioner of Dark Magic, she had been recruited and has remained a loyal member of the Obsidian Circle ever since, and she is a close confidant of Isobel. After some time, she persuaded the coven to buy the house for her and has maintained it ever since. It was purchased and registered in her name using her new identity, Cristiana Marinov. She still feared the KGB and had returned to her home only once to finalize the property purchase. She had little use for the cold of northern Russia, yet the house could be an asset for others, as it was being utilized in this manner now.

"It is beneficial to have such loyalists in our coven, Isobel. Is it not?" He asked.

"It is. You will find the home fully stocked, clean, and quite comfortable. I will dismiss the driver for this evening and call him when we are ready to go to the airport. I will bring your bag to the master suite."

"Very well, " he replied as the driver opened his door. I will have time before the flight to finalize the last-minute details. I will call Gunther.

"It's safe," Himiko said after examining the locked iron box. "Can you sense it, Gaea?"

"Faintly. It appears that the precautions we took are working well. With the earth around us, it's no wonder it can't be sensed from a distance."

"Should we open it to make sure?" Marc asked.

"No!" The two girls replied in unison.

"That would break the spell I put on it, Himiko explained, "and if even for a few moments, it would be open for those that search for it."

"I told you it would be safe," Aerin said.

Gaea had allowed him to come with her to check on the Grimoire. After Aerin spoke out, everyone in the house knew where it was. She hoped that finally seeing the box would satisfy his desire to find it and that he would leave it alone.

"Now that you have seen it, you stay away from it. Understand?" Gaea instructed.

"It's just a box, not the book." He complained.

"You heard Himiko. We can't open the box. It's too dangerous. Can't you see that?"

"I guess." Aerin had become bored and excused himself, running back up the stairs.

"I hope that puts an end to that," Mark said. "It's very damp down here. Won't that harm the book?"

Gaea rolled her eyes at his comment. "Really, Marc? Think for a minute."

He shrugged.

"What do you think would happen to it if we tossed the box into the Atlantic Ocean?"

"Right. We are trying to get rid of it. If the dampness destroys it, all the better."

"I wouldn't count on that happening." Himiko placed a burlap sack over the box. "Now that your parents and the Peppers know of our hiding place, there will be more eyes on it and Aerin if he decides to try something foolish like trying to open the box."

"True. Why the burlap sack?" Gaea asked.

"No reason. It just looks more hidden. Silly, huh?"

Marc laughed. "It looks safer to me."

Both girls laughed at his remark, and he led them out of the root cellar.

Once outside of the garage, Gaea turned to her friends. "Let's go get a bite to eat. I'm starved."

"You need to pronounce the incantation more succinctly, and your hand movements are not quite right, Seraphina," her father instructed.

"I'm trying," she replied, taking a stance he had shown her at the start of the session.

"I know. You have been practicing hand casting a bit, haven't you?" Gunther asked.

"A little, when I've had the time. It's difficult without instruction from someone who knows how to do it."

"If you had been here, I would have taught you. But you headed off to school."

"I did."

"And then dropped out. Why?" he asked.

"It was boring, and I didn't feel like it was getting me anywhere in life. Practicing black magic is more fulfilling. Why do I need to study psychology in the first place?"

"You and I chose that because of your abilities as a medium. The schooling was intended to help you hone those skills. I don't think you fully grasp how beneficial being a psychic medium is for a Night Witch like yourself. The two used together can be a powerful combination."

"So can the knowledge contained within the Grimoire." She sat down in a nearby chair. "Can we take a short break?"

"Yes, but time is short, and I need you to learn this spell. It can save your life."

"I have other ways of defending myself." She said flatly.

"Those ways can be more harmful than beneficial. I can't say I approve of you associating yourself with a demon. He cannot be trusted. He has no concern for you or what you desire, and he will use you for his own ends. You are disposable to him," Gunther said, sitting down next to his daughter.

"I was going to break ties with him after I had the Grimoire," she explained.

Gunther laughed at her naivety. "You think you can do that so easily? If you do, then you are a fool. Once a demon has you in a blood bond, you become his, in this life and beyond. You will be his servant for eternity."

"How can I get out of the pact?"

"That is beyond me, but there is another- a powerful necromancer- who might know a way. He is the High Priest of our coven, a highly powerful magus. Perhaps he has an answer." He paused momentarily, then grasped his daughter's shoulders and turned her to face him. "You don't know how your mother died, do you?"

"You told me she died in a boating accident in southern Portugal."

He shook his head. "I fabricated that lie because you were very young, and explaining the real cause would have been impossible. Your mother died because of a powerful demon. Abaddon beguiled her with promises of power and the honor of serving beside him in the afterlife. At first, he granted her powerful spells that enabled her to achieve things she could not have done on her own." He paused, standing and gazing out the garage door, lost in thought and memory. Snowflakes continued to fall silently to the ground. He took a deep breath and continued. "Initially, she remained the caring and thoughtful person I had met. She adored you and took great pride in watching you as a young child. But then the demon began to demand things from her in repayment for the gifts he had given her. At first, those tasks were menial, but soon she began traveling outside the country, leaving you and me alone for days and weeks at a time. When she returned home, I begged her to tell me where she had been and what she had been doing, but she refused, insisting it was none of my concern. But it was.

"Did you finally find out?" Seraphina asked, her fascination growing as her father revealed more about her mother.

"I did as there were clues such as plane tickets and such, but let me continue," he said. "You didn't know your mother was a psychic medium, did you?"

She shook her head.

"A potent one. She believed that with the demon's help, she could control and master the dead to do her bidding—build an army of zombies."

"You have to be joking," she said, incredulously.

"No, I am not. The association with the demon began to warp her mind, leading her to believe that the impossible was possible. If anyone desired an army of mindless creatures, it would have been the demon himself. However, that is not how demons operate; those desires were your mother's. She claimed to have managed to revive the dead one evening, but it didn't last, and the corpse soon crumbled to dust. She was determined to keep trying. I felt like I was losing her to madness, and there was nothing I could do to stop it. Had I known about her blood pact, I would have intervened before she committed to it. But I didn't realize until it was too late.

"How did it happen?"

He smiled weakly and returned to his chair. "It was during a Black Sabbath not unlike the one we are attending. She had been planning the overthrow of the High Priest, but she had no support within the coven. She assumed that the demon would assist her in killing our leader."

"The demon did not help, did he?"

"Your mother had outlived her usefulness and had become a mere annoyance to the demon. Instead of assisting in the gruesome task, he betrayed her. He informed the High Priest of her intentions, which infuriated him. As you may come to learn, Count Boris Sergev has little patience for disloyal members. While he has no love for demons, one did save him, although it was also beneficial for the demon. As I mentioned earlier, demons do not offer help without expecting something in return. That 'something' is often much more than the beneficiary initially planned. Demons are known to be liars, and any pact they make cannot be trusted, as it is likely to be broken at their convenience. This is why I am so concerned for you and the pact you made. Which demon was it, and was there blood involved?

"The demon is Belphegor the Defiler, and no, there was no blood involved. I summoned him and conveyed my desire for the Grimoire. He seemed only too eager to help me obtain it. That was pretty much it. He was the one who showed me the location of it in Bar Harbor, but that is all that he showed me."

"I see," Gunther said. "Save whatever else you think of regarding your pact with Belphegor for High Priest Sergev. Let us hope he has a way to free you from the demon's grasp before you face a fate like that of your mother."

"I'm sorry." She said and gave him a brief hug. "Teach me this spell once and for all. I will try my hardest to perfect it."

CHAPTER 4
The Return of Douglas Blanchard

Cinnamon Woodfire buzzed with activity, even though summer was still more than three months away. Locals and residents from nearby towns had discovered the restaurant primarily through word of mouth, quickly establishing it as a favorite weekend dining spot. Weekdays were busy as well, with Vicky and her winter staff managing orders for baked goods from stores, delis, and other restaurants. Both of her delivery vans were always on the move throughout Hancock County. When summer arrived, Vicky anticipated that deliveries would take a back seat to the influx of patrons dining at the restaurant.

"Five minutes on the loaves of raisin bread," Catherine Driskoll called out. Vicky had hired the twenty-year-old sous chef just a week ago, and she was already thrilled with her choice. Although Catherine wasn't officially a sous chef, Vicky viewed her as one thanks to her impressive cooking knowledge and skills in the kitchen. She adapted well to the fast-paced environment required to fulfill daily orders. In addition to the standing orders, Vicky had set up a makeshift bakery at the front of the restaurant where she displayed her goods for walk-in customers. It seemed she could never bake enough pies, as they typically sold out quickly after opening.

Two other girls worked alongside Vicky and Catherine, providing help as needed, washing dishes, and assisting with any other tasks that arose throughout the day. Debbie and Daisy Hanson were twins living in Bar Harbor. They had graduated from high school the previous year, and neither of them knew what career they wanted to pursue, although they seemed to enjoy their work at the restaurant. Being twins appeared to be an advantage, as they understood each other's thoughts—at least, that was the impression. They proved invaluable in Vicky's kitchen.

Daisy rushed to one of the large ovens and checked the bread. Satisfied with her observation, she removed the bread trays and placed them onto a cooling rack. "Get the cinnamon rolls ready. This oven is ready for its next batch."

"I'm on it!" Debbie called back, rolling a multi-shelved kitchen cart full of rolls over to her sister. Together, they loaded the oversized cinnamon rolls into the oven.

Vicky looked around the kitchen and assessed the situation. Everything was running smoothly, and they were in a lull as the kitchen was in cooking and cleaning mode. She gave a few instructions and then retreated to the back of the building.

Vicky's office was accessible by a staircase leading to the second floor, which served as an extra dining area, a bar, and a piano bar. A balcony on the second floor provided a view of Agamont Park and, beyond that, the Bar Harbor Narrows—a waterway that flows into the Atlantic Ocean. Fishing boats dotted the water as they moved in and out for the day's catch. During the summer months, Vicky envisioned the lively space filled with customers enjoying meals, drinks, and sing-alongs at the piano.

She needed to remind the restaurant manager, Denise LaFrance, to confirm whether the pianist she had found would accept the job; if not, they would have to continue searching for a musician, which was proving unexpectedly challenging. There was so much to accomplish, and time was passing quickly. Vicky noted that Denise was currently visiting her parents in Springvale, a small town east of her hometown of Cape Neddick.

As Vicky started up the staircase, she paused briefly to look into the hallway leading to the dining room. She had installed a door for easy access to this area, as going down to the front of the building and then climbing the newly built staircase meant for guests to reach the dining room felt like a waste of time.

She felt the hairs stand up on her neck, and a chill ran down her spine. Although she couldn't see it, she could hear a piano playing. She had just left everyone in the kitchen, and none of them knew how to play. Taking a deep breath, she prepared herself to move toward the music. She wasn't sure who might be playing, but she had a sinking feeling it could be someone she hoped wasn't there.

The piano rested in the far corner of the room, a baby grand designed to accommodate ten people, essentially functioning as a piano bar for her patrons to enjoy.

The hallway also led to the customer restrooms and another door that opened to a staging area. This staging area was equipped with two dumbwaiters for delivering food from the kitchen. A wall separated this space from a long bar that could accommodate an additional thirty guests.

From where Vicky stood on the staircase landing, she could see only a small portion of the dining room, with a couple of tables and chairs neatly arranged. Out of her line of sight was the piano bar. The hallway opened into a large area that featured an upstairs dining space capable of accommodating fifty additional guests.

She slowly made her way down the hallway, glancing around nervously, afraid that something might suddenly leap out at her.

"Calm down," she whispered to herself. "Don't be silly." Perhaps one of her employees played the piano after all.

Although she didn't recognize the song playing, its vintage style suggested it was from the 1940s or 1950s, which only strengthened her suspicion about who it might be. She was nearly at the bar when the door to the staging area burst open. Startled, Vicky shrieked and dropped the notebook she was carrying, coming face to face with a very frightened Daisy. "Oh my!" Daisy exclaimed. "You scared me half to death!"

"You? I think I peed my pants!" Vicky said shakily. "What are you doing up here anyway?"

"Catherine sent me up to get the paddle off the old mixer. The one in the kitchen broke."

"It's ok, Daisy. Calm down. Did you hear a piano playing by any chance? She asked.

Daisy shook her head no. "I didn't hear anything except for the exhaust vents from the kitchen.

Vicky knew all too well the racket her ventilation system made when operating at full capacity. Her ovens and stovetop exhausts were funneled into a large duct that ran from the kitchen to the third floor, finally venting to the outside through the roof. She had it on her to-do list to insulate the soffit that housed the duct to help dampen the sound, yet another task on a very long list. "You had better get that to the kitchen," Vicky said, watching the girl run toward the back stairs. "And remind Catherine that we need to order a new paddle." She called after her.

"I will!" Daisy answered and disappeared down to the first floor.

Vicky was still trembling as she walked into the dining room and glanced at the piano across the room. It stood in silence, drawing her in. Approaching it, she examined the keys that had been meticulously restored by a conservator of fine musical instruments in Bar Harbor. The fallboard was lifted, revealing the newly installed keys. She remembered that it had been previously closed and locked. As she scanned the floor, she spotted the missing key. She bent down and picked it up, inspecting it closely. Turning her gaze to a black-and-white photograph of a man standing at the piano, which hung on the adjacent wall, she read the plaque beneath the picture. It paid tribute to the pianist who once played this instrument and entertained patrons decades before Vicky's time. She had found the picture in a first-floor closet and, with some sleuthing by Bob Pepper, identified the man as Douglas Blanchard, who had died while playing this very piano. Blanchard had also been the resident ghost when Vicky took ownership of the restaurant. He had vanished for reasons she didn't know and had not returned. Now, she was contemplating the possibility of his return, which did not make her happy.

"Douglas." She said out loud.

No one answered.

"You will never guess who that was," Cathy said to her husband as she hung up her cell phone.

"The Pope or the President. Had to be one or the other." Bill said, grinning.

"Stop, you fool." Cathy plopped down next to Bill on the sofa. He folded the newspaper he was reading and tossed it onto the coffee table.

"Tell me."

"My brother and Rollie wished us a belated Merry Christmas and a Happy New Year. How nice."

"Where are those two?" Bill asked.

"On another shipwreck, this time in the Gulf of Mexico. The US Government has hired them to research and document a World War

Two destroyer that suck there. It seems no cause was ever found for the ships' foundering."

"Never a dull moment with those two," Bill said, sipping his coffee. "It's too bad they couldn't make it up this year. Maybe next?"

"Jeffrey said they were sorry they couldn't make it and would try to make amends after they finish with the wreck."

Jeffrey Tarpon and Rollie Brambilla, two renowned marine archaeologists, had become acquainted with the Penders when they discovered Constance, a fishing vessel once captained by the owner of Shaw Manor—the house Bill had purchased for him and Cathy. It was only recently that Jeffrey learned Cathy was his sister, and they had been separated at a young age. Now, they were trying to catch up during Jeffrey's scarce free time. Jeffrey and Rollie were colleagues and a gay couple who married after overcoming the stigma that coming out might hurt their careers, when, in fact, it had no effect whatsoever. Their discoveries far exceeded any potential criticisms. Cathy was overjoyed to find out that she had a brother.

Bill's phone rang, and he retrieved it from his back pocket and answered it. "Pender." He spoke.

He listened, then answered, "Gaea is out with Marc, taking a walk, and I think Himiko is in her room meditating. Why, what's up, honey?"

Cathy looked at Bill questioningly.

"Gaea must have left her phone here. Can she call you when she gets back?"

"Bill," Cathy whispered impatiently.

He motioned for his wish to be quiet. "I see. That is disturbing news. I will have her call you right away, ok? I love you, too." Bill hung up.

"Tell me!" Cathy demanded.

"Well, Vicky seems to think the ghost is back at Cinnamon Woodfire."

"Oh God." She reacted. "That's all we need now."

Festival preparations were progressing well, or so believed Beverly Shatts, the event organizer. Postponing it due to the weather was quite a hassle. Nevertheless, with the support of her staff and volunteers, she successfully reorganized everything and got ready for the start of the three-day event. She had been informed that at other venues for the Winter Solstice, the celebration extended for days afterward. She took this advice to heart and arranged for specific amenities, such as Porta-Potties, to be available just in case.

Betty Shatts was no stranger to managing and organizing significant events. The forty-two-year-old fiery redhead had done so on numerous occasions and was always considered when a township or city needed an event organized. The town council of Van Buren learned about her through a friend of a friend who had hired her for a concert in upstate New York.

There were many factors to consider when planning a large gathering, like the Winter Solstice, and each of them required her careful attention to ensure everything was managed properly. The police force in Van Buren, for example, was too small to handle such a large influx of people into the town, so she enlisted the support of the Maine State Police. The fire department's EMT division was not equipped to manage multiple emergencies at once. Neighboring towns had been called in to assist the local departments, including some from the Canadian side of the border. With hospitals on standby in and around the town, she was confident that any emergencies that arose would be covered.

The festival would take place on the outskirts of town, where space was ample. Unused farmland had been cleared of snow, and tents were set up to accommodate the various vendors and attractions associated with the Winter Solstice celebration. All the tents were equipped with propane space heaters to combat the winter chill. Numerous tents throughout the field featured food courts, restrooms, information centers, and aid stations. Hanson Field, located at the northern end of the festival grounds, would offer space for the dozens of RVs expected to arrive. Lodging was limited on both sides of the border, and the Canadiens across the St. John's River also set up amenities for the visiting revelers.

Little did Betty Shatts know what would descend on the small village of Van Buren, Maine.

"She said what?" Gaea was in disbelief. "Vicky thinks that the spirit of Douglas Blanchard has returned to the restaurant?"

"That's what she said on the phone." Bill related. "She wants you to call her as soon as possible."

"The heck with calling, I'm going over there." She stated.

"I'm going too." Himiko chimed in.

"I'll tag along." Marc offered.

Thirty minutes later, they entered Cinnamon Woodfire, and Gaea stopped as soon as she entered the dining room.

"He's back," she said, "And he's not happy."

CHAPTER 5
Kindred Spirits

"I know damn well, Father, but we are talking about a demon here," Bob said into the phone, angrier than he should be. It seemed that the guard had changed at the Archdiocese of Boston, and the new management had no clue who Bob was or what he was talking about. "Can you tell me where the previous Cardinal was transferred to?" Bob asked, pacing his office.

Bill sat in a chair facing Bob's desk, listening intently. It never ceased to amaze him how his former publisher managed situations, commanding and intimidating with a hint of false sincerity. He couldn't help but smile.

"Yes, it is wonderful that he was transferred to the Vatican, but that doesn't help me much now, does it?" Bob looked at Bill and rolled his eyes. "What about Father Setzler? Is he still at the archdiocese? He went with the Cardinal as his assistant. Great. Therefore, you can't take action without initiating an official inquiry and following the proper channels. The whole thing will be over by then. Well, thanks for nothing."

Bob slammed down the phone, walked over to his liquor cabinet, removed a bottle, and poured himself two fingers of scotch.

Bill raised his eyebrows. "Don't let Dottie catch you," He warned, half joking. I didn't know you started again."

"I didn't," Bob said, dumping the alcohol down the sink. "I'm just pissed off. I've lost my contact in Boston, so we're on our own on this, Bill."

"So, I gathered." Bill picked up his can of beer and took a drink. "They only assisted with the exorcism last time. Do you think we might need another one?

"No. Probably not, but there might have been other things they could have helped with. I don't want this situation to spiral out of control, Bill." He sat at his desk and put his face in his hands.

"Priests deal with demons, not witches and warlocks," Bill said, standing and walking to the window. "This is such an amazing view. Better than mine in the widow's watch." He looked out over the Atlantic, which was crashing against the rocks below. A lone seagull drifted on the air currents, calling out perhaps for a lost mate.

"I don't like the idea of those three kids going to that gathering without a backup plan. It scares me to death."

"You? Afraid? I don't believe it."

"You know how much I adore them, Bill, especially Gaea. It would break me if something happened to them."

"I'm her father, Bob. It's tearing at my guts something fierce." Bill sat back down and finished off his beer. "I have been giving this some thought, however. What if we take a little trip ourselves? Just you and me. Say an ice fishing excursion to, say, I don't know, Northern Maine?"

Bob looked across at his friend and grinned. "You are one sneaky sonofabitch, Bill Pender. Spying on your daughter. Aren't you ashamed of yourself?"

"Should I be?"

"Hell no. And I love the idea. Ice fishing, the women won't want to go; even if they do, we can talk them out of it. Male bonding, guys-only trip, you know that sort of bull crap."

"You think Dottie will buy it?" Bill asked.

"Will Cathy?"

"Hell no," Bill replied. "So, what do we tell them?"

Bob thought for a moment and took a deep breath. "I don't know yet. We'll think of something. So, we first need to get lodging, which might be next to impossible this late in the game." He picked up the phone and punched in a number. "Driscoll? I need a favor."

Bill listened to Bob with utter fascination. Bob was truly a master at getting things done, and within ten minutes of Bob hanging up and receiving a return call, he confirmed that he had secured a suite at the best hotel that Van Buren had to offer.

"Driscoll?" Bill asked.

My go-to guy here in Maine. It pays to know someone who has connections and whose fingers are dipped into a little of everything.

"Impressive. Now, what exactly is our plan once we get there?"

Bob grinned as the two began to scheme.

"So, he is back?" Himiko asked.

"Unless a piano can play by itself," Vicky said, walking into the dining room from the kitchen. "Hiya, Sis." Vicky gave all three a brief hug.

"He's pissed," Gaea said again. "And I don't think he is alone. I sense another presence."

"Two ghosts?" Marc asked, exasperated. "If one wasn't enough. Geeze."

"Thanks for coming so quickly, Gaea. I'm hoping it doesn't mean he is here to cause problems." Vicky was remarkably calm, considering the potential situation. The spirit of Douglas had caused problems in the past when Vicky moved into the restaurant. Acting more like a poltergeist, he made noises, moved things, and created messes that Vicky had to clean up, and she quickly grew tired of his antics. With Gaea's help, a sort of deal had been struck concerning the possible removal of the piano. Douglas was upset that she might get rid of the instrument. Vicky, after careful consideration, decided to keep it, have it restored, and hire a pianist to entertain her patrons. With the addition of a picture of Douglas and a commemorative plaque hanging next to the piano, the ghost seemed to be appeased, and things calmed down considerably. Then the Grimoire problem arose, and now it seemed that the activities had resumed. Vicky had hoped Douglas Blanchard had departed along with the book, but now she was reconsidering that thought.

"No problem. Give me some time upstairs, and I will try to talk to him and find out who the other spirit is," Gaea replied. "Marc, Himiko? Why don't you help in the kitchen while I investigate?"

Her two friends nodded and followed Vicky. Gaea tuned and headed toward the stairs that led to the second-story dining room.

"I hope she can get this figured out," She heard Marc say as they disappeared into the kitchen.

She climbed the stairs slowly, reaching out with her abilities to sense who or what might be nearby. She could immediately detect Douglas above her, along with something else she couldn't quite identify. She believed it to be a woman, but couldn't discern much more; however, as she ascended, more and more became clear.

As she entered the dining room, she had a clear view of the piano bar. Douglas sat at the keys, while a woman of perhaps thirty stood next to him, as if she were listening to him play. Her hair was nearly white, which Gaea believed to be a premature condition brought on by some trauma—an experience that ultimately caused her death. Neither of the two acknowledged her presence as she stood watching them. Douglas appeared to be leafing through some sheet music placed on the piano.

"Douglas?" Gaea spoke up. "Who is your companion?"

He turned and faced Gaea. "Ah, she is here, my darling," Douglas said to the white-haired woman, then turned his attention back to Gaea. "Did you bring my book? Did you bring the Grimoire?"

"I did not." She replied, stepping forward in a manner that showed she was not afraid of the two spirits. "Your claim on that book seems to be in dispute, Douglas. Others seem to be after it as well and are claiming it belongs to them."

"They lie!" He said angrily.

His companion leaned forward and placed a finger over his lips—a gesture to calm him down. "There is no need to get upset, my love. I'm sure that this girl will cooperate."

"My name is Gaea. And yours?"

"Don't give her the time of day!" He barked. "She is nothing more than a thief. She stole the Grimoire from me!"

"My name is Lillith. Is it true? Did you steal the Grimoire?"

"The book was removed to prevent it from falling into the possession of those who desire what it contains. Witches and warlocks who intend to use it for ill intent." Gaea partially lied.

Douglas stood up. He was fuming with anger. "You had no right! I was guarding the Grimoire from such a fate! It was safe here!"

"No, it wasn't," Gaea said, trying to convince herself. What if the Grimoire had been safe left in the closet? Perhaps Douglas had been a powerful warlock in life and retained his powers in death? She quickly dismissed the thought. He would have used such power when it was first taken, but he had not. She suspected he had acquired the book from the thief who had stolen it from the museum. The circumstances seemed to fit, although the details remained hidden from her.

"Maybe it was you who stole it from the museum?" Gaea taunted. "Maybe wanting to sell it to the highest bidder? Or maybe you didn't realize what it was you actually had?"

She could instantly see the effect of her words on him. The ghost grew calmer and took his seat at the piano again.

"I am no thief, but I did know of the man who did steal it." Douglas seemed to deliberate and resolve himself to telling Gaea some of what had transpired if he had any chance of retrieving the book and achieving his own goals. "The man was a petty criminal, a drunkard, and would do almost anything for a small fee. I was the one who brought him into my employ to remove the Grimoire from the museum and bring it to me. Luckily, he was able to complete the task before he was caught. The simpleton could not even remember who I was when the police questioned him about the book. He claimed to have lost it, which greatly benefited me. The Grimoire disappeared as far as the authorities were concerned.

"But why did you want the book to begin with?" Gaea asked. "Are you a warlock?"

He looked up at the woman.

"Tell her." She said, smiling at him. "There is no shame in what we intend to do."

"Very well." He nodded, taking her hand in his. "I am a necromancer. I used to be a member of a powerful coven and was ordered to obtain the Grimoire and return it to the High Priest, who claimed it was his. There were conditions under which I insisted on performing the task of retrieving the book. Stealing an artifact from a well-known museum was no easy task."

"Go on." Gaea urged.

"A rival wizard had killed Lillith, sacrificing her to a demon, and she became trapped in the afterlife, unable to move on. She was condemned to relive her defeat on the anniversary of her death as punishment for challenging the warlock over the Grimoire. It was a powerful spell that he had used to destroy her."

"And you didn't help her?"

He shook his head. "I was not there when it happened, although I wish I had."

"You would have been killed as well." Lillith seemed moved by her husband's recall of her fate, and a ghostly tear fell down her cheek.

"Perhaps." Douglas agreed. "I thought my love was lost to me forever, and I became a recluse, hiding from my coven and my practice of dark magic. I came to Maine to escape my peers and found myself here, the new pianist, losing my sorrows in music. When I did gain the Grimoire, I did not give the book to the High Priest and cast a spell upon it to hide it from him. I hid it in the back of the closet here in the restaurant and hoped it would never be found."

"Then you died here at the piano," Gaea stated.

"Yes. My broken heart failed, causing my death. It wasn't until years later, after what seemed like an endless search, that I found Lilith still trapped in her eternal struggle in the afterlife. I used the book to partially free her, but the task is not yet complete. Part of her soul remains bound to the altar upon which she was sacrificed. I have not been able to complete the spell."

"But she is here, standing in front of us? I don't understand?"

"It is but a part of her. Her free will to choose is still held captive. There is a spell hidden in the Grimoire that will break the curse that keeps her, an addition to what I have already performed, but I have yet to find it within its pages. I am not an evil man, Gaea. I only wish to free Lillith so that we can both move on from this world."

Gaea looked at the woman, and for a moment, Lillith partially faded. She gazed at Douglas with a questioning expression.

I can only hold her here for a short time before the curse recalls her. I am not powerful enough to break what calls her back. Her appearance is unpredictable, as she can escape at any moment. When she is able, she comes to me. The curse eventually catches up to her and ensnares her again.

Gaea sighed. "This complicates things a lot, Douglas. What I said about other people seeking the Grimoire is true. They know it is out of hiding, but they don't know exactly where. They do know it is in Maine and probably close to here. I fear that moving it now will attract their attention, and we will have a conflict."

"You are correct to think that will be the case. Whoever is after it will stop at nothing to possess the Grimoire. Even if it means bloodshed. What are you planning? I need access to the book one more time," Blanchard pleaded. "I can't bear not being with my beloved."

As he spoke, Lillith faded and vanished.

"Can't you feel my grief?"

Gaea could truly feel his grief, and the pain was almost unbearable for her. "I'm not sure I can promise anything. I am going to the Winter Solstice to seek help on this matter. My friends and I are ill-equipped to handle the Grimoire. We are hopeful to find help there that would take it and keep it from evil hands."

"You might find a powerful witch or warlock who would agree to take the Grimoire, or you might find yourself in despair at the hands of a powerful necromancer who will not take kindly to your attempts to rid yourself of the book. Either way, I need access to the Grimoire, even for a short time. Please believe me, I have no intention of keeping it or any desire to possess it. My only wish is to free my wife. I can reach the book if you tell me where it is. I cannot take it, as I am only a spirit. To move the Grimoire, I would need someone to assist me with the task. So, you see, I am no threat to take it from you."

"Let me give this some thought." Gaea needed time to process what the Ghose of Douglas Blanchard had just told her. The appearance of Lillith was new and introduced a complication in their goal to rid themselves of the dreaded book. She would need to talk to Marc and especially Himiko. She wished her witch friend could speak with Douglas, but she lacked the ability to do so. Himiko would have to trust what Gaea told her. Together, the three would need to make a decision. "I'll be back in a day or two and let you know the plan, ok?"

"Please don't take too long," the ghost pleaded. "I'm not sure how long Lillith has before she is gone from me forever. Her appearances are becoming fewer and fewer."

Gaea nodded. "A couple of days."

Gaea headed back down the stairs. She had a lot to discuss with Himiko and Marc, and not much time to make some decisions.

She found the two in the kitchen, busy washing the baking pans Vicky had used for some freshly baked pies. She had boxed one and gave it to Marc to take home to the Peppers. Bob had a fondness for apple pie and considered it one of Vicky's unmatched in taste.

"We need to talk," Gaea said.

CHAPTER 6
A Choice & Dire Consequences

Cathy arrived in Kennebunkport just before noon. The impromptu trip was necessary to help catalog some artifacts that her store had acquired through a donation from the estate of a deceased man. Her manager, Denise Bastien, had come down with the flu, so Cathy had to cover for her, even if only for a few hours. Otherwise, the store was only open by appointment as it was off-season. The addition of new items was crucial to the stores' productivity. Cathy was to understand that the items were ancient and rare. It would take her expertise to identify and price them accordingly.

"Hi, Doctor Pender!" an older woman said, pausing from cleaning the front counter. She was well into her 60s and had been a friend of Cathy's for years, having been her first hire when she opened her first antique shop.

"Hi Angela. Everything okay?" Cathy replied, walking behind the sales counter and tossing her purse onto it.

"Oh yes. I thought I'd tidy up a bit while I waited for you to arrive. The items are in the back, laid out on the table. Denise was about to start on them, but she was so sick, the poor soul."

"Great. This shouldn't take too long. I need to return to Bar Harbor this afternoon. Thanks for doing that. You can leave when you're ready."

I was just about done. I have a roast in the oven; I'm cooking for supper back at the house. I can't trust my Frank to look in on it so it doesn't overcook.

"Don't I know about that. My husband can be useless in certain areas as well. I'll lock up when I leave."

"Ok, have fun!"

The back room of the shop was multifunctional, serving as a storeroom, office, and laboratory. It was one-eighth the size of the sales area, but it fulfilled its purpose well. Cathy still hadn't quite grasped why another store manager couldn't have managed a routine task, such as identifying and cataloging, until she laid eyes on the objects on the table. One of them took her breath away. Lying before her was a book that bore an uncanny resemblance to the Grimoire. But it couldn't be, as it was in a steel box in a root cellar.

She took a pair of surgical gloves from a box on the table and put them on. Carefully, she began to examine the book. Although it was the same size, it was very different. It was a grimoire made from human skin. She was sure of that, but that was where the resemblance ended. The writing in it and on it was in Latin, and after examining it, she thought it was a kind of history book, not some evil book of spells. She would need someone who could read Latin to be sure. Sighing, she placed the book back on the table and started examining the other objects. An hour and a half later, she was ready to leave.

As she donned her coat, she had an idea and returned to the back room. Picking up the book, she tucked it under her arm, locked the front door, and walked to her car. She tossed it into the back seat, started the Land Rover, and headed for Pepper Mansion. She wasn't quite sure why she decided to take the book; she just thought maybe it might come in handy. As she drove onto the on-ramp of I-95, snow flurries began to hit the windshield.

"Just great." She said to herself and turned on the radio.

Snow was falling heavily when Air Svensk Flight 2811 taxied onto the runway in Stockholm. The pilot, a forty-five-year-old blond-haired man from Germany, and his co-pilot, a thirty-two-year-old woman from Canada, guided the Learjet for takeoff into a stiff wind. The snowstorm had not yet escalated into the expected blizzard forecast by the Swedish Meteorological and Hydrological Institute; thus, the plane was cleared. The pilot glanced once more at his instruments, then pushed the throttle to full. The jet rolled down the runway and into the air.

"He what?" Himiko was beside herself. Gaea had waited until they returned to Pepper Mansion before telling them about her conversation with Douglas and Lillian. "Tell me we are not going to trust the Grimoire with him. He's a necromancer for Pete's sake!"

Marc stood stunned at what he was hearing.

"I didn't say we are going to," Gaea said in her defense. "I told him we would consider it."

"Do you believe him?" Marc asked. "It's sad that his wife is trapped, if she really is."

"She's already dead, Marc," Himiko said to him.

Gaea took a cookie from a jar on the countertop and sat down at the kitchen table. After taking a bite, she stood back up. "I forgot the milk."

"Gaea!" Himiko was clearly upset at the recent developments.

"What? I'm hungry."

Marc tried to hide his grin.

After pouring herself a glass, she took two more cookies and sat back down. "Ok. From what I saw and sensed, I believe what he told me, and it makes sense—the robbery and what happened after that. He is sincere. He can't hide that from me. I'd know if he was lying. He is in love with Lillith, even in death, and is desperate to help her in any way possible."

"It's whatever way possible is what scares me, Gaea." Himiko helped herself to a cookie and offered one to Marc, who accepted it. "He wants to come here to find the incantation in the book?"

"Either that or we take it to him. He's a ghost, Himiko. He can't carry it."

"We can't move the book now," Himiko stated. "It would be super dangerous even to try."

"It will be seen?" Marc asked, raiding the cookie jar again.

"More likely than not," Gaea answered. "I would think that whoever is seeking it would know of its movement immediately. Right, Himiko?"

"Right. Then all hell would break loose. Moving it is not an option."

I agree. However, if we want to help Douglas and his wife, it means he needs to come here. We would have to reveal the Grimoire's location to him.

"What if he squeals to one of them? You know, one of the bad warlocks?" Marc proposed.

"Possible, but doubtful." Gaea reiterated her belief in his sincerity. "His only thoughts are concerning freeing Lillith. He even told me he does not want the Grimoire for himself. He left his coven and intentionally hid the book from them, risking his life in the process. He kept it hidden for years until he died. Then Lillith began showing up."

"What about Lillith?" Himiko asked. "Is she trustworthy?"

I can't read her very well, probably because she is only a kind of mirror of her ghostly self, being trapped by the spell. Douglas trusts her explicitly.

"Ok, let's just say we take the chance," Himiko began, "how would we go about it? You will need to go to the restaurant and inform him of the location, and you may not return here before he arrives. We can't see ghosts."

"No, you can't let alone talk to them. But I know someone who can."

"What the hell is that doing in here?" Bill said to his wife when she dropped the book on a desk in the Pepper library. Bob was equally concerned about the Grimoire's presence in his home. Cathy had returned before Gaea and decided to reveal her intentions to Bill and Bob before they arrived.

"It's not the Grimoire," she explained, a grimoire, yes, but not the Grimoire."

Both Bob and her husband had confusion written all over their faces.

"This book was part of the items I went to Kennebunkport to examine. Take a closer look." She offered.

"I didn't get a good look at the one in the root cellar," Bill admitted, looking at the new arrival. "It looks the same."

"But it's not, Bill," Bob said, reaching to open the book's cover. "May I?" He asked Cathy.

"Be my guest. I think it's harmless. Made of human skin but harmless."

Bob opened it to the first page that had text and read the Latin aloud. "Caligulae Cesaris historia de vita et morte".

"You read Latin, Bob?" Cathy asked with a laugh. "What don't you do?"

"It came in handy as a publisher." He replied.

"What does it say?" Bill asked.

"History of the Life and Death of Caligula Caesar." He replied. "I am assuming that the skin is his?"

"Unknown but possible," Cathy said, looking at the script.

Bob flipped through the pages of the book, careful not to damage it. "It's all written in Latin. Nothing special about this book, be it bound in human skin." "It does resemble the Grimoire." Bill agreed. "They are nearly the same size. Someone might mistake it for the spell book if seen only for a moment or from a distance."

"Mom? Dad? We're home." Gaea called upon entering the mansion.

"We're in the library, honey," Cathy called back. "Can you come in here? Bring Himiko and Marc with you."

"That was an interesting visit to Cinnamon Woodfire," Gaea said, stepping into the library. "It seems our ghost has returned and brought a friend with him. What's up?"

Bob held up the book for a brief moment, flashing it so the three could catch a glimpse of it.

"How the hell did that get in here?" Himiko blurted out? "Did Aerin take it?"

Bob glanced at Cathy and Bill. "It seems your assessment was correct, Bill."

"What is this all about?" Gaea said, approaching the desk, Himiko and Marc in tow. "How did the Grimoire find its way into the house?"

"Take another look," Bob said, handing her the book.

Gaea's jaw dropped.

"That is not the Grimoire," Himiko stated. "But I could have sworn when I saw it that it was."

"I know, right? So what is this, and where did it come from? Is it a grimoire?" Gaea asked.

"Yes." Her mother replied. "It's a biography of sorts written in Latin."

"A biography of one Caligula Caesar, to be exact." Bob took over. "We were debating whether the cover is of Caligula himself before you three arrived. But that is of no relevance to the question at hand."

"Which is?" Marc asked.

"Well, we just tried our theory on the three of you, and you fell for it. This book could pass for the real Grimoire if it were shown quickly." Bill said, walking to a mini-fridge and taking out a Diet Coke.

"Ah, use it as a diversion," Marc said enthusiastically. "I love espionage stories. I read them all the time growing up."

"You are still growing up, dork." Gaea poked him in the ribs.

"We think you should bring this book to the festival. You might be able to use it as a distraction if you need to make a run for it." Bill took a big gulp from the can.

"Wouldn't that be dangerous?" Himiko was concerned. "If someone thought it was the Grimoire, they might take some violent action. Someone could get hurt."

"We are assuming that you are all in trouble and need to get away," Bob answered. "This book might buy you the time needed to escape."

"It sounds like a plan," Gaea picked up the book and studied it for a moment. "But, we have another problem that has arisen, and we need to talk about it."

"Oh?" Cathy responded. "What might that be? We have enough problems as it is."

"Well, we have one more," Himiko warned. "Douglas Blanchard wants access to the Grimoire, and the three of us are considering it."

Bob, Cathy, and Bill looked at one another.

CHAPTER 7
Degelis, Quebec

Kenneth Burpee lived a short drive from Van Buren in Canada. He was a fledgling magic user who had joined the Obsidian Circle just over a year ago, with his great-aunt as his sponsor. Sharon Burpee was an elderly woman in her late eighties, and she wanted a Burpee to uphold the decades-old tradition of having at least one family member in the coven. She served as the direct contact for coven members in Canada and took her position seriously. It was her responsibility to report directly to the High Priest, who was second in command, or in this case, a woman. Sharon was also tasked with informing those under her supervision about some of the coven's business, including the upcoming Black Sabbath.

She hadn't held out much hope that many would attend, and of the few members in Canada, two had confirmed, one being Kenneth. The other lived in a small town outside Vancouver, British Columbia, on the West Coast, someone she had never had the pleasure of meeting. The response she received felt more like an "I'll come, but it's somewhat inconvenient" attitude. Kenneth, on the other hand, was ecstatic. At twenty-two years old and fresh out of college, he was thrilled to begin learning and practicing black magic. Having the chance to meet the High Priest of the Obsidian Circle was not only an honor but also an opportunity to impress the man and demonstrate that he intended to be very active in the coven and strive to rise through its ranks.

His great-aunt had warned him not to get too close to other witches and warlocks he would encounter at the Black Sabbath. Most, she explained, were recluses who did not appreciate mingling with their fellow coven members.

Practicing the occult and black magic was not looked upon favorably by the general public, and white covens despised those practitioners because they did not engage in magic for the benefit of the Earth and its people. Instead, they practiced to better themselves, forging pacts with creatures from the underworld. She had strongly warned Matthew not to approach this, or he would undoubtedly lose his soul.

Wars have raged throughout history among covens, often pitting black against white and sometimes black against black. Some conflicts were driven by religion, while others, particularly those involving a black coven, centered around power. There were instances when a person was suspected or caught practicing witchcraft by the public, and upon conviction, they faced hanging or burning at the stake. The practice of seeking out and punishing witches and warlocks has faded into history, at least for now.

Sharon had been tasked with organizing the initial event for Black Sabbath, and it was her responsibility to determine where it would be held. Although the invitations stated Van Buren, the exact location would not be revealed until the day before. Ultimately, she chose her property near Degelis, Quebec, just a short drive from downtown Van Buren. Crossing the border would not pose an issue, as the remote location was not monitored by either the US or Canadian border patrol. The old potato farm featured a large barn that once housed the season's crop, now standing empty except for a few old farming tools. After her husband's death, she decided not to continue farming, sold most of the acreage to another farmer, and retreated into solitude. It was rare for her to mingle with the public; however, occasionally, she would go to the doctor or the farmers' market to buy herbs, which she used in her practice. Now, with Kenneth back from school, he handles most of the trips to pick up her necessities.

His nursing degree was also beneficial to her. His part-time job at the clinic in town left him plenty of time to care for her needs, which were few. Thanks to the Canadian government, she qualified for home care, and the funding they provided allowed her to pay for his services. Not that she couldn't afford it herself, but those were the perks of growing old in a socialist country. At her advanced age, she was no longer allowed to drive her Buick, so she gave it to Kenneth. Overall, she managed exceptionally well and remained active in her coven.

The Winter Solstice was primarily a gathering of white witches and warlocks, along with individual practitioners. However, something had emerged that required a gathering and the cooperation of any member of the Obsidian Circle who could attend. The Grimoire, it seemed, had reappeared after being lost for years. Details were scarce, but what Sharon could gather indicated that it was located in Maine, although the exact location within the state remained largely a mystery. It was also believed to be in the possession of a white witch and psychic medium. It wasn't the witch that worried her; it was the medium, who would sense her presence and immediately recognize that she was a black witch. The medium would also realize that she was searching for the Grimoire, and obtaining it was of the utmost importance. The members of the coven were instructed to discreetly mingle with the crowd and try to ascertain if the book had been brought to the festival. If it had, the coven would intercept and retrieve it quietly to avoid drawing attention to themselves or the Grimoire—a task easier said than done. Still, the High Priest had commanded it, and he was not a man to refuse what he demanded. In many ways, he was a warlock to be feared.

Sharon pushed aside the curtain and looked out the window of her kitchen, briefly catching a glimpse of herself in the glass. Long gone were the sharp brown eyes and smooth alabaster skin, now replaced by the wrinkles that crossed her face. White hair had supplanted her black locks, and she now walked with a slight hunch, as kyphosis had affected her with age. Her upper back curved forward, making her feel as though she resembled a witch from a fairy tale—the hag that sought to kill the young princess. She laughed for a moment, then turned her attention to the car driving up to the house. Kenneth had returned with the herbs and other ingredients she needed to mix a protection potion that would shield her and Kenneth from being discovered by the psychic medium.

She let the curtain drop back into place and went to greet her great-nephew.

Gaea had been contemplating the Douglas Blanchard problem for two days and remained uncertain about allowing the spirit near the Grimoire. She believed in his sincerity regarding his desire to save his wife's spirit and also that the Grimoire held the key to achieving it. Her parents and the Peppers were firmly against it, and Himiko was too, though she agreed to support whatever decision Gaea made. Marc was ambivalent, as he often was when it came to decisions about the book. He felt that engaging with the magical book was beyond his grasp and that his opinions would be irrelevant. Therefore, he left the decision-making to the two girls. He was there to lend his strength when needed and to provide emotional support.

Gaea had important considerations regarding the Grimoire, the most significant being its discovery at the Pepper Mansion. This could ultimately place her entire family in serious danger, as she was convinced that witches and warlocks would invade to reclaim the book. She was unwilling to endanger anyone unless it was absolutely necessary. The only ones who fell into that category were herself, Himiko, and Marc, although she secretly hoped he would return to the University of Maine and wait for her. However, she knew that this would not happen. He was as devoted to her as a newborn puppy is to its mother.

One of her biggest concerns was her brother Aerin. Though very young, Aerin was a powerful psychic medium who was vulnerable to an attack from the Night Witch, another medium. Gaea felt the Night Witch's abilities while on campus and was unwilling to put him in harm's way. Fortunately, her mother was preparing to take him back to Cape Neddick. Christmas vacation was nearing its end, and he had to return to school. That was one less problem she would have to face. Her father, on the other hand, had chosen to stay in case she found herself in trouble. Then, as Bob Pepper put it, the cavalry was coming to rescue the trio. She was hoping against hope that they would stay out of it, as they were ill-equipped to handle what might occur. According to Himiko, the witches and warlocks in Van Buren were not to be trifled with. They were powerful and dangerous. She would put nothing past what he or Bob might do.

Himiko had devised an option involving the grimoire her mother had brought from her shop in Kennebunk Port. She claimed that she could cast a spell on the book that would make it appear to have magical properties, even if only for a short time. "Consider it something like wearing perfume," she explained. "It smells pretty until it wears off."

Gaea could see the usefulness of having a diversion that would mimic the real thing. It would also allow them to kill two birds with one stone. First, if Douglas waited until they were at the festival and Himiko cast the spell, he would be able to access the real Grimoire with little chance of it being discovered, as attention would be focused elsewhere. Second, the doppelganger would draw in people interested in the book, and hopefully, they would be in a position to help. On the flip side, it would also attract the dark witches and warlocks who were originally seeking it. The two-edged sword that this situation created was dangerous, but also essential if they were to rid themselves of the Grimoire without handing it over to undesirables. It seemed to hinge on being in the right place at the right time, meeting the right person in that moment, and emerging unscathed. With Himiko's plan, giving Douglas the opportunity he desired appeared safe and feasible. Once again, timing was everything. She had made her decision, and it was time to talk to Marc and Himiko.

"Lucky bastard, Bill," Bob said. "Your wife is leaving and bought the ice fishing trip hook, line, and sinker. Mine saw right through me. She knows we are going up Maine to keep an eye on the kids."

"She's ok with it?" Bill asked, reaching into the fridge, plucking a Coors Light from its depths.

"No. Of course not. But, Bill, she is a good woman. She cares for the kids as much as you and I do. Maybe even more. She believes this trip is necessary. She says if action is needed, we won't be able to act quickly enough from here."

"I tend to agree," Bill said, popping the top on the can and letting a quick burst of cold vapor escape into the air. "That is why we have to go up there. You can't muster a reaction fast enough, even with your array of contacts."

You're right. I'd have to hire some experts, and it's too late for that. Besides, this time I want to be there if something goes down.

"Me too."

Bob walked up to a picture on the wall and swung it open, revealing a hidden safe. Spinning the dial, he quickly unlocked it and reached inside, pulling out a handgun, followed by another.

"When you said cavalry, you meant it, Bob."

"He handed Bill one of the weapons. "It's not loaded. They are collectors' items," he said. "Colt 45s from World War II. Commanders' pistols."

Bill examined the gun. Its body was silver, and the stock appeared to be made of ivory. The gun Bob held looked identical. "Did you steal these from Patton?" he said half-jokingly.

Bob smiled and pulled a box of ammunition from the safe. "I am hoping we will not need these; however, having them with us as backup will make me feel better. Do you know how to use it, Bill?"

"I've done some shooting. Primarily with a long rifle. I hunted with my grandfather as a kid in upstate New York."

"That's good—no training needed," Bob replied, opening the box and handing Bill a handful of shells. "I just hope to God we don't have to use these."

Bill removed the clip from the gun's hilt and examined it for a moment before loading bullets into it, each one locking into place with a sharp click. "I'm not excited about carrying this, Bob. Accidents can happen."

"Don't you think I have thought of that very thing?" Bob dropped his gun onto his desk. "I have weighed the risk carefully, and not having them if the need arises could be worse than having them with us." Bob turned and walked toward Bill. "I have a strong box that I bought made especially for these guns. I suggest we keep them locked away and only take them out if a situation warrants it."

"I can live with that plan." Bill placed his gun next to Bob's. "I hope I don't have to lay eyes on it again."

Bob returned to his desk and took a seat. "You know something, Bill? I've never fired either one of these weapons. I'm not sure they even work."

Kenneth parked the Buick Regal under a solitary maple tree in front of the old farmhouse, hopped out, and opened the rear door of the sedan. The car was nearly ten years old but had extremely low mileage since his great-aunt rarely drove it except to go to town and back. Even the metallic gray paint shimmered in the sun, as if it had just been applied. There were no signs of wear on the interior, and he could swear it smelled factory-fresh. Not a cigarette had been lit in it, and thankfully, the heater worked like new, too.

He opened the rear driver's side door and took two paper bags from the seat. He pushed the door closed with his hip and turned to enter the house. Pausing for a moment, he surveyed the old building. Like the car, it had been meticulously maintained. Even the old wooden clapboards on the side of the farmhouse were in excellent condition. Not a single one was out of place or missing. Built in the mid-1800s, the five-bedroom home would eventually belong to him, or so his great-aunt had told him. She had no other family members she considered worthy of the house, and she adored Kenneth. When that day arrived, he made a vow to himself that he would uphold the home as she had done.

He struggled to open the front door when it swung open, revealing a smiling elderly woman dressed in a black dress, with a purple shawl draped over her shoulders.

"Let me take one of those before you drop it." she said, taking one of the paper sacks from his arms.

"Thanks, auntie." He replied and followed her into the kitchen. "I was able to get everything on your list, even the Blackthorn and Mugwort. They had them at Crosby's Five and Dime like you said."

"Of course they did, dear." She began to unpack her bag. Kenneth eagerly helped her. What the boy did know, although he soon would, was that Catherine Crosby, who owned the store, was a practicing Wiccan and the go-to place for witches and warlocks alike. She didn't seem bothered by who was purchasing her herbs and supplies and was glad to sell them to practitioners of both black and white magic.

"I can't wait for the upcoming festival, especially my first Black Sabbath." He was nearly bursting with excitement, and gathering ingredients for his auntie doubled his emotional state. "What are the herbs used for?" He asked, picking up the Mugwort.

"That is used for a protection spell," she answered, taking it from him and placing it into a jar. The Blackthorn is meant to ward off evil spirits, such as demons. Do you remember what I told you about entities from the underworld?"

"Leave them alone, or I will regret it." He replied. "I promised you I would not attempt any kind of summoning."

"That would make me a happy witch." She smiled at him and placed the herb into another jar. Both were meticulously labeled with a white piece of tape, the names of the herbs written in her hand.

"Can I help with anything else?" He asked.

"As a matter of fact, yes. George Reynolds and his two boys are coming by to clean the barn this afternoon. I'd like you to go out there and reverse the boards in the back. I don't think it would be a good idea for them to see the pentagram on the floor, do you?"

"No, it wouldn't. I'll take care of it now." Kenneth kissed her cheek and ran out the door.

"When they start, I want you to be with them in case they stumble upon something they should not find." She called after him.

"Got it!" He disappeared out into the cold.

The pentagram had been laid on the floor years ago when she held Black Sabbaths for a small group of witches and warlocks, all members of the Obsidian Circle. As the years passed, they either moved away or died, leaving her alone. The board that was burnt with the pentagram could easily be reversed to conceal the symbol if necessary.

The practice of black magic didn't used to be a solitary thing, and a few people would occasionally gather to celebrate one occasion or another. Then, for reasons unknown, people drifted apart and began choosing solitude over gatherings. She hadn't used the barn for a gathering in several years. The barn was in dire need of cleaning, and she was too old to do it; she didn't want to burden Kenneth with it. Reynolds could handle it quickly, and it would be clean for both the coven members and the High Priest.

Sharon Burpee sighed and sat at her kitchen table. She felt tired and had been growing fatigued more easily lately. She wondered if her time might be nearing its end. If so, there was much to accomplish before that day, including teaching her young warlock all that she could.

And if she didn't have enough to worry about, the High Priest himself, Count Boris Sergev, along with Sharon's direct superior, Isobel Argante, had contacted her with a request that she took as an order. The two were going to be guests at the Burpee farm, and keeping Kenneth away from them would be a daunting task.

She placed her hands over her face and sighed.

CHAPTER 8
The Night Witch & Aerin

Being home at Shaw Manor neither excited nor depressed young Aerin. School was about to restart, and he would return to his daily life where he would reunite with friends, especially his best friend Logan, whom he hadn't spoken to in what felt like forever to a young boy, and do what boys do: get into trouble.

Logan was the son of his father, a professor at a local college, and his mother, who was the literary agent for Bill Pender. The family had moved to Maine for a change of lifestyle, although Logan's mother was often away working in New York. When his dad wasn't available, Logan had Aerin and the Pender family. However, this Christmas he didn't have them, as Aerin's family was in Maine visiting their grandparents. So, Logan was excited when his father answered the phone and handed it to him.

"It's Aerin." He said, smiling, and returned to reading his newspaper.

"Hello?" Aerin said into the receiver.

"I'm home," Aerin replied. "Yeah, a couple of days early. My mom thought I could use the time to study and get ready to go back to school."

"Yuck," Logan said, making a sour face. "We're still on vacation and we haven't had any time to enjoy it. You can't just study. We have a lot of things to do and catch up on. Remember, we're supposed to go explore the Shaw Cemetery?"

Logan's father gave his son a stern look and shook his head.

"Well, ok, maybe not the cemetery, but we can explore the woods around your house."

"That would be a lot of fun. Let me ask my mom if you can come over tomorrow. It's kind of late now."

Logan put the phone against his chest. "Dad, can I go over to Aerin's tomorrow? He pleaded.

"Well, let's see, technically, you are still on vacation. Okay, when you're done talking to Aerin, have him put his mother on, and I will okay it with her. Maybe you can do a sleepover if she's ok with the idea." He had work to catch up on before returning to college, and having the house to himself sounded like a splendid idea.

"Yay!" Logan exclaimed, and quickly shared the idea with Aerin, who then hurried off to find his mother.

Fifteen minutes later, the details had been finalized, and Doug would drop off Logan before breakfast. It seemed Vicky was home because her restaurant was being fumigated, and her offer to cook breakfast was one he couldn't refuse. Therefore, the two would be at Shaw Manor at 6 am.

Cathy hung up the phone in the kitchen.

I heard you, and no problem, Mom. Breakfast will be ready at 6:30 am on the dot. It will be nice to cook in my home kitchen for a change and not have to cook as much. I miss it.

"You can always sell Cinnamon Woodfire and move back home. Your father would be overjoyed."

"Ha, not a chance," Vicky said, picking up a dish towel and polishing a glass before placing it into the cupboard.

"What's on the menu?" Cathy asked, raiding the cookie jar on the counter.

"I'll whip up something."

"I can't wait. Now, where did Aerin run off to?" She said, looking around.

"No idea. He ran off once he heard you approve the sleepover."

"Ok. I need to run into town. Do you need anything?"

"I thought you'd never ask," Vick said, producing a shopping list. "If I'm going to be here for a couple of days, I will need what is on this list."

"Grocerics. I should have known." Cathy said, rolling her eyes. "Hey, sure you don't want to come with?"

"No thanks. Things to do here like calling Bar Harbor and checking on the restaurant. My manager came home early from vacation and is seeing to the fumigation."

"Suit yourself. I'll be back soon." Cathy left.

Vicky was a last-minute addition to the trip back to Cape Neddick. After discovering rat droppings in the pantry, she promptly called a fumigation company that, thankfully, could do the job right away. She decided to have the building tented, which took three full days with the treatment she chose. The guarantee stated that nothing would be alive once the tent was removed. The poison gas was both efficient and deadly to anything living inside. Her father joked, asking her if it killed ghosts. Vicky didn't find the comment funny at all; she had work to do, and this was an unnecessary distraction. She resolved to make the best of it and drive home for an extended weekend. It would be beneficial to get some rest and spend time planning the restaurant's future. She left the kitchen, tossed the dish towel into a hamper in the laundry room, and headed upstairs.

Seraphina had mastered the spell, and to her father Gunther's satisfaction, she was casting it by hand as well as he was. Not only had she learned the initial spell that could knock an opponent unconscious, but she had also perfected two others: a confusion spell and a protection spell that would be useful when trying to hide or defend herself against an attacking magic user. There was still more to learn, but the time had come to leave for Van Buren. He had received word that the Black Sabbath would be held in a town in Canada called Degelis, Quebec, at a farmhouse. He hoped it was not too far from the Winter Solstice so that he could continue his search for the Grimoire. With his coven present, he and Seraphina would have support, but the extent of that support remained a mystery. The dark warlocks and witches would undoubtedly mostly keep to themselves and their own affairs unless the High Priest commanded otherwise. It amazed him that they could all gather together at all, but with Count Sergev and Argante present, he expected no issues or problems with the other members.

He had never met the old woman who was his superior and was appointed to organize the Black Sabbath, as she lived near the festival. She had been in contact with him, but only to inform him about the upcoming Black Sabbath. He had never discussed the Grimoire with her, so he had no idea if she was aware of it. He kept quiet about the subject. There was no reason to mention the book unless she asked about it and the search to find it. Members of the Obsidian Circle received information that was relevant to them specifically and were expected not to share unnecessarily.

Discovering his daughter's awareness of the Grimoire was not part of his plan. She had informed him that she was aware of the book and had summoned the demon Belphegor to assist her in finding it. Gunther thought differently. He suspected that she had summoned the demon in an attempt to gain power. Belphegor recognized her desire and her vulnerability and exploited them for his purpose: to reclaim the Grimoire that was written in his hand. Unable to execute the task himself, the defiler chose Seraphina to carry out his wishes, promising her power and the Grimoire, which he had no intention of giving her. After all, demons were untrustworthy liars.

However, she was convinced that the demon was helping her, and although she denied it, Gunther believed she had made a blood pact with Belphegor. If that were true, she was in dire danger, if not already lost. Time would tell, and the truth would be revealed when the Grimoire was found. It depended on who discovered it and what they planned to do with it. A fight for it would undoubtedly ensue; he was sure of that.

Seraphina appeared, carrying her duffle bag, which she tossed into the trunk of the Mercedes-Benz. He noticed that her hair was unkempt and that she didn't seem to have taken the time to shower. Her clothing also looked disheveled, as if it had been pulled from the dirty laundry hamper and thrown on halfheartedly.

"You look like crap." Her father said matter-of-factly." You didn't bother to shower, did you?"

"I didn't sleep very well. Can you cut me a break? Please?"

"Sure. Right after you take a shower and make yourself presentable, you are not going with me looking like you are now."

Seraphina was not happy but gave in to her father's wishes. "I'll be right back."

After watching her leave, he unzipped her bag and searched through it. Finding no evidence of what was necessary for conjuring, he zipped it back up and returned it to the truck. The last thing he needed was Belphegor showing up unannounced, summoned by his daughter. There was already enough to worry about, and he was eager to hit the road. Her delay in their departure was frustrating. The sooner they reached Van Buren, the better. He hoped to find the Grimoire, return it to the High Priest, and wash his hands of the unpleasant situation. By doing so, he might be able to save Seraphina and himself.

An hour later, they were on I-95 heading north, with a three-hour drive ahead of them. Seraphina had quickly fallen asleep against the car door, leaving Gunther to himself and the radio. Thankfully, it wasn't snowing.

Gaea, Marc, and Himiko arrived at Cinnamon Woodfire just as the exterminators drove up. The manager was standing outside the building, waiting to greet them, when she noticed Gaea.

"What are you doing here?" She asked. "Didn't your sister tell you that we are closing for three days to fumigate the restaurant?"

"She did, but she forgot something in her office, and she sent us to get it. She is working on some paperwork and needs it." Gaea lied.

Sure, you have time. But make it quick, ok?"

"We will," Gaea replied, and the three went inside.

"We will wait here," Himiko said. "If you need us, just call."

Gaea nodded and walked upstairs, heading for the piano bar. Upon entering the dining room, she immediately saw Douglas sitting at the Piano. His wife was nowhere in sight.

"Hello, Gaea," Douglas said to her. "Unfortunately, my wife cannot be here. She was recalled a short time ago. It is tiredly repetitive."

"I can imagine it is. Look, Douglas, we have considered your request, and I believe you to be sincere. You claim that you and you alone will know of your visit to the Grimoire, and that no one else, including my family, will be in any danger. Do I have your word on this?"

"You do. As I have said, I will only seek the knowledge from the book to free my wife from her imprisonment. Once done, I will leave this place forever. Your sister will be rid of me."

"Very well. We are traveling to Van Buren and will not be there when you visit the Grimoire; however, my brother is a powerful medium and will be watching from a distance. I will know if you deceive me, Douglas. I hope that will not be the case."

"I am in your debt for helping. I will not do anything to destroy the trust that you give."

How long do you think it will take you?" She asked the spirit.

"I believe no more than an hour. I know now which passage in the book contains the text to perform the spell that is needed to break the hex. I will cast the spell while at the Grimoire, then immediately leave."

The spell hiding it from unsavory eyes will be broken, making it visible for all to see. Can you cast another spell to return the book to the shadows?

"I can and I will," Douglas said, relief spreading over him. His long quest to free his beloved was nearly at hand.

There is a specific time you need to adhere to, as we have another grimoire that we are using as a diversion.

"Another Grimoire?" Douglas was confused. "How can there be another?"

"It is not a magical book, Douglas. "It is bewitched to seem that it is, but in actuality, it is just a simple book bound in human skin."

"When can I approach the Grimoire?" He asked.

I will reach out to you sometime tomorrow night as we near our destination. Please make yourself available to me. You will know when it's time, and then you can go to the book. I will tell you then where it is. Fair enough?

"More than fair. I am truly grateful for your trust, Gaea."

"Be aware, tomorrow evening when I reach out to you, be quick to act. The longer you take, the more dangerous it becomes for the living."

"Gaea?" Himiko called from below. "There is a man down here asking us to leave. They are ready to tent the building."

"On my way." She called back. "They are exterminating vermin in the building with poison. I don't think you are in any danger." She said, smiling. Look for me."

"I will"

Gaea ran down the stars, holding a thumbs-up for Marc and Himiko to see.

Aerin had gone to his room and began practicing reaching out to the Grimoire hidden in Pepper's root cellar. He was unable to see it with his abilities but believed he could if he tried hard enough. If only his parents had let him stay in Bar Harbor, it would have been a simple task to monitor the ghost as it executed whatever he was planning to do with the book. As it stood, they had decided to remove him from potential danger while his sister and friends went off to figure out what to do with the Grimoire.

He concentrated and let his senses drift, finally honing in on the Pepper Mansion. Finding his way into the root cellar was a simple task, but he could neither sense nor see the book. He was blinded by the spell cast upon it to conceal it. However, he was determined and would concentrate, keeping at it all night if necessary. If the worst came to worst, he knew when the ghost would be at the Grimoire, and the spell would certainly be broken. He would then be able to see all that was happening in the dark space.

Pulling his blanket over his head to block out the daylight, he began to concentrate on the Grimoire to break through the magical fog that obscured it from him.

CHAPTER 9
Pre-Festival Arrangements

Flight 1028 had been on the tarmac for nearly two hours, held in limbo with its engines powered down due to sudden high winds from the mountains. The forecasted snowstorm had not materialized, much to the relief of the two passengers who sat patiently aboard. At least one of them was being patient; the other was visibly growing increasingly frustrated with the delay and felt helpless to change the situation. The Learjet, however, was lavish in its design and interior layout, making the wait somewhat bearable.

A single flight attendant had offered the two refreshments several times, yet Isobel Argante dismissed them with a wave of her hand. Important details needed discussion before their arrival in Maine. Therefore, the delay was proving beneficial.

"Have you confirmed our lodging with Magister Burpee?" He asked Isobel.

"I have, and she is expecting us." She replied.

"Tell me."

"She lives on a farm that no longer functions as such with her great nephew Kenneth, a recent addition to our ranks. His knowledge of black magic is minimal, so he will not be of much use in locating the Grimoire," she began. "She is an elderly woman, yet a powerful witch, which is why you promoted her years ago to Magister of Canada."

Yes, I remember. That was many years ago. I found her to be inquisitive, intelligent, and eager to help the Coven. I believe I made a justified choice in selecting her for the position.

"You did, Boris. She is also a very skilled alchemist and potion master. We have made use of her skills numerous times for various reasons, including your surveillance of the KGB. A most useful task."

"Which is extremely important, Isobel. We must be vigilant about what that notorious police force is doing at all times. We can't have them intruding on our affairs. And, yes, she has been most useful."

"She is getting very elderly." Isobel reminded him. "Who will take over for her when she is no longer able to serve you?"

I haven't decided, and it's not important right now. As long as she can perform her duties, she will remain Magister.

I believe that her great-nephew helps her with many things, such as gathering her supplies and transporting her to and from necessary appointments. Perhaps he may grow into the role? It's just a thought.

"The boy is still very weak in his skill and needs to learn much before being promoted to such a high rank in the Obsidian Circle, Isobel. However, it may be useful in gathering information when needed. There are times when the naive can be most useful, as their ignorance feigns innocence and they can be easily trusted."

The flight attendant reappeared, and this time Sergev ordered tea. Isobel requested vodka neat. One drink would not cloud her judgment, and Sergev seemed unconcerned.

The overhead speaker came to life, and the captain of the jet addressed them.

"This is Captain Johansson with an update. We will be cleared for takeoff within the hour. The windstorm will pass us shortly. I apologize for the delay and hope to be in the air shortly." The intercom went dead.

"Finally," Isobel exclaimed. "I thought we would never get off the ground."

"Patience, my dear." He said, tapping her leg with the palm of his hand. "We will get to our destination eventually."

An hour later, the Learjet taxied to the runway and flew into the sky.

Reynolds and his boys arrived shortly after Kenneth had driven the final nail into the boards he had turned over in the barn. The pentagram was now hidden from view. He kicked a bit of dirt across the floor to create the illusion that nothing had been disturbed. He planned to reverse the process once the barn was cleaned. Kenneth had also found some items used in the last ritual his great-aunt performed: burnt black candles, cups of herbs, and a decanter of liquid he swore was blood, although it could have been anything. He disposed of all but the holder that had contained the candles, as new ones would be used for the Black Sabbath.

Before leaving the barn, he placed the crowbar and hammer he had used in a tool closet near the front doors. He stepped outside and brushed off the dust. The thought of a steaming cup of cocoa crossed his mind, and as he made his way to the house, an old pickup truck pulled up to the barn.

An older man was at the wheel, and two young boys were riding in the back. They jumped out of the bed as the man opened the door to the truck.

"Hi, Mr. Reynolds!" Kenneth said cheerfully. "The barn is open and ready to be cleaned. Thanks for coming."

"Ayuh, no problem." The man replied in a thick Down East accent. "George Reynolds had relocated from Augusta, Maine, after marrying his Canadian wife. Her desire to live near her own family, along with her natural beauty, made the choice an easy one. He had been a farmer, but now he was the local handyman for the community on both sides of the border. He didn't make a fortune doing odd jobs, but as he would say numerous times, "It's a livin'.""

His two boys were the spitting image of their father, with bright red hair and freckled faces. The old man's face was lined with wrinkles from years of hard work under the sun. Yet, all three wore smiles that most found contagious.

"Boys, get the tool out of the bed and take 'em into the barn. I'll be there shortly." He instructed, shortly sounding like *shotly*.

As the two jumped into action, George turned his attention back to Kenneth. "Tell Ms. Burpee I will be in to pay my respects when we're done. Shan't be too long."

"I'll let her know, Mr. Reynolds. I'm going in to get some hot cocoa, would you like some or some coffee?"

"We brought our own, but we could use three cups. Forgot ours back home, if you could."

"Sure thing. Be right back." Kenneth ran into the house, where he found his auntie in the kitchen, busy at the stove and standing over a steaming cast-iron pot.

"What's cooking?" He asked, reaching into the cupboard to get the cups. "Reynolds is here. He'll come in when he's done to say hello." Kenneth held up a cup. "He forgot his at home."

Sharon nodded at the cup. "I'm making a New England Boiled Dinner. We could use something hot that would stick to our ribs for supper."

"Sounds yummy! I'll be out in the barn like you asked, Auntie. Oh, and I found some things from the last ritual and got rid of them."

"Oh, what were they?"

"Just some herbs and some red liquid and a couple of burnt candles. I put the candle holders in the tool closet and threw away the rest. I hope that was ok."

"Just fine. Herbs lose their potency with time. It's best we use fresh for the Black Sabbath. You run along now, Kenneth."

She watched him leave and frowned. She had made a mistake by leaving the tools of her trade lying around, even if they were her own property. Leaving the blood vial was the worst of the transgressions, as, if it had fallen into the wrong hands, it could have had devastating consequences. The blood, although not from her actions, had come from a human—a child, to be exact. The infant had not been harmed and was not present at the ritual, but the power contained in the blood was not insignificant and did not fade with time. A necromancer could have used it to raise the dead. She had used it as an ingredient in a ritual to sever her ties with the denizens of the underworld. She had done this four years ago to protect Kenneth from anything that might arise from her dealings with those who inhabited it. Her dealings were neither extensive nor binding. Still, she needed to be cautious regarding her kin. She was glad that Kenneth had discovered her mistake and corrected it, and also that the incident had become known to her coven and the High Priest. Such a mistake could cost her position within the hierarchy.

She wiped her forehead with a dish towel draped over her shoulder and sat down. Her heart was palpitating again, a situation that had been recurring intermittently over the past couple of months. She had avoided going to the doctor as there was too much to accomplish in preparation for the Winter Solstice and the Black Sabbath. She couldn't afford to be sidelined when the game was afoot. There was far too much to do.

The palpitations began to fade, and the phone rang. Standing up, she walked to the old rotary phone that hung on the wall and answered it.

"Burpee residence." She said cheerfully. "Sharon speaking."

The voice on the other end of the line was one she recognized immediately, and she listened carefully to the instructions being given to her.

"I understand." She said and hung up.

At exactly 11:30 am, a silver Mercedes-Benz pulled up and parked outside The Loose Moose Hotel in downtown VanBuren, Maine, and Gunther turned off the engine. He reached over and shook his daughter awake.

"We're here. You slept the entire way," he said, opening the door and climbing out. The hotel was the only three-story building in town and one of a dozen in the area, all of which were booked for Winter Solstice. Signs of the festival were visible nearly everywhere one looked. Decorations hung from poles along the two-lane street that was Main Street of Van Buren. The street was not as busy as he would have guessed, yet dozens of people wandered in and out of the shops that lined the business district of the town. He looked and chuckled at a sign in the window of the hotel that gave a warm welcome, reading, "We welcome the friendly witches and warlocks for the annual Winter Solstice. Have a pagan good time!"

He shook his head and opened the trunk of the car. A sleepy Seraphina joined him and retrieved her duffle bag. "I didn't sleep last night."

"You mentioned that earlier. Look, let's check in, and then you can go back to sleep if you want. I have something I need to take care of. I won't be long."

"Wait, if it has something to do with the Grimoire, I should go with you."

"It doesn't, but it is coven business that I have to attend to alone. Like I said, I won't be gone long."

"You're lying, aren't you?" She asked slyly.

He crossed his chest in a cross. "I swear, not Grimoire business."

"She watched the gesture. "And I trust that?" She laughed.

"I'm serious, it has to do with Black Sabbath, okay? I need to meet with the Magister in charge of arranging the details for the coven meeting."

"Sure, okay. Maybe I'll take a walk around town and get my bearings. It would be nice to have a clue where things are in this backwoods town."

"Sounds good. You do that. Now, let's go check in."

Sharon wasn't used to having company, especially unfamiliar people. Still, the order had come from Isobel, and she was determined to follow through with it. A man named Gunther, a member of the coven on special orders, was scheduled to come to the house for a meeting. He was expected to arrive that very afternoon. Her instructions were to assist him in any way and with anything he might need until the High Priest arrived. Other coven members were also due to come into town, and she was to inform them solely about Black Sabbath. Nothing was to be mentioned about what the man would tell her.

She sighed and glanced at the pot on the stove. Supper might be late this evening. Standing up, she made her way to the bedroom. If she were to have a guest, she might as well freshen up.

"So, we are committed to the plan," Himiko said, stuffing her remaining clothing into a suitcase she had borrowed from the Peppers. Hers was back in the dorm room, and there was no time to go fetch it.

"Once it is 10 pm., we should still be an hour out from Van Buren." Gaea began verbally rehearsing their plan. "We will pull over, and you will cast the charm on the grimoire while I reach out to Douglas, giving him the location of the real grimoire and the okay to go do his thing with it. I gave him precisely one hour to accomplish what he had to, and he agreed to cast the spell to put it back into hiding. At the same time he is casting his spell, you will break the spell on the book we have."

"If the timing is correct, we should send out the signals that will confuse anyone searching for the Grimoire," Marc said, seeing to his own borrowed suitcase. "Clever."

"Correct." Gaea continued. "For a brief time, the Grimoire will be visible in Bar Harbor, but so will our doppelganger. We hope that a book closer to the festival will garner attention and be regarded as the true Book of Belphegor. The Grimoire will be overlooked in the root cellar, and before anyone can act, both will vanish as quickly as they appeared."

"It's a brilliant plan," Gaea said, "as long as the timing stays precise and there are no slipups, and Douglas does what he says he will do." Himiko was still nervous about the entire plan and didn't fully trust the spirit.

"I think Douglas is sincere." Gaea reiterated. "I can't put a finger on why, I *feel* as though we can trust him. I guess you will have to trust me."

"Oh, I know I do," Marc said, putting on a baseball cap that read I love New York.

Gaea looked at him and laughed. "Dork."

"Come on, we need to be on the road in an hour," Himiko said, closing and locking her suitcase.

"Let's move," Marc said.

Flight 1082 banked and came around on its final approach to Northern Maine Regional Airport in Presque Isle, Maine. This small airport, affectionately known as the gateway to Northern Maine, is the closest to Van Buren and just a 35-mile drive, which takes less than an hour. Isobel had arranged for a car to take them into Canada to the farmhouse where they would stay.

She would have to go into Van Buren to complete tasks, while Sergev would remain in the home's seclusion unless the Grimoire was found. The Magister's great-nephew has a car available for her when needed, and since he is local, he would assist her with the layout of the area. Additionally, being a coven member was a bonus.

The sun was beginning to set, which aligned with her intention to arrive discreetly. They would need to drive through the center of Van Buren to reach their destination, and she wanted to make the passage unnoticed. It was in her nature to be excessively cautious when it came to Sergev and the coven.

The pilot set the plane down gently, and it taxied to a building where a car was waiting, a man dressed in a suit standing next to it. Serge looked out at it.

"Our transportation?" He asked Isobel.

"Yes, and a coven member. He drove here from Minnesota for the Black Sabbath. He knows nothing of the Grimoire and has only been tasked with driving from the airport to the farmhouse and back to the airport."

"Impressive as usual, Isobel."

Isobel stood and stepped aside, allowing him to climb out from the window seat. She guided the way to the front of the aircraft, where the flight attendant was lowering the steps. The cockpit door opened, and the pilot emerged to greet his passengers.

"I trust the flight was satisfactory?" He asked.

"Very," Sergev answered, walking down the steps onto the tarmac. The driver was collecting the couple's luggage and loading it into the trunk of the car. Moments later, Sergev and Isobel left the airport, heading toward the US-Canadian border.

Upstairs at Cinnamon Woodfire, in the darkness, the spirit of Douglas Blanchard sat at the piano, anticipating the events that were about to unfold and would affect his and his wife's existence in the afterlife. If everything went as planned and the psychic medium came through as promised, he would be able to escape the purgatory in which he found himself. As it stood, he was condemned to relive her death again and again, as she returned to him only to be torn from his side shortly after her escape. The same scene played over and over endlessly. He could see her escape, her desperate attempt to free herself from the demon that held her. It let her go as if playing with her, ultimately reining her back in, crushing what was left of her free will, which was merely a flicker of a dying flame. If he could not free his wife soon, she would be lost forever. That was not an option for Douglas Blanchard.

He had contemplated using the Grimoire to bring life back to himself and his wife, but ultimately decided against it. They had lived their lives, and for better or worse, it had come to an end. His only desire now was to cross over with her once and for all and free themselves from earthly possessions as well as the torment of the underworld. He would do his best to uphold his agreement with the girl Gaea.

He glanced at the clock on the wall. Tomorrow, at this time, his wife would arrive, and they would both go to the Grimoire, where he would release her from the bonds of the Demon Belphegor.

In the darkness, his wife materialized and touched his arm.

CHAPTER 10
An Assault & A Change of Plan

Vicky smiled as she watched the two young boys devour the breakfast she had prepared. Bacon, ham, blueberry pancakes, and a loaf of fresh bread were rapidly disappearing from the table. Logan was especially enjoying the meal since it was a rare treat when Vicky was home to cook. Her mother and Doug had finished eating and excused themselves, taking their cups of coffee to the sitting room to chat.

"This is so good! Thank you, Vicky!" Logan said, stuffing the last piece of pancake into his mouth. "You are so lucky, Aerin."

"Was lucky." Aerin reminded him. "She is living in Bar Harbor, running that stupid restaurant now."

"Hey! My restaurant is not stupid!"

Aerin looked down at his plate. "I'm sorry. It's just that I miss you lots." He said apologetically.

"It's ok, I miss you too." she said, picking up the two empty plates. "You want some more orange juice?"

Both boys shook their heads no.

"Well, ok then. See you two at lunch, now scoot!"

Aerin and Logan ran off to prepare themselves for their assault on the enemy in the woods. There was nothing like a good game of playing war, and Aerin had all the necessary gear to stage a good fight, even though the enemy was imaginary. He would be Sergeant York, and Logan would be Corporal Strickland. Both boys knew who the famous Sergeant York was, as they had heard of the soldier's heroics from Mr. Pender one day while they were playing in Aerin's room. The boy had a complete set of toy soldiers. Aerin had invented the other name.

The sun was out, and it had warmed up making for a perfect assault on the Nazi scum camping on the far side of the woods near the Shaw Cometary of which was off limits for the boys to enter. They could skirt the outside, however, allowing them to flank the enemy unseen. Sergeant York always came up with the best plans.

The boys donned their winter jackets, and after Aerin handed out the cap guns and plastic helmets, Aerin called to his mom that they were going out.

"Be careful and stay away from the cemetery, ok?" She called back. "And don't go near the stone wall either."

"We will," Aerin answered, and they ran outside.

The stone wall ran the entire length of the Shaw Estate, separating it from the Atlantic Ocean below. Years ago, Bill had extended its height after the death of Cathy's best friend, who had fallen from the widow's watch. It had been a dreadful occurrence and confirmed that Shaw Manor was, indeed, haunted at the time. None of the children had been born yet, but Bill thought it prudent to have a mason extend the wall, as it was too easy for someone to climb over it or even trip and fall, tumbling seventy feet to the rocks below. The cliff on the opposite side of the wall provided a spectacular yet deadly view of the Atlantic below. There was no place to stand on the ocean side, as the structure had been erected directly on the edge of the cliff.

"C'mon," Aerin instructed. "We'll take the path up to the cemetery, then sneak along its fence so we can surprise the Hun when they least expect it."

"Ready, Serge!" Logan acknowledged with a salute.

Aerin led the way as the two began creeping up the pathway, hiding behind trees as they went.

"Need help with the dishes?" Cathy asked Vicky. She had seen Doug out and had gone back to the kitchen for a fresh cup of coffee, which she noted her daughter had just made.

"Nah, I'm done here anyway," She answered, taking the pot from Cathy and pouring herself a cup. The two sat at the kitchen table, busying themselves with small talk, when the phone rang.

"I'll get it," Vicky said, reaching for it behind her chair. "Oh, hi Dad. Hold on, she's right here." She handed the phone to her mom.

"Hey, honey. Anything new up in Bar Harbor?" Cathy listened to her husband.

Vicky could only make out her father's voice, but not what he was saying. She sat content to sip her coffee and listen to her mother.

"Oh, stop, the restaurant did not burn down." Cathy scolded. "You'll give poor Vicky a heart attack."

Vicky rolled her eyes.

Cathy talked with Bill for the next few minutes, then hung up.

"Well?" Vicky was curious.

"Gaea and her friends have left for Van Buren, the restaurant is tented and being fumigated, and your father is going with Bob ice fishing."

"Ice fishing? You are kidding me. I didn't know Dad was the outdoorsy type."

He's not. As far as I know, he's never even been camping. No, something is off. I'm not sure what, but those two are up to something.

Vicky scratched her head. "Beats me what it could be. Maybe with all that's been going on, they want to chill for a couple of days."

"Doesn't add up," Cathy said, counting off items on her fingertips. "One, those two are very nervous about Gaea going up to Van Buren and dealing with the book; two, Bob has been keeping an eye on the restaurant like a hawk; and supposedly your ghost is going to take a look at the Grimoire for some spell to free his dead wife from something."

"Yeah, I can't see them going anywhere with all of that happening. Something is most definitely afoot with those two."

"Well, we only have one person in that house who might know," Cathy said with a grin.

"Dottie." They said together.

"I think she bought it," Bill said, after he hung up the phone. "I don't think she suspects a thing."

Bob looked skeptical. "Bill, what you said didn't even convince me, and Cathy is a brilliant woman. I think she saw right through that lie."

"Well, if she did suspect something, she is not here to do anything about it. We'll be on our way well before she can drive back up to stop us."

"Bill, I wouldn't put it past Cathy to figure out something. We had better get a move on. Henry has your pickup truck packed with the fishing gear as well as what we are taking for our real mission. Cameras, binoculars, recording devices, you know, surveillance equipment. All but this." He said, laying his hand on the steel box.

"The guns."

Bob nodded. "We'll stow them in your bed box. It locks, doesn't it?"

"You bet. It's brand new. I've got the key on my key ring. I have two, so I'll give you one in case we get separated or lose one."

"Shouldn't you two be getting going?" Dottie interrupted them, opening the office door. "The day is wasting."

"Hi, sweetheart," Bob said, going to hug his wife. "How are you feeling this morning?"

"Nervous, you old fool. Now you promised me that you will be careful in Van Buren and keep those kids safe."

Bob looked at Bill. "I told you. In all these years, I have never been able to get anything past Dottie."

Bill laughed. "Dottie, we're just going to keep an eye on them and get them out of there if things start getting dodgy. We don't plan on letting them know we are even there."

Dottie walked up to Bill and looked him straight in the eyes. "Bill, are you that gullible or just foolish?"

"What do you mean, Dottie?" He asked.

Bob answered for her, "Bill, Gaea is a psychic medium."

"Oh, crap," Bill said taken aback. There was a very good chance that she would know when they arrived if she didn't know their plans already. "She will know we are there."

"Don't worry about it, Bill." Bob sounded reassuring. "If she cared, she would have complained about it when we came up with the idea. Let's go. Check-in time is 11 am at the Loose Moose Hotel.

Seraphina took another shower after checking in and decided to explore the town. With her father gone to run his errand, she had some time to spare.

To her amusement, most of the shops she browsed had altered their inventory for the upcoming festival to feature knick-knacks of paganism and witchcraft, along with other items to ensure the revelers had what they needed to celebrate. She discovered one store, Crosby's Five and Dime, that offered a selection of fresh herbs that she recognized immediately were not meant for consumption. They were intended for use in witchcraft. Whether or not they had been added for the festival, someone connected to the store was a witch.

The festival was set to kick off the following evening, and vendors were starting to set up along the street. A few were already selling their goods. Vicky stopped at a hot dog stand, where an older man was busy tending to hot dogs and sausages that slowly rotated on roasting rods. Seraphina, who hadn't eaten since yesterday, ordered two hot dogs, smothering them with mustard and relish while skipping the ketchup. After paying him, she walked across the street and sat on a bench. She watched as cars passed by, surmising that traffic must have increased with the upcoming festivities. She also noticed the significant police presence in the area, many in different uniforms indicating the various precincts they belonged to. She counted five already, including local, state, and town names she didn't recognize, plus one from Canada. She hadn't anticipated the police being there and hoped they wouldn't cause any issues while searching for the Grimoire. Seraphina pushed the thought aside; they were there for crowd control, not to look for a coven engaged in secret business.

She finished the second hot dog and tossed the cardboard container it had been served in into a nearby green trash can. "Van Buren Recycles" was neatly painted on the side of the bin. As she began to stand, a car drove slowly past her, its windows blacked out. For some reason, the car caught her attention. She brushed it off and resumed her exploration of the town.

The farmhouse was relatively easy to find, and Gunther pulled into the driveway just as an old pickup truck was pulling out. Two boys with fiery red hair sat in the back. The elderly man driving waved at him, and he waved back before proceeding to park his car. As he parked, he noticed an elderly woman standing at the front door watching him. He assumed it was Sharon Burpee, and he climbed out to approach her.

"Ms. Burpee," he said, forcing a smile and extending his hand.

She looked at it, ignored the gesture, and turned. "Come."

He followed her into the old farmhouse, and once inside, he noticed its décor, which was neatly arranged as one might expect. Items collected over the years she had lived there included family photos and other belongings typical of an elderly woman. There was no indication suggesting that a powerful witch practicing black magic resided in the old house.

She led him to a sitting room decorated in a similar fashion to the last one and motioned for him to take a seat.

"There has been a slight change of plans. High Priest Sergev and Archmage Isobel Argante will be here shortly. We are instructed to wait for their arrival before we begin. I alone will greet them. You are to remain here."

The woman was all business and offered no pleasantries as she left him. His dealings with the coven had been limited, originating from the Grimoire. Magister Burpee had contacted him because of the upcoming Black Sabbath. He realized that she might know about the Grimoire, but he intended to keep that information to himself. Let Sergev bring it up, not him.

Gunther didn't have to wait long as she led Sergev and Argante into the sitting room. He stood to greet them.

"Sit." Isobel commended.

Gunther sat.

Sergev looked at his Magister. "Tea, if you would be so kind." He asked Sharon.

She nodded and left for the kitchen.

Sergev and Isobel sat down in opposite armchairs, leaving an uneasy Gunther sitting on a settee between them. A few tense moments passed as they sat in silence.

"Have you any news of the Grimoire?" Sergev asked, taking a teacup from Sharon.

"Not as of yet, my lord. We have only just arrived," Gunther answered. Obviously, Sharon Burpee had been informed about the search for the book.

"We?" Isobel broke in.

"Yes, my daughter Seraphina. She is a member of the coven and is familiar with the Grimoire. Gunther filled her in on her separate search for the book, which had been unknown to him until it was discovered quite unexpectedly in the woods of Bar Harbor. He nearly struck her unconscious with a spell when he realized who his opponent was. As it turned out, she had outsmarted him and escaped until their meeting in the chapel. Unfortunately, the Grimoire was not there. An unknown individual had removed it.

Sergev nodded with the explanation. "Your daughter is now to be trusted?"

"Yes. She has sworn her aid to find the Grimoire and return it to you. She no longer seeks it for herself."

"That is yet to be seen," Argante said, standing and walking to a window. She scanned the grounds for anything out of the ordinary. A barn sat stoically some distance from the house, and a young man whom she presumed was Kenneth, the great-grandnephew of their host, was closing up its doors. Satisfied, she returned to her seat.

"I can assure you, Archmage Argante, she is subservient to me and will do what I tell her," Gunther said, accepting the cup of tea from Sharon.

The room fell silent as Sergev sat deep in thought. Isobel was used to him and his long thought processes; the other two were not and grew nervous.

"The girl may be useful to us," Sergev said at last, easing the tension that had been building. "She knows of the Grimoire and undoubtedly knows of the power it contains within its bindings. She will be able to recognize it if it presents itself."

"Presents itself?" Gunther asked, confused. He wondered how an inanimate object could do such a thing.

"The Grimoire is more than just a book, my young warlock," Sergev began. It was forged in the depths of Hell by a mighty demon who goes by the name Belphegor the Defiler. The book has been separated from its master and seeks reunification. Make no mistake, the Grimoire will do anything within its power to make that happen. It is deceitful, like its master, and will purposely hide from human eyes to evade capture. I believe that it is hiding as we speak. It is either in hiding or has been bewitched by someone who wishes it not to be found. Either way, I intend to locate it with you, and now with your daughters' help.

"Can you tell when it comes out from hiding, my Lord?" Gunther asked, fascinated with what he was being told.

"I will be able to if I am looking. You see, I have certain abilities that most do not."

"There is a reason that Lord Sergev has risen to the position of High Priest of the Obsidian Circle," Isobel said, taking a sip of her tea.

I believe I understand. My wife and daughter possess abilities. They are psychic mediums, or they were in the case of my wife. She is deceased.

"Yes, dead because of her deceit and her greed. I was the one who took her life. It was unfortunate, as she was a powerful necromancer in our coven. That is no longer a concern. What's done is done—only the Grimoire matters, Gunther. We must find the demon's book. Are you loyal to me or do you dwell on a dead woman?"

"I am loyal, Lord. I lost her when she still lived." Gunther replied.

"What is the plan?" Sharon Burpee asked Sergev, changing the subject.

Once again, there were a few moments of tense silence as he seemed to contemplate. Finally, he spoke and laid out a carefully planned, systematic method to find the Grimoire. An hour later, he had finished formulating it, giving orders to Gunther as well as instructions he wished Isobel to relay to the coven members when they arrived.

"And one more thing, warlock," Sergev said, addressing Gunther. "If Seraphina betrays us, it will be you who kills her."

Gunther swallowed hard and nodded his assent. "Let us hope it does not come to that."

"Let us hope," Sergev replied dryly.

The assault had been successful, and Aerin proclaimed another victory over the despised enemy of freedom. He and Logan raised their flag at the enemy German encampment, a blue pillowcase Aerin had borrowed from the linen closet, and began their march home. It was lunchtime, and Vicky was cooking.

CHAPTER 11
A Rival & A Broken Spell

Bill and Bob arrived at the Loose Moose and quickly checked in, hoping to avoid his daughter, whom he assumed had come to town before they did. They were whisked up to their suite, where the two men sat on the beds, testing the firmness. Both seemed satisfied, and Bill began to unpack his suitcase.

"Don't," Bob said.

"Huh?" Bill asked.

"We might have to make a quick exit from this town, and I for one don't want to have to take time to pack."

"Right," Bill said and put the shirt back. Let's unpack the surveillance equipment instead."

Bob picked up the case, placed it at the foot of his bed, and opened it. Carefully, he laid out the contents and examined them. "I'm hungry," he said, pausing to look over a camera. "We have to eat, so we're going to have to venture out sooner rather than later."

"People will be at the festival, and I am assuming that is where the kids will be," Bill considered. "We can eat here at the hotel or nearby. We do know that they are not staying at this hotel."

"True, and what you said would seem the proper plan of action." Bob agreed, "But we also need to familiarize ourselves with the town and its surroundings, again risking exposure."

"A double-edged sword, but necessary. How else can we keep an eye on them?"

"We have to find them first."

"I feel like the Hardy Boys," Bill said with a laugh, referring to the fictional sleuths created by Nancy Drew.

"Yeah. I read the books when I was a kid as well. My father tried to get her as a client for his publishing house, but she was committed and wouldn't budge. I met her once when I was very young."

"This is great! But it's quite early, and I'm feeling hungry now. How about we check out the restaurant downstairs?"

"Good idea. We can plan our next more over dinner."

As the two walked down the stairs, a strange-looking girl passed by them. She had white hair, and Bill could have sworn her eyes were black. She scurried past and disappeared into a room down the hall.

"Our neighbor," Bill said sarcastically, and continued walking down.

"This was a great idea, Gaea," Himiko said as Gaea pulled into the motel and parked.

"Well, we need a place to carry out our plan, and why not do it comfortably, an hour from Van Buren? We are close enough for your spell to be effective, and I will have the peace to contact Douglas."

"Perfect," Marc said, jumping out of the Jeep and unloading their luggage.

"I'll go get us a room," Gaea said.

"Hey, look. They have a mini-golf course." Marc tossed his backpack over his shoulder. "Too bad it's winter, or we could play a round."

Gaea shook her head and looked around. Snow was still predominant everywhere, but she could see Big Rock Mountain in the distance. She and Marc had gone skiing at the resort located there two years ago. "When things were normal," she mused. Her thoughts were interrupted by the return of Himiko, holding a set of keys.

"Room 8," she said cheerfully. It was somewhat expensive, probably because of the festival. We were fortunate to secure this room, as they had a last-minute cancellation right when we arrived. Lucky, I suppose.

"Now that's funny!" Marc exclaimed, pointing to the sign that advertised the Motel.

Gaea and Himiko turned and looked. Gaea read it out loud while Himiko began laughing. "The Broomstick Motel. We can't seem to get away from it!"

"It probably doesn't have anything to do with witchcraft," Himiko said, trying to control the remaining giggles.

"Then what's the hitch for?" Marc said clearly, losing it.

Indeed, there was a hitching post near room number 9, and beside a maid's cart leaning against it stood a broom.

"When the witches fly in, they can tie up their brooms!" Marc continued, causing them all to lose control with laughter.

"I have got to take a picture of that with the motel sign," Himiko said, pulling her camera out of her backpack. Get into the picture, you two."

Marc and Gaea posed as Himiko snapped a couple of shots.

"Perfect!" Himiko exclaimed.

"Ok, let's get settled in." Gaea was anxious to get prepared for the evening.

Marc unlocked the door, and they walked inside.

A bus transformed into an RV arrived at the designated campsite for festival-goers intending to camp during the event. It featured a black exterior adorned with yellow pinstriping, and its windows were darkened, preventing anyone from seeing inside. In the back, an Asian man observed the flurry of activity as people set up their camping spots. The RV's driver skillfully navigated to the back of the lot, parking at a respectful distance from the other campers.

Inside the RV, the man had a distinct reason for attending the festival, and he wasn't there to celebrate the Winter Solstice. He could sense Grimoire nearby; it tugged at his instincts, yet remained just out of reach. Another matter weighed on his mind as well, something he aimed to resolve. The Archmage he had once fought over the Grimoire was also in Van Buren searching for the elusive book. He had unfinished business with Boris Sergev and was determined to settle their score. Sergev's life would be the price.

High Priest Aoki adjusted his black robe around his muscular frame as if to fend off the cold that did not penetrate the RV's interior. A clan member approached and stood before him. "Lord, we have arrived in Van Buren. Tachi has chosen an acceptable place for the RV away from people. I believe we will have the privacy that you desire."

The man was in his mid-thirties and of Asian descent, as was his master. High Priest Aoki, a man who appeared much younger than his actual age, allowed only witches and warlocks of Asian descent to join his coven, ruling it with an iron fist. He tolerated nothing less than complete subservience; to refuse meant a swift death at the hands of the Necromancer.

"Very well. Send out two Magi to scout the area and have them return within three hours. Go with them, and as you question people, do not mention the Grimoire or anything about the Order of Mazoku. Our coven must remain secret and not be discovered by the Obsidian Circle until the time is right to do so. By then, I will have disposed of Sergev and his companion, Argante; we will possess the Grimoire and take our leave. Avoid law enforcement at all costs. Do not make yourself suspicious. You are here solely to participate in the festivities. Understood?"

"Understood." Tachi bowed and took his leave to select the two magi who would accompany him.

Aoki leaned back, closed his eyes, and thought of his daughter. He was grateful that she was away at university and would not become entangled in these dealings. Things could get messy, and she was not powerful enough to defend herself or be of assistance. She was not ready to join the coven. For now, Himiko was safe, and it brought him comfort.

"I thought as much." Cathy was angry. Not because Bill had gone to Van Buren to look after Gaea, but because he felt he had to lie to her. Yes, she would have complained about what they intended to do, but she would have eventually given in. She felt more at ease knowing that Bill and Bob were nearby and ready to jump in to help if needed. Calling Dottie was always the easiest way to find out the truth and what was happening. She had an inkling that something was wrong when she spoke with Bill but decided not to press him. Dottie was sure to know what her husband was up to, so she would, in turn, find out what Bill was up to. Upon learning of her husband's scheme, she had laughed about it with Dottie, but when it came right down to it, she was pissed off.

Cathy considered calling her husband to curse him out; however, after some thought, she decided against it. What they were trying to accomplish was admirable, but it could also be dangerous. Her involvement might confuse their plans. There would be plenty of time to chastise him once he came home. A week on the couch was a must. Cathy smiled and decided to drive to the antique shop to check on things and pass the time. After a quick check with Vicky, who didn't need anything from the market, she left Vicky in charge of the boys and headed for Kennebunk Port.

"It's nearly time," Gaea said, pulling the grimoire out of an old satchel. "Himiko, how long will it take to cast the spell on the book?"

"No more than a few seconds. It's a very simple identification spell that witches use to uncover information about items. It will cause the book to exude magical properties that should last about an hour. After that, I can cast the spell again if needed."

"One time should be enough if Douglas keeps his word. And we don't want to give ourselves away; that would put an end to everything we are trying to do."

"There is a diner across the street that seems to be," Marc said, putting on his coat. "I think I'll get a bite to eat while you two do this. I don't need to be in the way. Gaea needs to concentrate, and I would be another distraction."

"Thanks," Gaea said. Yes, I need to focus on this. Can you get Himiko and me something to go? Like a burger?"

"Chicken sandwich for me," Himiko said, taking the book from Gaea.

"Make that two."

"Three," Marc added. "That's what I was planning on getting for myself. OK, call me on my cell when I can come back."

"Will do," Gaea sat down on the floor in a meditative stance, crossing her legs. Himiko placed the book on a small desk centered against the wall across from the bed. Marc quietly left the room.

"Ready?" Himiko asked.

"I think so. Cast the spell on the book."

At the last moment, Himiko decided to use a different spell, one that would mimic the aura of the actual Grimoire. The spell wouldn't be exact, but she intended to let it last for only an hour. She was convinced it would be enough to whet the appetite of those who sought it—enough to prompt them to start searching for the magical signal. She chanted quietly, manipulating the very fabric of the mystic aura, calling forth the power that would bewitch the book. After a few minutes, she sat back and took a deep breath.

"It's done. Do your thing, Gaea."

The psychic medium nodded and began to reach out to Douglas.

In Cape Neddick, as Logan lay sleeping, Aerin reached out with his abilities and made contact easily. He could see the Grimoire and would be able to monitor the ghost when it manifested. If there were any issues, he would run down to the root cellar and interrupt whatever the spirit was doing and attempt to stop it.

In the depths of the root cellar, Douglas appeared next to the Grimoire. With a simple thought, he reached through the iron box, breaking the spell that Himiko had placed on it. The aura of the Grimoire was now visible to those who sought it. Slipping into deep concentration, he used his mind to search through the book. Somewhere within its bindings lay the key—a passage to complete a spell that would break the curse placed upon his wife. He would find it, no matter how long it took. The only thing that mattered was defeating the demonic curse.

CHAPTER 12
Where There Is Evil...

A hodgepodge of police officers gathered at the Van Buren Police Department, which consisted of a single building with three rooms: Sheriff Daniel Drisko's office, a reception area, and a solitary jail cell in the back. Van Buren didn't experience much crime, if any. The Van Buren police force included Drisko and two deputies, one of whom was on maternity leave, so he appreciated the extra help provided by outside law enforcement.

The Winter Solstice drew a large crowd, according to the event organizer. The last significant gathering the town hosted was the annual livestock fair, which attracted interest only from locals. He knew everyone who attended the event. The Winter Solstice Festival was enormous and covered a wide area in and around Van Buren. Drisko wasn't taking any chances with things getting out of control. He had even notified the FBI office in Bangor just in case they were needed.

The first official law enforcement briefing was held in the parking lot next to the station. Two hundred officers from a dozen surrounding towns were assembled, including four from neighboring Canada. Across town, a similar, though smaller, gathering was occurring for volunteer firemen who had responded to the call to stand by if they were needed. Sheriff Drisko believed he had everything under control. There would be three days of peace if he had anything to say about it. The last thing he needed was a crowd invading his town and trashing it.

What worried him the most were the crowds who came solely for the three-day music festival that coincided with the Winter Solstice. He understood the need for entertainment, but most of the people attending the festival didn't care one bit about celebrating the Winter Solstice. He recognized many of the bands scheduled to perform, and more than a few were heavy metal bands; he also knew the types of fans associated with that genre. Heathens, the lot of them. In his view, a good Christian shouldn't listen to such music. However, he didn't dictate what happened in town. That responsibility belonged to the town selectmen, who focused solely on dollar signs. The woman handling the event had assured him not to worry and that everything would run smoothly. After all, this sort of event occurred all over the country without issues. The sheriff thought otherwise, and he intended to manage the situation accordingly, regardless of what the event organizer had told him.

Another thing that annoyed him was that the sergeant of the Maine State Police might want to be in charge of policing the event, and he looked like just a kid, no more than twenty years old. He would be damned if he let some snot-nosed punk tell him how to run his town. Things would be done his way, or the staties could pack it up and go home. He could manage.

As it turned out, the State Police were content to take up their positions just outside town and would monitor what came in and went out of Van Buren. If needed, they were a stone's throw away.

After the hour-long meeting, all factions had received their assigned duties, which included crowd control, policing the neighborhoods, managing traffic and parking, overseeing the makeshift holding area being set up at the high school gymnasium, and various other tasks. The sheriff would oversee the command post from the comfort of his office, although he would be available to make final decisions on any matters that might arise in the field of operations.

With the police situation resolved to his satisfaction, the only thing left to do was go across town and ensure that the fire chief wasn't neglecting his responsibilities. Sheriff Drisko didn't trust the prick any further than he could throw him.

Beverly Shatts hung up the phone, mumbling her frustrations to herself. Sheriff Drisko was a nuisance, but she had to deal with him while the event was in progress. She felt relieved that he had assured her both the police and the fire department were prepared to handle anything that might arise—one more task checked off her list. Most of her to-do list had been finished. The event was set to kick off, although it was a couple of weeks behind schedule due to the weather. She had reservations about the success of an event tied to a specific calendar date. It was kind of like postponing Christmas. She hoped that people would still show up, and this year's winter solstice would be her best-organized one yet.

She left her temporary office at the town library and walked to her car. She wanted a cup of coffee and a donut, and Tim Horton's across the border had the best around. She started her car and headed toward the border.

For almost an hour, the essence of Douglas Blanchard flowed through the Grimoire until he found the passage essential for liberating his wife from the demon's eternal grasp. It spanned only fifteen words yet held the crucial component of a spell to nullify the curse. Drawing on his memory, he commenced the incantation.

Boris Sergev recognized the aura of the Grimoire immediately, but it was also perplexing. There appeared to be two, and he could not determine which one was the book he sought. The signals were not aligned and were many kilometers apart. It would take him time to identify the location of the Grimoire, as a mistake could have serious consequences. Others were searching for it as well, making time crucial. He could send a coven member to the location once he knew it, but there was another concern. Most people with power had yet to arrive. He only had the old woman, her grand-nephew Gunther, and his daughter. He dared not send Isobel as she was needed by his side. In any event, Sergev would have to wait until he revealed the Grimoire's location.

"The Grimoire is near." Sharon Burpee said, handing Sergev a fresh cup of tea. "I can feel it."

"You are correct. But do you feel the other?"

"The other is a diversion, but I cannot tell which is which." She said, sitting down across from the High Priest.

Neither can I. It will take me time to differentiate between the two. Someone does not want us to know what is happening with the Book of Belphegor. They are trying to deceive us.

Isobel stood by the fireplace, which was ablaze, casting a warm glow around the room. "We do not have the witches or warlocks to send yet, Sergev. To do so would be foolish."

The High Priest nodded. "Yes, I have considered that. It would be folly to send those that we have now. They are not strong enough to handle who or what they may encounter on such a task."

Gunther sat ignored in the room. He knew they were discussing him and his daughter, Seraphina. He believed he was powerful enough to handle perhaps one adversary, but not a group that would undoubtedly be sent from a rival coven, if there was one. He could not dismiss the possibility.

"My Lord, we cannot dismiss the fact that another coven may be searching for the Grimoire for themselves and may be in town as we speak," Gunther spoke up.

"I have considered that as well, warlock," Sergev said. "It is that possibility that keeps me from sending you to investigate either of the locations once they are identified. Either way, I would not send your daughter. She is too weak."

Gunther nodded and fell silent.

"Perhaps I should go into town with Kenneth and have a look around. If there is a coven, I will find it." Isobel offered.

"Do so," Sergev commanded.

Isobel bowed and left to find her companion. Her expertise would undoubtedly uncover a rat in the trash if one had entered Van Buren.

Gaea, along with Aerin, had been monitoring the Grimoire when the aura it radiated disappeared. Gaea hoped that Douglass had recast the protection spell on it and completed his task. She sensed no presence of the ghost and assumed he had left the root cellar. It would be up to Aerin to check if the Grimoire was still safe and hidden using his abilities. She picked up her cell phone and dialed her brother's number.

Himiko helped Gaea to her feet. "I'll go get Marc." She said and left the room. "I'm hungry."

Douglas Blanchard had not only kept his word but had cast a potent spell on the book that would hide it more effectively than the one Himiko had used. The book was there, safely locked in the iron box, and Aerin was able to detect its faint aura before Douglas bewitched it. He breathed a sigh of relief, then jumped when his phone rang.

"Dammit Gaea!" He answered. "You scared the living crap out of me."

"Is it safe?" She asked.

"Yes, safe and locked away like it was never touched," he told her. "I could tell because I could *see* Douglas doing it with my mind. But I don't sense it now."

"I think Douglas cast a more powerful spell on it than Himiko had. I can't sense it either. I'm glad it's safe. Keep checking anyway, ok?"

"I will. Be careful, sis." Aerin hung up.

Himiko and Marc returned as Gaea hung up with her brother.

"It's safe." She told them. "Himiko, you had better break the spell on our book before someone tracks it here. We don't need visitors."

"You got it." she said, and went to the grimoire on the table, where she began to chant.

Marc passed out the food he had bought at the diner. "I'm glad that's over with." He said, handing her a Coke. "I think I might sleep a little better."

"We are not staying," Gaea said as Himiko finished with the book. "It's too dangerous to stay. What if someone did figure out where this book is and is on their way to it? No, we are driving on to Van Buren and checking into our room there. Then I, for one, will sleep better."

"Good idea, Gaea," Himiko said, taking a bite of her sandwich. "No need to take chances.

"Ok then. While you two stuff your faces, I'll put the luggage back into the Jeep." Marc said, picking up his duffle bag. "We should be in Van Buren within the hour."

"Let's do it," Gaea said, swallowing the last of her chicken sandwich.

The Order of Mazoku was not to be trifled with; they were a coven determined to pursue their goals without interruption. Anyone who obstructed their path often faced severe consequences, even death. Their study of black magic had a singular purpose rooted in malevolence. They devoted themselves entirely to their High Priest, willing to sacrifice their lives for him, and he served only Belphegor the Defiler. Human sacrifices were a common occurrence in their rituals, as well as in those of their Black Sabbath.

The Grimoire held high value for Belphegor. Thus, it was of the utmost importance to High Priest Aoki, and he would stop at nothing until he had it in his possession. Everything else was secondary. The Demon had commanded him, and he would succeed.

The Grimoire had made itself known, and he could sense its calling. Confusion arose as there seemed to be two conflicting signals. He knew at once that one of them was a red herring meant to deceive. He had discerned the location of one of them, which was no more than an hour away, and immediately sent three of his most powerful Magi to investigate and retrieve the magical book if it was there. If not, they would extract the Grimoire's location from the deceivers and destroy them, whoever they might be. They would pay for their insolence. If the Mage could not discover the other location, Aoki would, given time, albeit time was something he did not have.

As the three Magi drove toward the area where the book had been found, they passed a nondescript Jeep. Inside, an unremarkable book was lying in the back seat. It was an ordinary tome, except that it was bound in human skin.

"Well, they accomplished the first step," Bill told Bob after a brief chat with his son. It seems that our ghost has done what he set out to do and left the Grimoire behind, wrapped in a protective spell."

"Bill," Bob looked around the room. "Perhaps it's better if we don't mention the, ah, item by name. There's no telling who might be in earshot."

"Right. Stupid me." Bill replied, heeding Bob's caution. "This town is no doubt crawling with witches and warlocks. No telling who is who."

"And it's not up to us to deal with the item. That is for Gaea's group. We are only here as backup and to ensure their safety."

"You're right, Bob. How do you think we should proceed?"

"I'm going to proceed to devour this steak to start," Bob said, cutting into the inch-thick piece of meat. "Then, I think we should look around town to get our bearings. After that, we should find the festival grounds and explore them. We need to figure out where the kids will spend most of their time and locate places where we can keep an eye on them."

"Yeah. I noticed that there is also a concert happening in town, and I'm guessing it will be at a different location. Freaking outdoor concert in the winter."

"It's probably part of the festival," Bob reasoned. "I would doubt that they will be wasting their time listening to music. There is too much at stake."

Bill cut into his porterhouse. "I will be more at ease once we establish their movements and find out what they are up to."

"Agreed," Bob said. "We will need to wear our parkas and keep our heads covered with the hoods. We don't need to get discovered by them."

"We'd better get started right after we eat."

"Bon appétit," Bob said, raising his glass of soda pop in a toast. "To success."

"To success," Bill answered.

High Priest Sergev had just discovered the first possible location of the Grimoire when both energy emanations ceased. He hadn't had enough contact to discern the location of the second. He was back to square one and would have to do things the hard way. He sighed, closed his eyes, and sat back on the couch. Perhaps Isobel would turn up a clue.

High Priest Aoki was not so disheartened when the two auras vanished. He had the location of one of them, and if needed, would soon have the second. He retreated to his private room in the rear of the RV. It was time to converse with the underworld.

CHAPTER 13
Exploration & A Change of Hotel

Gaea, Himiko, and Marc stood at the front desk of their hotel in disbelief. The room they had reserved was unavailable because the hotel had overbooked. To their relief, however, the hotel found them a room at another hotel down the street. The Loose Moose had a last-minute cancellation, so they could have that room. It was on the first floor and had two beds, which suited the trio perfectly. It was better than having no room at all in the winter.

As it turned out, the Loose Moose was a nicer hotel than the one that had been reserved for them by Bob. It even had a restaurant to Marc's delight.

As the trio settled in, Marc suggested they explore the town, but both Gaea and Himiko were too exhausted from the day's events. Tomorrow would mark the start of their quest. After all, people were still arriving for the Winter Solstice festival, so there was no point in covering the same ground twice.

"Where do you think we should start?" Himiko asked, folding down her bed. She had been the first to shower and was wearing her Bugs Bunny pajamas, which Marc immediately wanted a pair of himself. Gaea laughed at the sight of her boyfriend dressed in cartoon characters.

"We can start at breakfast in the restaurant," Marc suggested.

"That's a good idea," Gaea said, wrapping her wet hair in a towel. We can get a better idea of how exactly we will do this. We can't start walking up to people and asking them about the book."

"No. That would not be wise." Himiko agreed. "We would have every unsavory wizard beating on our door if we did. I, for one, don't need that headache. It's also hazardous to our health."

"Any hot water left?" Marc asked, picking up his shower bag.

"Plenty," Gaea answered.

"I'll be right back," Marc said and stepped into the bathroom.

"Himiko, when we were driving here from the motel, we passed a car."

Himiko's interest was piqued. "And?"

"I sensed that the individuals inside were searching for the Grimoire, and they were not friendly people. I sensed evil."

"Wow. That is not good news, Gaea. The spell I cast on the book in that room must have worked exceptionally well. I'm glad I broke the spell quickly."

"I'm glad we got out of there. There is no telling what might have happened if we had stayed."

"If they were unsavory wizards or witches, I am sure it would not have been pretty. Well, they have no way of tracking us," Himiko stated. "I signed the register with a fictitious name and address. Should they try to find who last rented that room, they will be searching for a Mr. and Mrs. Jones from Orlando, Florida."

Gaea laughed as Marc stepped into the room.

"What did I miss?" Marc asked, fluffing his pillow and crawling into bed.

"Nothing," Gaea said, hopping into bed next to Marc. "Let's get some sleep."

Himiko turned off the light.

Earlier that day, when Gaea was driving her friends from the motel to Van Buren, Bill and Bob had finished eating and were taking advantage of the remaining daylight by exploring the town. It was expected that Bob would lead Bill into a bookstore, where the owner recognized the author immediately.

"You're a real piece of crap, you know that Bob?" Bill said as the woman stepped out from behind the sales counter and approached them.

"The item is a book, Bill. I thought this was a good place to look around and listen," Bob explained.

The woman was in her fifties, short in stature, with graying hair and horn-rimmed glasses. "Hello!" she exclaimed. "I'd recognize that face anywhere!"

Bill feigned a smile. "Hello." He said politely.

"Who would have thought it! The famous Bill Pender is here in our little town. How wonderful!"

Bob tried to suppress his laughter while pretending to examine a book on the shelf beside him.

"Yes," Bill lied. "I came up here for the Winter Solstice festival. I might get some ideas for a new story."

"There is not much excitement in this little village," the woman said.

A customer had approached the counter with a book in hand, waiting to pay for it. Bill hoped it was not one of his. He didn't come to Van Buren to do a book signing. He pointed toward the woman. "It seems you have a customer."

"Oh, yes. Thank you!"

The two men watched her scurry away, and Bill sighed in relief.

"I hope that is not going to happen wherever we go in this town." He sounded concerned. "If it gets out that I'm here, it will certainly get back to Gaea, and our plans would be spoiled."

"That is true," Bob said, motioning toward the ongoing sale. The store owner had already informed her customer of Bill's presence. "Let's get out of here."

The two made a quick exit and disappeared into the growing crowd on the street. A light rain had started to fall, and the two pulled hoods over their heads.

"Let's head over to the festival grounds," Bob suggested. "There will be fewer people, and we can formulate our plans. Most of the vendor stalls will be set up, so we can figure out the lay of the land, so to speak."

"Sounds like a plan. Let's go."

Kenneth drove Isobel to Van Buren, as she had requested, and parked the car at Shaw's, the only grocery store located just off Main Street. She made him promise to go home and return in precisely three hours to pick her up. She did not want the fledgling warlock to be in the way while she did her job. The chance of uncovering any information was slim, as the day was nearly at an end, and there were still people who had yet to arrive. She was concerned about the actual witches and warlocks who predominantly practiced black magic, as well as any sign of a coven, whether it was a rival or not. Anyone could be searching for the Grimoire if they had the abilities to find it. A garden-variety witch who didn't practice actual magic would not even know of the book's existence, let alone have the power to fight for it. However, such a person might have come across the Grimoire by chance. At this stage, any information could be helpful to the Arch-Mage. If there was any information, Isobel intended to uncover it.

She watched Kenneth drive away, then walked toward the main street that separated the town. With the festival approaching, the street was filled with people wandering back and forth, popping in and out of the many shops. It was nearing dinner time, and the street vendors were busy selling hot dogs, hamburgers, and other fast food. Isobel was not hungry.

Isobel had limited information to act on. One person of interest was a young and powerful psychic medium. While her abilities could be advantageous, they also posed a potential threat to Isobel's quest. The medium could sense another psychic, but if Isobel attempted to use her powers, the medium would become aware of her. By casting a protection spell before arriving in town, she could safeguard herself from the medium's mental probing. It was uncertain whether this medium was a witch, but she traveled alongside a witch of unknown origin, who was presumed to be weak; Isobel remained cautious about that assumption. Isobel viewed every potential adversary as formidable and possibly deadly, so she would move forward with care.

Isobel decided to start by visiting the four hotels in town. It was logical to assume that her quarry would check into one of them upon arriving. Unless, of course, they had arrived in an RV, which she had seen many of since coming to town. All of them seemed to drive through and then out of Van Buren, possibly heading to a camping area—something else she would have to investigate.

The first hotel she entered was the Van Buren Arms, a small two-story building with a sign in the window that read, "No Vacancy." After a brief conversation with a young man at the front desk, she dismissed the possibility of it accommodating the psychic medium or the witch. She wandered around the lobby for a few moments, searching with her abilities, before walking out. There was no one of interest nearby. A visit to two more locations yielded the same result.

She was struggling to focus on whom she was searching for among the many people wandering about town. Each of them had individual thoughts, and most came to her as a jumble. Discerning a single train of thought was nearly impossible. She would need to be very close to either of the two to identify them, and Isobel did not have time for a random encounter.

As luck would have it, her conversation with a desk clerk at the Loose Moose provided some information.

"Yes, we have had four parties of young people check in this afternoon. I can't give you the room numbers for privacy reasons, I'm sure you understand," he explained. "I can, however, tell you that one was a party of two girls and a boy, another was of two girls, and the other two check-ins were accompanied by their parents."

Isobel thanked the man and left the hotel. She didn't need him to tell her the room numbers in question; she had plucked the information from his mind. She did not have concrete evidence that either of the two parties was who she was searching for, and she was not ready to start knocking on doors. She would need backup to do so. Instead, she planned to return tomorrow during the day. The rooms would be empty since the occupants would undoubtedly be out attending festival activities. She would bring the boy Kenneth as a lookout and search the rooms. Perhaps the warlock could be of some use. A quick search through the rooms could reveal much or nothing at all.

There was still an hour and a half before her ride would arrive to pick her up. Her next stops were the shops serving the witches and warlocks attending the festival. Perhaps there was something to learn from them. Isobel fully expected to find mostly the garden variety that had no power whatsoever.

Kenneth was closely monitoring the time. He didn't mind being assigned menial tasks by the coven. He was happy to contribute in any way. Still, he wished for a chance to speak with the High Priest, even if only briefly. Kenneth had told his Auntie that he would not be a nuisance to the visitors and would comply with any requests made of him.

He decided not to drive back to the farm and instead pulled the Buick into a parking spot at the far end of the grocery store lot. He would wait for the Archmage here in town, confident he would be on time to return her to High Priest Sergev. While he waited, he listened to the oldies station on the car radio.

The three Magi quickly handled the situation at the motel where the Grimoire emanation was discovered. After being denied any information about the guests, they resorted to alternative methods to obtain it. It would be well into the morning before the crime scene was identified, and their search of the room yielded no results. The previous occupants had left, with the room key resting on the side table next to the bed as evidence of their departure. Whoever Mr. and Mrs. Jones were, if found, they would not be returning to Florida anytime soon, if at all. They did not get a full description of the couple; the woman was young with dark hair, but the husband remained undescribed. The three Magi started their drive back to High Priest Aoki with limited information and scant news.

The festival grounds, as Bill and Bob had anticipated, were extensive and covered several acres of land. None of it was devoted to parking, and the only vehicles present were those belonging to vendors, support trucks and vans, police, and fire rescue. Managing the entire festival with just the two of them would be nearly an insurmountable task. Bill could not fathom what the concert venue looked like. Fortunately, they would not have to address it unless necessary.

"My God," Bill said, looking around. "Where do we begin?"

"This thing is humungous." Bob agreed, pulling his parka tighter around his body to shield himself from the rain, which was coming down harder. "I think there's some rhyme and reason to how this is laid out. People have to be able to find things; otherwise, it would be one giant mess."

"There has to be a guide to the festival along with what is being offered as well as the planned activities," Bill said. "Now, where do we get hold of one?"

The two examined each other, and Bob shook his head. "The hotel lobby, of course. I think I even saw a display full of them, but I didn't pay close enough attention to realize it and take one."

I didn't even notice it. Well, I don't think we can accomplish much without it. How about we head back and call it a night? The festival kicks off the day after tomorrow, and we need to finalize our plans before then. That gives us tomorrow.

"Sounds good to me," Bob said. "Let's get out of here."

High Priest Aoki received the news from his three Magi without any distress. He suspected that Mr. and Mrs. Smith might be a fictitious name used by the guests at the motel. It was evident that their stay was solely intended to mislead anyone searching for the Grimoire. Furthermore, if only two individuals were involved, one of them was likely a witch or a warlock, although their exact level of magical power remained uncertain.

Aoki pondered other questions that had arisen. Were there only two individuals, or more? Were they in possession of the Grimoire or simply a diversion for someone else? If they did have it, what did they intend to do with it? The Obsidian Circle immediately came to mind. If Sergev had found it, perhaps it was on its way to him. If so, intercepting the book before it reached his hands was imperative; otherwise, there would be bloodshed—and a lot of it. A coven war would be inevitable, and Aoki would not welcome such a conflict. Not here and not now. He was ill-prepared for such a battle, and the Winter Solstice Festival was too public for violence. Police would descend on Van Buren from both the United States and Canada if such a conflict were to occur. No, it was best to continue acquiring the Grimoire as a covert operation, keeping it as far away from the public as possible. He would devise a plan to snatch it from under their very noses if need be and make a quick escape with Belphegor the Defiler's tome of dark magic. Once clear of Maine and the United States altogether, he would then finish his blood bargain with the demon. He would have what was rightfully coming to him, either by his hand or with the help of Belphegor. The Grimoire was a fair exchange for the revenge he sought.

Aoki closed his eyes and dropped into meditation.

Isobel Argante returned to her High Priest with somewhat better information. She had possibly found the psychic medium and the witch who was believed to possess the Grimoire. However, she was unable to sense the book at all and could not confirm whether it was even in Van Buren. She informed him of her plan to return to the town in the morning to search the two rooms she suspected. One, she believed, would be where the medium and the witch resided.

"Your plan seems sound enough," Sergev said to Isobel upon her return. He had retreated to the bedroom provided to him by his hostess. It was simple yet suited his needs, as it had its own bathroom. He inferred from the décor and pictures in the room that she had given him her room for his stay. Isobel was to sleep directly across the hall in a similar room. "Perhaps some information can be obtained from searching it, such as the identity of the two in question."

"There is a third with them, I believe," Isobel said, looking out a single large window set in the wall. "Who he is, I do not know, but I intend to find out. If he is some Archmage, I need to know it. Before I accidentally stumbled on him."

The remaining members of our Coven will arrive tomorrow, and I plan to hold a meeting in the barn to explain why we are here and what our intentions are. I will need you present, along with your skills as a medium. I want to know if anyone plans to be disloyal and attempt to take the Grimoire for themselves. Our efforts require the complete subservience of all members we intend to involve. One rogue witch or warlock could cost us our prize.

"Understood," Isobel said, pouring herself a cup of tea from a pot on the table. She held up the cup, motioning for permission. Sergev waved his hand to continue. "The festival does not begin until the day after tomorrow, so I do have time for further investigation. What time tomorrow do you intend to call the meeting?"

I have informed Magister Burpee to relay the time of 11 pm to everyone. They will need time to arrive and settle in, so I will give them the day to do that. You will also have the day to conduct your investigation. I hope you will uncover something valuable.

"Me as well. I am bringing the boy Kenneth with me to serve as a lookout, if that's okay with you."

"He is far from a boy, Isobel. He holds a degree in medicine from a college. Our last physician died years ago. Perhaps he should be referred to as Mage Kenneth. It seems he has earned the title."

"As you wish, my Lord. He will be addressed as Mage Kenneth Burpee by your order."

CHAPTER 14
Magic Users & Musicians

Kenneth was ecstatic when he was called in to see the High Priest and did his best to stay calm and professional as he faced the older man, listening intently to what he had to say.

"Magister Burpee has seen fit to induct you into the Obsidian Circle, and all that remains is for me to formalize it. There is no ritual or fanfare involved in joining our centuries-old coven, but there is a vow of complete service and sacrifice when called upon. I understand that you have a degree in medicine?" Sergev asked. The young man before him was visibly shaking.

"I have an advanced degree in nursing." Kenneth clarified for the High Priest. "I am not a doctor."

Nursing still requires the understanding of medicine, does it not?"

A basic understanding, yes. I can bind broken bones and treat minor injuries that don't require surgery. I also know how to treat conditions such as the flu and other viruses that can affect people and cause illness. I have a solid understanding of medications and their uses as well.

"Very well. It is within my discretion to bestow upon you the title of Sage. Do you know what a sage does in the Coven, Kenneth?"

He shook his head.

A Sage performs healing magic and offers various services, including the skills you possess. They are called upon when a coven member needs assistance. By accepting this role, you will advance your education in conventional medicine and learn spells as necessary. You might also be asked to travel to fulfill your responsibilities. Do you accept the opportunity I present to you?

Kenneth didn't need to think for more than a second before he blurted out his answer. "I do and will to the best of my ability, my Lord. I will seek to reenter university to obtain a degree as a physician. I will earn a doctorate."

That is up to you to decide whether to continue your schooling. My concern is that you learn the magic required to be a contributing Mage in our coven.

"I will certainly strive to learn every spell, incantation, and the herbs needed to perform my duties."

"Very well. I, Boris Sergev, High Priest of the Obsidian Circle, bestow upon you the rank and title of Sage, along with all the associated rights. You shall be referred to as Sage Kenneth Burpee, Magician Doctor of the Obsidian Circle, by all members of the coven with the respect that the title commands."

Kenneth bowed and waited for Sergev.

After a moment, he spoke. "You may leave me. Archmage Isobel Argante waits for you downstairs for your trip into Van Buren."

Kenneth bowed once more, turned, and left, closing the door behind him. He could hardly wait to share the news of his becoming the Sage of the coven with his Auntie, but it would have to wait since Isobel needed to get to town.

The increase in traffic was clear as Gaea, Marc, and Himiko crossed the street toward the local library. They had picked up a festival brochure from the hotel lobby, and the multi-page document had a lot of useful information, except for the map, which Marc thought was poor. Their options were to find a nearby gas station and hope they sold maps or to visit the town library to check one out. Libraries always carried many maps of their own townships as well as the surrounding areas. The three decided to go to the library, which was within walking distance of the hotel.

They were pleasantly surprised by the size of the building that served as the library, meeting hall, and town museum. Gaea had noted that her mother would have become enthralled with exploring the items on display. Once a history buff, always a history buff, her dad had said more than once. Gaea would have loved to browse through the artifacts if they had had the time, which they did not.

The librarian was a gentleman who looked the part—balding, middle-aged, wearing glasses and a tweed sweater draped over his shoulders, with sleeves tied in the front. He was eager to help them find what they were looking for. Within minutes, the three of them sat at a table with two maps spread out before them. He quickly mentioned that the photocopier, if needed, was ten cents a copy. Gaea smiled and thanked him, then turned her focus to the maps. One was a detailed map showing every street in town, including alleys and cul-de-sacs, though there weren't many. The second was of the outskirts of Van Buren, showing the areas used for the Winter Solstice festival as well as the field where the concert was held. According to the map's legend, they were about six miles apart. One wouldn't interfere with the other.

"This road." Marc pointed to it on the town map. "Runs from the hotel to the edge of town, then it merges with the main road to the festival. We could use it to stay low if needed."

Himiko leaned over, examining the route. "I like it. We don't necessarily want to stay in hiding, but it could be used as an escape route."

Gaea pointed out, "I'm not sure I want to be on a dark back street if we are running from someone." I think I would rather try to lose myself in the crowd.

Marc shrugged. "Good point."

I'm more interested in where we might find help in town, with all the shops. The one thing this town seems to have is shops," Himiko said.

"This is the last town before crossing into Canada," Gaea pointed out. "It would make sense to try to take advantage of the visiting Canadiens before they head back home."

Here's one that looks interesting—Crosby's Five and Dime. Hm, I think I have shopped in stores like this once, looking for herbs. If they do sell herbs, then I would bet a witch owns the store and some of the patrons practice magic. Himiko said, taking a pen and jotting down the address. Of course, we have to go there to know for sure.

"We'll make that our first stop," Gaea agreed. "And this one. It's a fruit and vegetable market. They probably also sell herbs."

Himiko nodded. "Maybe."

Marc had been examining the second map. "I don't think this one will be very helpful. It only shows the field used for the festival. I believe the hotel brochure will be more useful. It lists vendors, what they're selling, and their locations." He rotated the map so the girls could see. "Look, vendors are assigned specific areas based on what they sell. This spot over here," he pointed to a different part of the map, "is for anyone promoting witchcraft. It seems they're covering a lot of ground, like magic, herbs, and even various covens. I think this might be the area where we should spend most of our time."

"I think you're right," Himiko said, reading it for herself. "If there is someone with knowledge of the Grimoire, I think we will find them at the festival."

"Ok, let's do this," Gaea suggested. "Let's spend the day in town today. Tomorrow the festival starts, and we can move our attention fully to the festival grounds."

"Sounds good to me," Himiko said. 'I'm getting low on Mugwort. If they have that, then I know the owner is a witch. Let's head to Crosby's."

As the three walked down the street, Gaea thought of something. "Himiko, you left the book in the Jeep, right? I mean, you didn't take it up to the room."

It's in its bag in the Jeep. I figure it can stay there unless I need it. No point advertising it. It might be mistaken for the real thing. Plus, it might be emitting a little of the spell I put on it. Though, I doubt it.

"Good. I was worried for a minute."

Bob and Bill got up early and headed for the fairgrounds using a convenient side street that ran perpendicular to the main road. Bill found it by accident while looking around the outside of the building. He doubted that his daughter and her friends would use it, as they aimed to be around the crowds, not hide from them. The street led them onto the main road on the outskirts of town, and overall, it was a very short drive to reach the fairgrounds. Bill spotted what looked like a logging road near the festival, pulled onto it, and parked in some bushes, effectively hiding the pickup.

"Well done, Bill," Bob said, putting on his parka. The rain had stopped, but it was still cold, and the goose down jackets made the weather bearable.

"Who the hell goes to a festival in the dead of winter?" Bill asked, zipping up his parka.

"It is Winter Solstice." Bob reminded him. "Not Summer Solstice."

"I think I would have preferred summer to this crap."

Bob took out the brochure and unfolded the map portion. "Let's see, it seems we are here at the northwestern corner of the grounds," he said, showing the map to Bill. "I'm no expert, but I would think that the kids will be searching this area." He said, pointing to an area on the map that was shaded in blue.

Bill looked. "That seems logical. The area is dedicated to witchcraft and various covens. I don't think they would find much help at the food court."

"No. They wouldn't," Bob answered wryly. "We need to identify some areas where we can keep an eye on them."

"Covertly spying on my daughter and her friends. I wish we could have put a wire on her," Bill chuckled, stomping his feet and rubbing his gloved hands together. "I hope they have a heated tent for guests to go into to warm up."

I'm sure they do. Let's get moving. Hopefully, we can find a couple of spots and get out of here. I don't think the kids will show up today. There won't be many people here until tomorrow morning.

"Yeah, just idiots like us that want to pre-scout out the area planning for what they are going to do."

"Grab the camera, will you?"

"Sure," Bill replied, reaching into the truck.

Bob led the way as they entered the grounds.

Isobel sneaked past the desk clerk at the Loose Moose Hotel and headed upstairs to the first room she planned to search. As she neared the door, it swung open, and two young girls stepped out. One of them closed and locked the door behind her. Isobel guessed they were in their mid-twenties and both had blonde hair.

She reached out and touched their minds with hers, then withdrew. These two were not who she was looking for. It had immediately become clear that they were there to attend the concert and had no interest in the festival or witchcraft. Isobel smiled and let the girls walk past, then, turning, she followed them back downstairs and walked to Kenneth.

"They are not who we seek," she said quietly. "Has anyone come or gone in that room?" she asked, pointing to a door a few steps down the short hallway.

He shook his head. "No one."

I will have to assume they've already left. It's a risk, but one I'll take. If you see two girls about the same age as the ones who just passed by, but brunette, delay them until I can exit the room. Understood?

"Understood." Sage Kenneth answered. He maintained a cool, calm demeanor, but inside he was bursting with excited nervousness. He watched as Isobel approached, knocked softly, and after a moment, mouthed something he couldn't hear. She then opened the door and slipped inside.

The room seemed to be occupied by young people. The beds were unmade, and clothing was scattered across the beds and a chair in a messy way. She quickly searched through the backpack and duffle bags on the floor, then checked the bathroom. She left the room, which looked untouched, and locked the door from the inside, pulling it shut.

"I have the information I was looking for. Take me back to the farm. I need to speak with High Priest Sergev."

"Immediately, Archmage Argante." He whispered and followed her out of the hotel.

As they left, two large buses pulled up in front of the Loose Moose Hotel. They side-stepped them and headed for Kenneth's Buick.

Gaea led the way as they left the last shop on their list. They had decided to save Crosby's Five and Dime for last. Although the owner wasn't present, she was indeed a witch and provided herbs to local people practicing witchcraft. When Himiko asked if they sold Mugwort, the girl behind the counter smiled and led her to the back, where she was shown an array of herbs and other magical items not meant for everyday customers.

"I knew immediately you were family." The girl said, pointing out the Mugwort.

"Family?"

"A witch." The girl answered. "You are one, aren't you?"

"Oh, yes, I am," Himiko said happily. "I'm glad that you have this. I was nearly out. Are you the owner of the store?"

No, my mother is. She is a witch as well and very powerful. She will be here tomorrow if you want to stop by and meet her. I'll tell her that a new witch stopped by. She will be thrilled.

"I'm just here for the Winter Solstice festival. I go to school at the University of Maine in Orono."

"Of course you do. My name is Nadora."

"I'm Himiko."

"Are your friends…"

"No, they are not as you said, family. Just my friends from school."

"I see," Nadora said, and a bell chimed at the front of the store. "Customers. Come here, let me ring you up."

A man had entered the store and was looking over the fresh vegetables as Gaea and Marc joined Himiko at the counter.

"Find what you needed?" Gaea asked.

"Yup." She answered as Nadora pushed a small brown envelope toward Himiko.

"Great!" Marc said, tossing a Snickers bar next to it. Gaea held up a bottle of Coke.

Himiko paid for all three, and they left the store, with Himiko telling Marc and Gaea about the owner and Nadora referring to her as a powerful witch. They agreed to come back to the store the next day. A lead was a lead.

Let's head back to the hotel. I'm hungry, and it's time for supper," Marc's stomach was growling, and the girls readily agreed.

"More likely than not, I have identified where the medium and the Night Witch are staying." Isobel had returned to the farm and was briefing Sergev. "And there is another development."

"I see, go on."

"The two women are not alone. They travel with a man."

"A warlock?" Sergev asked.

Unknown, but I wouldn't rule it out. I quickly checked their room at the Loose Moose Hotel," Isobel continued. "One of the bags had herbs and a spell book. But there was no sign of the Grimoire. I did a mental scan as well, but couldn't find anything."

"And how do you know there is a man who travels with them?"

"There was a shaving kit in the lavatory that contained men's cologne as well as men's clothing in another bag."

"I don't like the idea of a potential warlock. He might need to be dealt with, and we don't know how powerful he is." Sergev stood up from where he sat on the edge of his bed.

"If he is a warlock," Isobel reminded him. "There is a chance he might just be a companion."

"What do you suggest?" He asked the Archmage.

Surveillance. We can assign three members to monitor their every move. If they make a move with the Grimoire, we respond.

"We do not know if they are the ones possessing the Grimoire," Sergev said thoughtfully. "What if they are not? No, just one coven member for now. We can assign another if needed. We are spread too thin as it is. Magister Burpee has informed me that two members who were to arrive from France have canceled due to health issues. We will have to make do."

"Very well. With your permission, I will pick the coven member for the task."

"You may do so. Oh, Isobel, how did our young Mage do in the field?"

"He performed adequately, my Lord."

Upon entering the hotel lobby, Gaea, Marc, and Himiko found it crowded with people. From their looks, Gaea guessed they were all musicians, as some carried guitar cases. After a quick conversation with a waitress in the restaurant, her suspicions were confirmed. The entire hotel, except for a few rooms, had been booked by the bands performing at the open-air concert.

"I wish we had time to check out the concert," Marc said, glancing at one of the menus the waitress had placed on the table. "I recognize one of the bands advertised in the brochure."

"Another time," Gaea answered, picking up a menu. "No time for self-enjoyment this time around."

We have three days to find someone to help us with the Grimoire, or we're stuck with it. Speaking of which, we haven't discussed what to do if that happens." Himiko sipped her iced tea, which the waitress had delivered.

"How can you drink iced tea in this weather?" Marc asked, blowing on his hot cocoa.

"Want some of my ice?" Himiko teased.

Marc stuck his tongue out at her.

Gaea ignored their banter. "I have been giving thought to just that scenario."

"Any ideas?" Himiko asked.

"The Atlantic Ocean comes to mind." Marc broke in.

Gaea nodded. "That might be an option, but I don't think we can do it until spring, which means leaving the book in my grandparents' root cellar. I'm not willing to keep it any longer than necessary. And I will not put them or any of my family in danger."

"Then we had better come up with another plan, then," Himiko said.

Their starters had arrived, and they each began eating their spring salads, unaware of who was seated at a table across the restaurant. Bill and Bob had returned from their trip and decided to dine at the Loose Moose. It wouldn't be until both parties finished their meals that they would realize they had been close to each other.

CHAPTER 15
Convening of the Obsidian Circle

Dottie hadn't heard from her husband in a while, and she was feeling worried and annoyed. Not knowing what was going on with him was one thing; not knowing about the kids was another. Bob had a duty to keep her updated on any developments, no matter how minor. She had thought about calling him but decided against it. He might be somewhere or doing something that could endanger him if she did. She would wait for him and also planned to give him a piece of her mind when he finally arrived. Still, she needed to keep Cathy informed about the situation. Although she had promised not to, she had told her about Bob and Bill's plan to go to Van Buren. When she first heard about her husband's perceived betrayal, she was upset. But as she calmed down, she understood why the two had to do what they were doing. The three of them did need someone watching out for them, even though Gaea was a gifted medium who could look out for herself as well as Marc and Himiko. If trouble arose, she would know about it well in advance.

In Cape Neddick, Aerin was becoming an issue that Cathy had to deal with, so she couldn't return to Bar Harbor. School was still a week away before it was time to start classes again, so she spent most of her time controlling Aerin's actions. Still, the boy found ways to get into trouble both inside and outside. His latest mistake was in the garage. He and Logan had decided to make a snack for themselves in the upstairs apartment. Luckily, they were interrupted by Carl, the Penders' handyman and gardener. After a swat on the backside and a scolding, Cathy sent her son on his way, wondering what he would do next. Once he was back in school, the house staff could take over for him. She fully trusted Mrs. Douglas, their Scottish head housekeeper, to keep order in her absence. Unfortunately, she was away on her Christmas vacation and wouldn't return to her duties until a week after Aerin went back to school. She finished eating the breakfast Vicky had cooked, poured herself another cup of coffee, and sat back down at the table.

"No word about Gaea?" Vicky asked, drying a plate with a dish towel.

"None," Cathy answered. "Dottie said she would call when she heard from Bob.

"I still can't believe Dad didn't tell you they were going to go spy on Gaea and her friends."

"Vicky, it's not really spying. He and Bob went to keep an eye out for trouble."

"And you don't think Gaea can take care of herself? C'mon, Mom, she is a psychic medium. Gaea would see trouble coming from a mile away."

"I know she can. Your father and Bob decided to do this on their own. If you ask me, they both feel the need to fulfill their fatherly and grandfatherly duties in protecting Gaea and her friends. If I had been consulted, I probably would have agreed to their plans. Whatever those might have been. I guess Dottie saw right through Bob, and he confessed to her before they left for Van Buren." Cathy said, picking up a brush and running it through her hair.

"I would be pissed if I found out Dad was spying on me."

"Vicky, stop it! He is not spying!"

Vicky shrugged. "I need to go pack. I have to drive back this afternoon. The restaurant is almost finished being fumigated, and I need to be there to reopen it and make sure everything is in order."

"Drive safe. Oh, and come say goodbye when you are leaving."

"I will."

Cathy watched her daughter dance out of the kitchen. She couldn't believe how much time had passed since she and Bill adopted her after her father's death. Without the Penders' intervention, Vicky would have ended up in some orphanage in Massachusetts, and there's no telling where she might have gone after that. She and Bill did the right thing. The girl had grown into an educated young woman who was well on her way to becoming a successful restaurateur. Cinnamon Woodfire was going to be a hit in Bar Harbor; Cathy was confident of that.

Upstairs, Aerin was using his abilities to reach out to the Grimoire. He was trying to ensure the book was safe and sound. If only his mother had let them stay at Grandpa's and Grandma's for another week. Since the spirit that had last been with the book had left, he could no longer make contact. There was a faint trace of an aura, but he couldn't be sure it was the actual book. Gaea had told him that Douglas would cast another protection spell on it when he finished with the book and that it would probably be stronger than the one cast by Himiko and that he might have trouble reaching the Grimoire. As it turned out, it was nearly impossible. Aerin could swear that the book was no longer there.

High Priest Aoki needed a new plan. The three Magi he had sent to investigate the aura from a possible Grimoire location had not returned with concrete information about who was in the room at the motel. It was clear to him that Mr. and Mrs. Jones did not exist and that the name was used to hide the true occupants. The man they interrogated gave only a vague description of the woman who checked in, which was not very helpful. A young woman with black hair and brown eyes matched half of the women attending the Winter Solstice. He needed more details, which meant sending his Magi to the festival. He didn't expect the person he was after to be at the concert venue across town, but he couldn't rule it out completely. He would need to send a Magi with psychic abilities to cover the concert since the loud music would make it impossible to hear any conversations. He shook his head, thinking it was most likely a complete waste of time.

There was one solution he knew would work. He would need to go out into the public himself. Aoki's skills were excellent, and he could find either the Grimoire or the person who claimed to have it. Once he located that individual, it would be easy to gather information or retrieve the book. He would give his Magi two days, and if they found nothing, he would go alone into the crowds.

"I don't believe it. You have got to be kidding me!" Gaea said to Marc. "Where? How come I haven't detected them?"

Marc pointed to the other side of the restaurant. "They are sitting at a table around the corner," he replied.

Marc had gotten up to use the restroom, which was conveniently near the table where Bill and Bob were dining. As he exited, he had a clear view of the two men deep in conversation. Too far to hear what they were saying, he quickly moved behind a partition to shield himself from their view and returned to his table, where Gaea and Himiko were digging into their baked salmon.

Gaea was beside herself with anger. "I can't believe they followed us." she said, tossing her napkin onto her plate. She had lost her appetite and started to stand up.

"Busted," Himiko said, reaching for her iced tea.

Marc grabbed Gaea's arm. "Let's not be hasty," he said, guiding her back into her seat. "Maybe they are not here for us?"

Gaea looked at her incredulously. "So what? They are here on an ice fishing trip?"

Marc shrugged. "Possibly."

"Don't be an idiot," Gaea said, allowing him to sit her down.

"What do we do now?" Himiko asked, shoveling a piece of salmon into her mouth. She, for one, had not lost her appetite.

"I have half a mind to go over there and give both of them a piece of my mind." She retorted.

"Maybe not such a good idea," Marc advised. "At least not here in public. We need to approach them in private."

"You're right," Gaea admitted. She was starting to calm down and listen to reason. Something could be said about the Grimoire and overheard by someone. Someone not meant to hear it. It was wise to wait. "I'll be right back." She said, standing up.

Marc grabbed her arm again.

"I'm not going over there. Trust me."

Marc and Himiko watched as she walked to the front desk. After a brief conversation with the front desk clerk, she came back and sat down.

"Dad and Bob are staying in suite 6. We will ambush them there." Gaea said, grinning evilly. "Tomorrow morning, before breakfast."

Marc smiled, and Himiko giggled.

Bill and Bob took their time eating and spent quite a bit of time reviewing what they had learned during their short visit at the festival grounds. There were plenty of spots to keep track of the kids, and the digital photos Bob took helped them refine their surveillance plans. The two locations allowed them to not only monitor the vending tables and the kids' movements but also spot anything suspicious near Gaea, Marc, and Himiko, unless they split up. Bill mentioned the possibility, but Bob dismissed it. When the three told them about their plans back in Bar Harbor, they were firm that they should stay together for safety unless they absolutely had to split up.

"We can't get too close to them, Bob," Bill warned. "We will be found out in a second if she senses us."

"Her abilities." Bob agreed. "I have been thinking about that. What do we do if we are found out? I don't think the ruse of going ice fishing is going to work, do you?"

"Not a chance," Bill answered. "Dang abilities."

I suggest that we come clean. We tell her that we are more than worried and couldn't see it clearly, just to let them go on this dangerous trip without some backup that could offer them a way out.

Bill thought for a moment. "I think that she will buy that excuse, but she is going to be upset nonetheless."

Bob laughed. "Upset? Try down right pissed off."

Bill smiled. "You're right, she will be, and I think I'm going to bear the brunt of her fury. She will let you slide. She loves you too much to be mad at you."

"And she doesn't love her father?"

"Of course she does, but 'Old Dad is also a punching bag when need be. Don't worry, Bob. I can take it."

"Let's hope we are not discovered."

"Let's hope." Bill agreed. We should hit the hay. Early day tomorrow."

Sergev received word that the members of his coven had arrived in town, totaling ten—six witches and four warlocks— all of whom were senior members with considerable skills and powers. He scheduled a meeting in the barn at 11 pm. It wasn't the Black Sabbath gathering, but a meeting to explain why they were summoned to Van Buren and to assign specific tasks. Aware of their skills, he knew the assignments would not be overly complex. Tasks would range from simple surveillance to detective work, involving discreet inquiries around the festival and possibly searching specific locations, which would require tact since he didn't want any of his coven members arrested for crimes like breaking and entering.

He had assigned Sage and Magister Burpee to prepare for the meeting. Unbeknownst to the High Priest, Kenneth had already set up most of the area, including placing the hidden pentagram boards face up so they were visible. After a quick trip into town, he bought the needed candles from Crosbys and the herbs his Auntie requested. The barn was ready before Sergev even ordered it to be prepared.

Rental cars started arriving and parking at the farm around 10:30 pm, and Kenneth made sure to act as a valet, either indicating where to park or parking the vehicles himself. Some of the coven members acted privileged and treated the Sage as if he were just a laborer, to see to their needs. They would learn differently during the meeting.

Black candles lit the alcove at the back of the barn, casting light on the pentagram and sending shadows dancing across the walls and a podium where High Priest Sergev was set to address his members. Other items were arranged strategically, symbols of the Coven along with objects connected to deities that the Obsidian Circle considered worthy of their devotion. One such item was a black iron book that contained no text and could not be opened. It served as a reminder of the Grimoire and the demon that created it. At that moment, none of the witches or warlocks present knew that the book had resurfaced, and they were tasked with finding it. Only the High Priest, Isobel, Magister Burpee, their new Sage, Gunther, and his daughter were aware of the recent events. That knowledge would soon change.

As the coven members filed in, they all wore black ropes that signified they were part of the Obsidian Circle. Around their necks hung pendants, each different, even though similar. These pendants indicated the witch or warlock's rank within the coven. Gold was worn by the High Priest, purple by Magisters, red by Archmagi, and others as well. Blue was reserved for the sage in the coven and would be given to Kenneth in a small ceremony during the meeting.

As the members took positions according to their rank around the pentagram, High Priest Sergev arrived and stepped into the center. He assessed his members, then led a chant in Latin before moving to the podium. Archmage Argante took her position at his side on the right, one step behind him, while Magister Burpee stood to his left.

"Welcome, witches and warlocks of the Obsidian Circle," he began. "I have called you here for more than just a Black Sabbath. I have called you for a purpose, a vital purpose that I have kept to only a few. Today, I will reveal everything to you and only you. My words will not go beyond the ten of you, and you will remain silent even to other coven members, for this matter does not concern them."

A murmur ran through the coven, and the High Priest silenced it with a raised hand. "But before we start, a matter of coven business—since we have a new member. He's trained in medicine and will take on the role of Mage. Kenneth Burpee, step out of the shadows and come forward."

Kenneth had indeed been standing away from the other members as he had been instructed to do by Archmage Argante. He stepped into the candlelight, and another murmur arose, only to be silenced again by Sergev. Isobel walked over and stood behind Kenneth, holding a black robe ready to put over his shoulders. After a few words spoken in Latin, she draped it on him and went back to her position. Sergev then produced a green pendant and placed it around his neck.

"You are now Sage of the Obsidian Circle. Take your place among us," he said, motioning to an opening in the circle.

Sage Burpee took his place, trying his best to mimic the other members and to control his nervous excitement.

"Is there any witch or warlock that would like to speak?" Sergev asked.

He was answered with silence.

Very well, you may break the circle and prepare yourselves for instruction.

The members stepped forward to face their leader, who took the black book from Isobel and raised it up. "As you all know, this is the semblance of the Grimoire, Book of Belphegor the Defiler, but it is not the actual book."

"The book is lost," a witch said. "It's been that way for decades."

The other spoke in agreement.

"Ah, but it has resurfaced and is nearby," Sergev said, handing the book back to Isobel, who returned it to its place.

The members began to speak all at once, and Sergev silenced them.

"How long have you known of this, my Lord?" a warlock asked. He was tempted to ask why they had not been informed earlier but held his tongue.

I have known for some time that it had resurfaced, but not its exact location. Only recently have I started to believe it is here in the State of Maine and perhaps even right under our noses in Van Buren.

"Surely, no one would bring such a powerful artifact to a festival packed with people?" a warlock asked, his pendant that of an Archmage.

"Perhaps the one with the book does not know what they have," a Magister suggested.

"I believe that the person really knows what they possess and that this person is, in fact, a witch, although a weak one. I believe her purpose is to rid herself of the burden of the Grimoire and not to try to use what is written inside of it."

"I cannot believe that a child of magic has come into possession of the most powerful book of black magic in existence." Another Magister spoke up.

"It has, I am sure of that. I also believe that this very witch is here attending the Winter Solstice to seek advice on what to do with it. She fears it will fall into the hands of someone who might use it to do harm. I, for one, do not want that either. The book needs to be found and stored in a place where it cannot be used for such purposes. I plan to embed it in Russian and cast a spell on it, hiding it forever from those who might be corrupted by what it offers."

"Why not use it for the Obsidian Circle? It would make our coven great again, as it once was." the Magister said. "Would it not be wise to do so?"

"It would not," Sergev replied. "None of us, including myself, can use the spells it contains, because doing so would mean falling into what its creator intended for it to do. It would capture our souls and hold them captive for Belphegor the Defiler. The Grimoire was never meant to be used by mortals; it was designed to lure them, ultimately destroying them. No, we cannot wield the power of the book, but we can keep it from those who want to do so. That in itself will save our coven."

The members discussed among themselves for a moment, then an Archmage spoke up. "I speak for everyone present. The orders of High Priest Sergev, leader of the Obsidian Circle, will be obeyed. If possible, the Grimoire will be found and taken to Russia, where it will disappear from humanity and be kept in a place known only to you and those you consider worthy of such knowledge. Please share your plans and intentions so we can fulfill your wishes."

For the next two hours, Sergev explained how to find the Grimoire, and as each member received their instructions, they left the circle and barn. The last to go bowed to Sergev before disappearing into the darkness.

CHAPTER 16
Opening Day & Intervention

The next morning brought light snow and a brisk wind that dropped temperatures into the single digits. The first day of the Winter Solstice festival was here, and the expected turnout matched expectations. Most people didn't appear bothered by the weather.

Vendors and visitors rapidly filled the fairgrounds and town streets. Concert-goers were scheduled to begin their festivities the next day. Multiple tents had been set up in and around both venues, which were heated, and most were already being used. The concert lacked the luxury of the Winter Solstice festival. Part of the grounds designated for the Solstice featured large tents, like those used by circuses, housing some attractions and being heated. One of these tents served as the central food court; others accommodated attending Wiccans, offering their crafts, herbs, books, and other items. Vendors who had not reserved space inside a heated tent or chose not to pay the extra fee were relegated outside and exposed to the elements.

Just before sunrise, Gaea and her two companions positioned themselves outside her father's and Bob's room, eager to catch them before breakfast. They were lucky—they had barely arrived when Gaea raised her fist to knock, and the door swung open.

Bill stopped dead in his tracks. "Uh oh," he said. "Bob?"

"What is it, Bill?"

"We're busted." Bill stepped aside to let the three in.

"Bet you're sneaky rear ends you are," Gaea said, pushing past her father and into the room.

"Come on in, Honey," Bill said nervously. "We can explain."

"We?" Bob said. "This was all your idea."

"Why you…"

"This is no joke, Dad," Gaea said, turning to face him. "Why did you follow us? This is very dangerous, and I didn't want you involved."

"That is precisely why we are here," Bob said grimly. "Did you think we would just stand by while you two headed to Van Buren, not even knowing who or what you were after?"

"It wasn't any of your business," Gaea said.

Marc wandered to the side of the room and looked out the window, not wanting to take part in what was unfolding.

"The hell it's not," Bob said, walking up to Gaea, his face nearly touching hers. "You three brought that cursed book into my home. Once we found out about it, it became our problem just as much as yours. If I'm not mistaken, it's sitting in my root cellar inside one of my iron boxes, isn't it?"

Gaea stepped back and looked to Himiko for support, but found none. Himiko shrugged, looking defeated.

"Sweetheart, it's against everything inside us and how we feel for you kids to just stand by and do nothing but wait for a phone call," Bill said. "We decided to come and try to watch out for trouble and help you escape if needed. Not to interfere."

"Indeed," Bob added. There is no intention to prevent or hinder what you are trying to accomplish.

"Maybe it's a good idea," Marc said. "I, for one, feel safer with your dad and Mr. Pepper doing what they said they planned to do. There's nothing wrong with them watching our backs."

"True," Himiko agreed. "And the two of you wouldn't be suspected of anything. Gaea, we might. We are going to ask around and hint about the Grimoire, and that is bound to raise suspicion. Maybe from dangerous people."

"Ok, let's say we agree to this, not that we have much choice in the matter. How do you two plan to watch our backs?" Gaea sat down on one of the beds in the room.

"We have a plan all mapped out, literally," Bob said, reaching into his coat pocket and retrieving the brochure of the festival. He unfolded it on the bed. "Have a look."

The five of them huddled around the map as Bob laid out their surveillance plans.

The phone rang, and Cathy hurried to answer it, nearly tripping over a kitchen chair. A sharp pain in her thigh and a bruise served as a reminder not to rush, and they would last a few days.

"Hello, Dottie?" She answered excitedly.

"Hi, honey, it's Bill." Her husband's voice came over the phone. "I'm in Van Buren with Bob and the kids."

Of course you are. I've known what you two were up to ever since you left Bar Harbor. Dottie told me everything she knew.

Bill covered the phone and muttered the words "Busted again" to Bob, who nodded knowingly. After all, he had confessed to his wife, and he was fully aware that she would confide in Cathy. It was just a matter of time.

"Yes, Bill said. "We are going to help them by keeping an eye out for trouble."

"You are not going to get in the way? Are you. Bill"

"Not at all," he replied. "Simple surveillance from a safe distance. But, if there is trouble, we will whisk them out faster than you can say escape."

"Well, I do feel better knowing that the kids know you are there. That way, they can keep an eye on you two as well."

It will be good. Look, Cathy, I have to go. There's a lot to discuss here, and time is running out.

"Bill, promised me you'll be safe."

"I will, I mean we will. Gotta go, bye." He hung up the phone. "Well, it seems that everyone knows where we are in Bar Harbor as well as Cape Neddick."

"Let's finish going over the plan," Bob said.

Cathy hung up and called Dottie.

Members of the Obsidian Circle had blanketed the town in search of something, but they weren't quite sure what it was. They were sure of one thing: they were searching for anything related to the Grimoire, its possible location, and the person who possessed it. How they would accomplish the tasks assigned to them by High Priest Sergev was left to each individual; however, they would all answer directly to Archmage Argante. They had little to go on except for what Archmage Argante had discovered. Two girls and a man traveling together were suspects and needed to be found and questioned. Finding them amid the sea of people that had descended on Van Buren would be no easy feat.

Three were sent to cover the town itself, one to the concert, and the remaining six to the Winter Solstice, which Sergev suspected might bring the best results. They were searching for a witch and a possible warlock, after all.

Isobel had stayed at the farmhouse coordinating the search, and everyone was using cellphones to stay in touch. If needed, she could reply within minutes. Magister Burpee would also remain at her home, while her great-grandnephew would be at Argante's disposal if she needed anything. After sending a quick text to each member, Argante was satisfied with the plan and released them.

Bill returned from a quick run to the local hardware store carrying a sack full of walkie-talkies. Granted, they were models made for children, but they had an advertised range of two hundred yards, more than enough for their needs. As Marc examined the piece of green plastic Bill handed to him, he turned it on. Nothing. "It doesn't work."

"Did you get batteries, Bill?" Bob asked.

Bill slapped his forehead. "I'll be right back."

Gaea stopped him, holding up her cellphone. "We have these, Dad."

"Ah, right," He replied. "I guess I'll save them. Aerin will love to play with them."

Gaea rolled her eyes.

"Let's grab a bite to eat, then head to the festival," Marc suggested.

"We need to stop at Crosby's," Himiko reminded them.

"What's at Crosby's Five and Dime?" Bob asked, handing his toy back to Bill.

"The owner is a witch and our first possible contact. I have a feeling that she knows every witch and warlock in the area and is meeting more of them as we speak. She seems to be the only source for herbs around," Himiko explained.

Gaea picked up her coat, slipped it on, and added, "As well as other items that a practicing Wiccan would need."

"True," Himiko said. "Let's go eat."

High Priest Aoki did not allow his Magi to operate independently and issued explicit instructions that he expected to be strictly followed. Unlike his counterpart, Aoki did not send out all of his followers; instead, he kept half in reserve. There was secrecy in small numbers, and he did not want to be discovered. The few he sent out were a risk, but a risk worth taking. If discovered by the Obsidian Circle, he faced the possibility of war. If any of the Magi made a mistake in judgment, they could be arrested and imprisoned. Neither outcome was acceptable to the High Priest.

Once the Magi were dispatched, Aoki retreated to the rear of the RV, assigned two guards to stand outside his quarters, entered, and approached an altar that sat to one side of a small bed. He lit the black candles on it, then arranged a small onyx bowl along with a matching dagger between them. Engravings on the dagger's hilt were carved in

Japanese. Translated, they spelled out the name of the deity he and his followers worshiped — Belphegor the Defiler.

He rolled up his sleeves and knelt at the altar. He began to chant and reached for the dagger, holding it to his palm and drawing it across, leaving a thin line of blood that dripped into the bowl's contents. The blood darkened the herbs of his offering to a dark ochre color. Aoki started chanting, summoning the demon. He would need help in finding his master's quarry.

The mixture in the bowl began to emit a thin trail of black smoke rising toward the ceiling. Closing his eyes, he started the incantation he had used countless times when summoning the greater demon. As he had done many times before, a figure started to form in front of the High Priest, gaining solidity as Aoki continued with his chant.

Outside the room, the two magi exchanged glances, a flicker of unease about what was happening behind the closed door. Inside, a fully formed Belphegor stood before Aoki, bent over because his great height didn't fit the space where he was summoned.

"Why do you summon me?" The demon spat. He reeked of sulfur and burnt flesh that assaulted Aoki's nostrils. He bore the stench with resolve and addressed Belphegor.

Master, I believe I have traced the Grimoire to the very Winter Solstice event that occurs nearby. A young witch, a psychic medium, and possibly a warlock have the book, that I'm certain of. I don't know if they currently possess the book, but if not, they know its location.

"What is it you want from me, warlock? You know I cannot reveal the exact location of my tomb. That information must remain secret and can only be discovered by the seeker of the Grimoire. Otherwise, the magic inside it cannot be used, as the book will not accept the one who finds it. That must be earned. Such is the command from Haides himself. But you know this. So again, why do you summon me?"

I only need help in identifying and locating the three individuals, my Lord. I have Magi searching the area, but our knowledge is limited. I beg for your assistance in this matter.

My patience is running thin, Necromancer. I tasked you with finding what's mine, yet you still come to me. You seem unable to follow my commands. Maybe I should bring in someone else?

"No, my Lord. It is my greatest desire to please you and fulfill your commands. I apologize for disturbing you."

Belphegor paused thoughtfully. "I can tell you this. The answer to what you seek is closer than you think. Search with your mortal heart and soul, and you might find more than you expect. Find what belongs to me. I leave you."

Belphegor vanished, leaving a confused Aoki to consider the demon's words. "More than he bargained for" could mean many things, whether reward or danger. He would double his efforts.

Seraphina listened to her father as he explained the commands imposed on the coven members in the search for the Grimoire. He had decided not to take her to the coven meeting since Magister Burpee had not officially invited her. He was also worried about her past dealings with the demon Belphegor, as Sergev had interacted with him before, which hadn't ended well. He thought it was best to keep her away from the High Priest until the Black Sabbath.

"You have dyed your hair brown, Saraphina," Gunther said, touching her hair. "That is your natural color if I remember correctly.

"I was sick of it being white." She responded. "People were staring at me."

"It looks good. A favorable change for a beautiful young girl."

"So, where are we to look, Father?"

We have been assigned to the Winter Solstice grounds, specifically the Wiccan tent. It's big but not impossible to search for three people, and I believe you have an idea what they look like?

"I have seen the weak witch twice and the psychic medium once," she replied, running a brush through her hair. I have no recollection of the man. The witch is Asian, and the medium has dark hair. I can recognize the witch, but I'm not sure about the other.

We find the witch; I am confident we will find the others. High Priest Sergev believes they travel together.

"And if they don't have the Grimoire?"

"Then," Gunther said, tucking a loaded pistol in his belt behind his back, "we get the location of it from them."

"Is that needed?" Seraphina asked about the gun.

"I feel safer for both of us if I have it." He replied. "Don't worry, it's only in case of a dire emergency. Sergev wants to keep this entire thing low-key."

Me too. I'm starting to regret even beginning the search for the Grimoire. So far, it has only brought me trouble. And now, you tell me I might have sold my soul to Belphegor? Sergev was supposed to help with that, you said so.

"And I believe that he will help you at the Black Sabbath. He has no love for Belphegor the Defiler and would not want to see any of his coven to be involved and swayed by his lies. You will be fine. Trust me, ok?"

Seraphina nodded and stood, taking her coat that Gunther was holding for her. "By the way, there is a store down the street called Crosby's Five and Dime. It's owned by a witch who sells to the local Wiccans in the area. We might want to check it out on the way to the Winter Solstice. I found it while exploring when you went to meet High Priest Sergev."

"Ok, good job. We will do just that." He said, opening the door for her. Together, they left the hotel.

CHAPTER 17
The Red Headed Witch

The owner of Crosby's was a woman in her forties with bright red hair that caused Marc to giggle. "She looks like a witch out of a fairy tale he said quietly to Himiko.

She was helping a customer, so the three pretended to browse around while they waited. She wore a long black dress and a traditional pointed hat, which Gaea guessed was because of the festival and for the visitors. Her skin was stark white, and her blue eyes were piercing. Gaea could feel the power radiating from her, yet even with her abilities, she was shielded from learning more about her. The woman was not someone to trifle with; she was sure of it.

A few moments later, the woman approached the three who had come together near the counter.

"Hello there!" she chirped. "Welcome to Crosby's. How can I help you?" she looked directly at Himiko. "You are family, aren't you?"

"Yes, I am. My name is Himiko. These are my friends Gaea and Marc."

"You seek something, or someone." She looked directly at Himiko, giving Gaea and Marc only a brief glance. "Come to the back of the store with me."

Marc and Gaea looked confused.

"You two as well," the witch said, leading them into a room filled with fresh and dried herbs. A table stood in the back with four chairs around it. On it, a black candle, unlit, sat alongside a cup of lit incense and a small bouquet. She motioned for them to sit, then called out for her daughter to mind the store.

She sat and addressed Gaea. You are a medium and a strong one, but you," she said of Marc, "are closed to me. You are not a warlock or have abilities as do your friends."

"I am just a friend." He said, feeling somewhat belittled by the remark.

"And a devout one, no doubt." The witch seemed to sense his unease. "Now, it is safe here away from prying eyes, I assure you. I have placed a protection spell upon this room to shield it. No one, so far, has had the strength to break it. My name is Tasha.

The three introduced themselves and looked nervously at each other, and Tasha spoke again. "Tell me what you seek. You have found it, haven't you?" she asked bluntly.

Himiko was clearly rattled. It wasn't supposed to be this easy. "Found what? Tasha?" She asked.

Gaea tried to break in. "Himiko seeks some specialty herbs." She lied.

Tasha ignored her. "You have found the Grimoire, and now you seek counsel."

"How do you know?" Himiko asked.

"The boy is transparent in his thoughts," she replied. "Again, do not worry. You are safe here, and I have no desire for the demon's book. It was made for evil purposes, and only those with such intentions can wield what it contains within its bindings of human skin."

"How do you know about the book?" Gaea asked, reaching over to touch Marc's hand, trying to comfort him. The witch was clearly a psychic with unknown abilities.

"I know of it. How and why are of no concern. Just be content that I have no desire to possess it. My question for you is, why do you seek counsel on it?"

"Didn't you read that from my mind as well?" Mark said sarcastically.

Tasha smiled. "I am sorry for the invasion. It was necessary so that I would know how to help you and your companions."

"We want to get rid of it and prevent it from falling into the wrong hands," Himiko confided. "We've had others try once before to take it from us. We managed to hide it and believe it's safe."

Tasha sat quietly for a few moments. "I have seen witches and warlocks in town with questionable motives. I had not quite discerned what until now. There are two covens here. One is at the RV parking lot, and another is up the road at a farmhouse. Both practice black magic, one more malicious than the other, but I believe both are after what you have. You didn't bring it with you, did you?"

"Gaea shook her head no." Let's say it is well hidden and under a protective spell."

Tasha looked at Marc. "Do not worry, Marc. I will not invade your mind again, or yours or Himiko's, Gaea. What you tell me will be of your own free will. I want you all to trust me."

"How can you help us?" Gaea asked.

I know of a coven that has powerful members and is large in number. They do not wish to possess the Grimoire; however, they do not want to see it in the hands of black magicians or returned to its creator. This coven goes by the name of Guardians of the Grimoire and is dedicated to protecting the book. They had been doing so until it was taken from its hiding place by one of their own who had turned to darkness and black magic. The Magi was eventually hunted down and killed for his wrongdoings, but the Grimoire had already been lost. It simply vanished without a trace. Many believed it was destroyed, while others thought its maker had reclaimed it. The mystery remained until a few decades ago when it reappeared in a museum. It was assumed that some archaeologist had found its hiding spot and discovered an unassuming, yet rare, book. It was donated anonymously to the museum and then stolen a few years later, disappearing once again. The coven I mention did not have the time to recover it. That brings its story to you three. I can connect you with the High Priestess of that coven.

Gaea still wasn't sure she could trust Tasha, but if the offer were sincere, it would rid them of the dreaded book. More time was needed to build that very trust. She decided to provide some more information.

"The book was found in the closet of my sister's restaurant in Bar Harbor." Gaea began.

Tasha raised an eyebrow. "A strange place for such a powerful book. I imagine how it got there is just as strange a story."

When my sister bought the building, it was discovered during cleaning. It seems that it was once owned by the restaurant's pianist, who died of a heart attack while playing the piano in the bar. He had obtained it from a thief who had stolen it from a museum. I found out he is a spirit haunting the restaurant.

"Interesting," Tasha said, reaching to accept a tray of coffee and cups that her daughter had brought into the room. She thanked her as the girl hurried away. "Coffee?"

As the four sat and sipped, Gaea explained Douglas's need for the book and how he planned to free his wife from the clutches of Belphegor the Defiler by using its power against the demon. He had died before completing the ritual and had been waiting, regaining the power he once had in life. The book was taken from the restaurant before he could finish the task.

Gaea intentionally left out some details, such as Douglas using the book in the root cellar to free his wife, if he even succeeded, which was still uncertain. She also withheld the location of the Grimoire out of caution. That information would be revealed at the appropriate time.

"So, that's it in a nutshell," Gaea said, finishing her story. The book fell into our hands, although we didn't know what it was at the time. Himiko had an idea, and my mom, who is an expert in antiquities, identified it as a grimoire.

"But not the Grimoire," Tasha said, pouring more coffee into her cup.

"No," Gaea said, glancing at her watch. "We need to leave. My dad and grandfather are going to be worried sick." She partially lied. She needed time to process everything they had discussed and decide if Tasha's intentions were truly sincere.

"Very well," Tasha said, standing. "If you wish, I will contact the High Priestess of the coven and inform her that the Grimoire might have been found, but that's all I will tell her for now. The decision about the book is yours to make. Let me know what you decide after you've made it."

"I will let you know tomorrow, okay? Please?" We need time to think all of this through.

"Of course. Take your time, but do not forget that others who are not so kind actively seek what you have and are nearby. Do not delay for long."

The trio thanked the witch and left. They hurried to the Winter Solstice to find Gaea's father and grandfather, wanting to learn what had just happened. As they rushed down the street, away from Crosbys, they passed a brown-haired girl with an older man entering the store. For a brief moment, Himiko and the girl's eyes locked onto each other.

Bob had just settled into his surveillance spot when a policeman asked him to move. As he stood to go, he recognized the officer. The patch on the man's uniform, indicating he was with the Bar Harbor police department, confirmed his suspicions.

"Martin? Martin Shultz?" Bob asked.

"Bob Pepper? What the heck are you doing sitting there?" the sergeant said with a laugh. "What brings you all the way here for this witch festival?"

Bob laughed, stood up, and dusted his pants off with his hands. "My granddaughter and a couple of her friends are here. Bill and I came along for the fun of it. I was waiting for them, so I thought I'd take a load off for a minute."

"That's fine and dandy, but you can do it right there," Shultz said, pointing to a metal box. "Electrical access point. You might get a jolt sitting on it."

Bob looked down, and sure enough, the box he had been sitting on was marked "Do not sit or stand, electrical hazard." "I didn't even see that. Thanks, Marty."

"No problem. Say hi to the kids for me." He said and resumed his patrol.

As he left, Bill walked up. "Gaea just texted me. They said to meet them in the food court and that they had made progress."

"Really?" Bob was intrigued. "That was fast. A Bar Harbor cop just busted me." He said, laughing.

"For what?"

"Unauthorized sitting." He replied, pointing to the box.

Bill glanced at the notification and grinned. "C'mon, they will be waiting, and I want to know what they have found out."

"Me, too."

The two men quickly moved towards another tent located some distance away from where they were standing.

Seraphina impatiently waited for her father to finish talking with the red-haired woman who owned Crosby's Five and Dime. He had disappeared into the back, leaving her to fume in anger. He hadn't even taken her back there with him. Wasn't she a member of the same coven as him and part of the mission to find the Grimoire? He was treating her like a little girl, and she didn't like it. To make matters worse, she believed she had just seen the weak witch along with her two companions, both of whom resembled the people they were looking for. "Fine," she thought. If her father was too busy to even include her in matters like this, then she would wait with what she had discovered. With every passing minute, they were getting farther away and lost in the crowd. Seraphina bided her time by browsing through the shop.

Tasha had read carefully about the man standing before her. He was a member of the Obsidian Circle and was part of a large group searching for the Grimoire. He didn't seem threatening or menacing and actually appeared friendly. Still, being a member of a coven that practiced black magic worried her. She had learned years ago that such people couldn't be trusted, even though her abilities suggested otherwise.

There was a young girl who came in not long ago," she spoke. There was no reason to reveal why they were in the store, and doing so could prove dangerous for them. "A young girl in need of some herbs for the Winter Solstice."

"Were there three of them? Her, another girl, and a man?" Gunther asked. "The girl may have been of Asian descent, perhaps Japanese."

Tasha paused for a moment to think. She had determined that he had no abilities, although the girl who came in with him did, but they were not very strong. A simple spell cast before they started talking shielded her from any attempt to read her mind.

She was only here a few minutes, but I believe she looked Asian, though I'm not sure if she was Japanese. Her English was perfect, and I didn't notice any accent. I remember her saying she was a college student here with a couple of friends to attend Winter Solstice and maybe catch some of the concert," Tasha added to her story. It also occurred to her that he had no idea she was a witch. As far as he knew, he was just talking to a shopkeeper.

I believe that she is in possession of an antique book that I have been looking for. I am very interested in purchasing it for my personal collection. You see, I am an avid collector of old books, scrolls, and tomes.

"How fascinating." She lied. "What makes this book so special?"

"The book was bound in human skin." He started but omitted that it had magical properties. "The skin of a very notorious convict that dates back centuries. It's not worth much to most people, but to me, it is priceless."

"Well, if she comes back in, would you like me to tell her of your interest?" She noticed that he had become increasingly nervous when she offered to help.

"Ah, no. I don't think that will be necessary. I am bound to run into her sooner or later. There can't be that many young Asian girls running around town now, can there?"

"No, I wouldn't think there would be."

"Well, I'll be going then. Thank you for your time."

Tasha watched as he gathered his young companion and left. It didn't take much to infer that the girl was his daughter as well as a psychic and a witch. A witch who was in a lot of trouble, having dabbled in areas of Black Magic that she should not have. Tasha could tell that the girl had, or at least had tried to summon something of immense power, and that was pure evil. A demon. If such a union had occurred and she was in allegiance or indebted to the monster, then the three, as well as the Grimoire, were in more danger than she had previously thought. This new development had made up her mind on whether to call the coven she had discussed with Gaea. She had initially promised to wait until they requested help, but now, knowing that the stakes had risen considerably, she would call and do so immediately. The fate of the Grimoire trumped everything else, including the well-being of three kids who didn't realize what they had become involved in. If the demon was Belphegor, then the situation was even more dire. Yes, intervention by the Guardians of the Grimoire would be necessary to reclaim the book and return it to safe storage. She would call the coven's High Priestess. She would call her sister.

CHAPTER 18
Guardians of The Grimoire

Deep in the mountains of Vancouver, British Columbia, an old, converted monastery was kept away from the public eye, as the members had intended when it was built. The main building and its outlying structures had fallen into disrepair for decades until a small group of people convinced Vancouver to lease it to them free of charge, on the condition that they restored and maintained it and offered it to visitors as a museum. The High Priest at the time signed the lease, and they embarked on the challenging task of restoring it. Fortunately for them, the Canadian government provided a substantial grant to help with the restoration, and within ten years, it opened to the public.

Unbeknownst to the government, not all of the convent was open to the public. The coven set the rules for the museum and its grounds, but deep beneath it lay secret catacombs, tunnels, and rooms built for their rituals and practices. One area was designed for a single purpose: to house and hide a specific item—a book not displayed among the museum's artifacts but kept in the shadows within a room carved from granite: The Book of Belphegor the Defiler. A powerful tome containing dark magic intended to destroy mankind.

The book was brought to the coven by a priest who oversaw the vast collection at the Vatican. After discovering the book's true nature, he looked for a way to eliminate it for himself and the church. He contacted the coven through questionable means known to his peers and arranged for its transfer to Vancouver.

Once the High Priest opened the package, he immediately knew what it was and what needed to be done. The Book of Belphegor had to be erased forever. No man or woman should ever be able to try to use what was written inside the book. The newly renamed Guardians of the Grimoire began carving a chamber into the stone on which the monastery sat. It became the coven's sworn duty and purpose to guard and keep the Grimoire hidden from anyone who might try to find it.

As the years went by, the book stayed hidden and safe until a warlock, a member of the coven sworn to protect it, became fascinated with the possibilities of what the Grimoire offered. He diverged from his coven's beliefs, betrayed them, and stole the book, escaping into the darkness of night. However, by the time it was discovered missing, the book was far out of the coven's reach and beyond the High Priestess's ability to locate it. The Grimoire had disappeared, and the coven's new mission was to find it and restore it to its stone prison. It would be up to the Guardians of the Grimoire to travel around the world and search for it. Some would settle in certain locations and adopt unassuming professions, allowing them to search for clues to its whereabouts. Others would constantly travel from place to place as nomads, seeking the lost book.

During the winter months, the monastery was closed to the public, allowing the coven to send more witches and warlocks into the field. Coincidentally, this winter the Grimoire resurfaced about 3000 miles to the east in a scenic state called Maine. It was also fortunate that a member of the Guardians of the Grimoire had taken up residence there: Tasha, the sister of the High Priestess, whom High Priestess Riana now spoke to on the phone.

"Yes, I am sure of it," Tasha reiterated to her sister after explaining the situation. "The three I told you about seem to know what the book is and its risks, but they don't have a way to get rid of it. They're already being chased by several witches and warlocks trying to claim the book for themselves. I believe they are from two covens, both of which practice dark magic. One of their members came into the store today. I think he's part of the Obsidian Circle."

"High Priest Segev's group," Riana confirmed. "I know of him because he is from the same ancient order that we once belonged to. His coven practices the dark arts; however, in recent years, he has become more softened, perhaps because he has seen his country suffer under communist oppression. I believe that if he is seeking the Grimoire, his goal is not to use the magic it contains but to take it into protection away from others who want it. He is not well-equipped for the task, though. He lacks the resources that I have here in Vancouver. We have more members, and the place where it is stored was built specifically for this purpose. Sergev should not be trusted with the Book of Belphegor."

"I agree, my sister. But the other coven that seeks it, I don't know who they might be."

Leave that to me. I have contacts who keep track of all the known covens. If one is on the move, I will find out which one it is, where they are headed, and for what purpose.

"Very well, Riana. What would you have me do?"

Talk to the three who have the book again and explain to them what my coven does and what I plan to do with the book. Reassure them that what we offer is genuine and that we do not intend to use it for dark purposes, as any attempt to do so would lead to mortal ruin. I will come with a group of my most powerful and specially trained members to handle the situation. My main concern is the innocent people who might get caught up in a struggle for the Grimoire between three factions that want it. It would be best if they handed it over to me, and I would leave quietly and peacefully.

I believe Sergev would cooperate. It's the other unknown coven that worries me.

I'll keep my eyes and ears open here. Gaea and her friends are supposed to return tomorrow or the next day to let me know if I can contact you about their problem. Now that that's settled, I believe I will have your words to convince them that turning over the book to you and our coven is the wisest choice.

"Very well. I will call you when I know for certain who the third coven is. Be careful, sister."

Tasha hung up the phone and went to find her daughter. Perhaps she could go out and find Gaea before someone else did.

"Well, which way did they go?" Gunther was angry, not at his daughter, but at himself. His overprotection of Seraphina had cost him the chance to confront the girl who possibly had the Grimoire, and she slipped right through his fingers. Seraphina might have followed them, but doing so would have meant getting lost in the crowds flowing through the street all the way to the festival grounds.

All I know is that they headed toward the festival. They vanished quickly, so I don't know if they went into another store or are heading straight there.

"Did they have the book with them by any chance?"

"No. I don't think they would be that stupid, do you?"

"I guess not. Well, we'd better head off in that direction. We might come across them again."

"What did you learn from that red-headed woman?" She asked.

"Nothing. Not a damn thing. Let's go."

Bill and Bob saw the kids at a food stand, ordering tacos and sodas. They didn't seem in much of a rush to do anything related to the Grimoire and were casually chatting among themselves, waiting for their food.

"Oh, hi Dad," Gaea said as the two men strode up to them.

"Lunch so soon?" He asked, motioning to the tray of food that Marc was holding.

"It's 11 AM. We were hungry." She answered, pulling napkins from a metal dispenser, handing Himiko and Marc a few each.

"Dang, where did the morning go?" Bob said. "I'm getting one for myself. Bill?"

"Sure. Now, Gaea, what did you find out?" Bill asked.

We met a powerful witch at Crosby's Five and Dime who knows everything about the Grimoire. We were trying to decide if we could trust her when you two showed up.

"So, what's the verdict?" her father asked her, taking a taco that Bob offered.

Himiko responded while Gaea had a mouthful of food. "Gaea was able to determine through her abilities that she was genuinely sincere and truthful in what she told us. She also does not believe that any magic was used to deceive. The witch knows of a coven willing to take the book, although we don't have the details yet. We are supposed to go back tomorrow or the next day"

Bob was skeptical. "Let's just say this woman, witch or whatever you want to call her, can be trusted. How do you plan to hand over the book? I'm not keen on anyone knowing where my home is."

"Her name is Tasha, Mr. Pepper." Himiko offered. "And we haven't figured that out either."

"Obviously, the choice of disclosing the Grimoire's location is not an option," Marc said, picking up another taco. "It never was, was it, Gaea?"

"No, it wasn't. I am thinking of an exchange point, somewhere in public, where shenanigans are less likely to happen."

"What about using where it all started?" Bill suggested.

"Cinnamon Woodfire?" His daughter asked. It was a sound idea, but her sister might have objections. "I'm not sure how Vicky would take to the idea."

"I think it's a fabulous plan," Bob added. "The restaurant is not open yet; however, it is in a good location within the public eye. We could even consider inviting a few uniformed police to have lunch at the time of surrendering the book."

"Do you really want to involve the cops?" It was Bill's turn to be skeptical. "I'm not sure that is such a good idea."

"Maybe not." Bob agreed.

Gaea had been thinking and devising a plan. "One thing we need to consider is that once the Grimoire is moved from the root cellar, it will have one less cloak to hide it. Himiko, will the protection Douglas put on it stay intact?"

I can't be certain. I don't know the spell he used or how long it lasts. Most spells fade over time. But it's possible that it will last at least until the box containing it is opened. After that, all bets are off.

"Then, it would be open for anyone searching for it to be found," Gaea said.

"So," Himiko added, "the passing of the book would need to be quick, and whoever takes it should make a quick getaway."

"Who says the box has to be opened?" Marc asked. "Let them have the book box and all."

The others looked at one another.

"That's brilliant," Gaea said, placing her soda on the stand they used as a table. "Why even bother opening the box? They can trust us that it's inside. If they can't, that's their problem. It's not like they're paying for it. If they decide to open it, so be it because at that point, it's no longer our concern."

So, we have a plan to hand it over; now we need to talk to Tasha and get her to finalize things on her end and make sure that the coven she is talking about will, in fact, accept the Grimoire," Bill said.

Gaea brought her fingers to her lips to shush him. "Don't say its name allowed. Too many people are nearby, dad. We don't know who may be listening."

"Right. Sorry."

"I think we should return to the hotel and discuss it further there," Gaea suggested.

"Let's finish our tacos and go." Bob agreed.

The five of them changed the topic to idle chit chat and finished their lunch. Twenty feet away, a Magi passed by but did not notice them.

Gunther and his daughter searched the festival grounds and tents all afternoon, but they never had any further contact with the Asian girl or the others who were with her. They always seemed to be in the wrong place at the wrong time, or they had already left the festival grounds, or they hadn't even gone there. Maybe they had gone to the concert area, where things were starting up for the first act. He needed to check in with Archmage Argante, and he wasn't looking forward to making that call. He might have had the three of them in his grasp and let them slip away because of his mistakes. She would not be pleased.

"They are not at this festival," he said to Seraphina.

She nodded in agreement. "I don't get it. She is a witch, so why wouldn't she be at the Winter Solstice?"

They are kids, based on who you saw at the University and coming out of Crosby's Five and Dime. Maybe their intentions all along had been to go to the concert, and the Winter Solstice was never on their list. College kids do like concerts.

"But what about the Grimoire?"

"Maybe the witch is intending to keep it for herself. In that case, she had hidden it and had gone on as if nothing was amiss."

"I don't buy that explanation at all," Seraphina said as they started the walk back to town. "When I learned about the weak witch back at school, I mostly ignored her as a threat until I saw her with the psychic medium. I grew concerned for the place where I stayed and practiced my magic. I was sure they would find out about it eventually, and they did. That's when I found the new one in the old chapel. They not only found it but searched it, and I am positive they know I practice black magic."

"Why is that such a big deal?" Her father asked, popping a piece of gum into his mouth.

Because witchcraft of any kind is not allowed on campus, and I was no longer a student, I was afraid they would turn me in, and I was nearing my goal of locating the Grimoire.

"With the help of Belphegor."

Yes. With the demon's help. He promised me that if I found it and retrieved it, I could learn its magic before he took it back.

"He lies," Gunther said flatly. "He seeks only one thing: another human soul. That's why he made the book in the first place, Seraphina."

"I know that now, but then I was filled with the obsession of finding and taking the power for myself. I didn't consider the consequences."

"You promised me that you didn't make a blood pact. Are you standing by that or did you lie to me?"

I swear I didn't. He told me that to earn his complete trust and help, I would need to do the ritual, but I couldn't bring myself to draw my own blood. I never tried it, though I continued to summon him. Not often, but I did.

Your soul may not be at risk then, but only High Priest Sergev will be able to tell if it is. As I have told you, we will find out at the Black Sabbath.

The two walked along in silence for a while, then crossed the town limits and passed its first building—a small coffee shop filled with cold customers. Gunther considered going inside for a cup but thought better of it. He had to make the phone call soon. There'd be time for coffee later.

"Do you think any of them recognized you at the store?" he asked, stepping onto the sidewalk.

"I don't think so. I stood out like a sore thumb with my white hair. Now that I've dyed it, I think I blend in quite well. I would have appeared to her as just another girl."

"Let us hope so," he replied, opening the hotel door to let her in. "I need to call Archmage Argante. Let's go up to the room; you can listen in."

Seraphina followed him up the stairs.

Gaea, Marc, and Himiko parted with Bill and Bob upon returning to the Loose Moose. The two men went to their room since they both needed to use the restroom. Marc needed to do the same.

"So, we head back to Crosby's first thing in the morning, right?" Gaea asked her friends.

"Yeah." Himiko agreed.

Marc suddenly stopped in his tracks, and the two girls looked at him curiously as he pointed toward their room. The door was open, but barely enough that someone not looking wouldn't notice; it was just ajar.

He led the way as they approached the room and paused to listen at the door. Hearing nothing, Marc pushed it open. The room had been ransacked.

CHAPTER 19
A Rift Within

The first band to perform at the concert venue was greeted by a full house made up of people from various age groups, from teens to middle-aged adults. The lineup of bands featured a wide range of genres, covering four decades of music. Organizers chose not to separate the acts by age group, opting instead for a diverse schedule designed to draw a mixed crowd. The fans didn't mind that a rock band followed a folk singer and then a jazz group. Everyone enjoyed themselves and took it all in stride, making it a pleasant experience for families to attend and celebrate together. Gunther and Seraphina fit in well among the cheering crowd, which made it easier to find the Asian girl and her friends. The crowds were large, though, and Gunther cursed himself for not getting there before the grounds opened. He and his daughter could have scanned the fans as they entered.

His report to Archmage Argante went better than he had expected. Expecting a sharp retort to his mistake at Crosby's Five and Dime, Gunther was instead met with a surprisingly casual reproach and was told to pay better attention and resume the search. Her melancholy attitude toward his error took him aback, but he wasn't about to delve into the reasons why. He promised to do better and hung up.

"I can't believe she went so easily on me," Gunther said to his daughter. "I've never met the woman, but from what Magister Burpee has told me, she is a no-nonsense Archmage who stops at nothing to achieve her goals. I thought she would have tarred and feathered me or worse."

"Maybe she was distracted by something else?" Seraphina suggested as they moved forward in the VIP ticket line to enter the concert grounds. Her father had managed to buy two tickets from a scalper; however, the price was steep. Gunther had complained briefly before shelling out the five hundred bucks for them. VIP tickets gave them access to all areas except the backstage, which he believed would also be off-limits to the Asian girl. His main concern was the prime viewing spot. He and Seraphina would head to the front grandstands near the stage and scan the crowd. His daughter would use binoculars, while he would use his camera with a zoom lens. If he spotted an Asian girl, he could snap a few pictures for identification later in case they could not get close enough or had no way to approach. The crowd would be tightly packed, making it difficult, if not impossible, to move through.

"Our goal is to get a positive ID on the witch and take some pictures. I can shoot areas of the crowd with the zoom lens, and if we don't see her clearly, we might be able to pick her out later in the crowd." He explained to his daughter.

"Hopefully, we will find her today." Seraphina took the pair of binoculars from him.

"We need to find her soon. We're running out of time."

Gunther was not hiding the fact that their time was limited. Others were searching for the girls too, but his plans were different from theirs. He kept his intentions secret and hadn't let Seraphina know what he aimed to do if he found the Grimoire. Giving it to his coven was not part of his plan. The pages contained power beyond his wildest dreams, which he wanted for himself. With Belphegor's help, he planned to seize that power. Whether he would share some of it with his daughter depended on her reaction. If a power struggle arose between them, she was disposable, just as her mother had been. All that mattered to Gunther was the Grimoire. He was tired of pretending to be a caring father and a weak wizard. His blood bond with Belphegor the Defiler had made him powerful. He now knew spells, hexes, and incantations that matched those of the strongest magic users. Still, he wanted more. If it cost him his soul, so be it. His time on Earth would be glorious as he ruled the magical world—everyone would kneel before him.

Gunther believed the Belphegor didn't want his book returned; what he truly wanted was a dark wielder of the Grimoire to serve his will. Since he couldn't rule on earth himself, he would do it through a mortal man. Gunther would be that man.

"It's filling up," Seraphina said, breaking her father's thoughts. "We can reach the top of the bleachers that way."

He looked where she was pointing. A gap in the barricade revealed stairs that went upward. "Perfect. Let's go."

The room was completely messy. Gaea, Marc, and Himiko entered and navigated through clothes, bedsheets, and other items scattered on the floor.

"Whoever it was, they were thorough," Marc said, starting to sort through the mess and gathering his clothes. "We'd better get our stuff and head back to your dad's room, Gaea. It's not safe here anymore."

No, it's not. They were after the Grimoire. I'd bet lunch on it.

Himiko picked up her spell book. "Not the Grimoire, maybe, but they know now that a witch was staying in the room. I would bet they are looking for all three of us. Somehow, word has gotten out that we might know something."

Gaea frowned. "I would tend to agree with you. The sooner we can meet with Tasha and rid ourselves of the dreaded thing, the better I'll feel. Either way, we need to get out of town and soon for our good health."

"Can you sense anything, Gaea?" Marc asked. "Anything on who the intruders might be?"

She paused briefly and closed her eyes. She was so frustrated with the state of their room that it never occurred to her to use her abilities to find some answers. She raised her hand.

In her mind, shapes started to form, and she began to notice some details of what she was seeing and feeling, and what she felt was not good. It was pure evil.

"I feel evil." she said as she started to speak. "There are three of them, all male and all of Asian descent. They are not talking to one another and are searching quickly. One of them has found Himiko's spell book and is looking through it. He is holding it up for the others to see." Gaea paused for a moment, then opened her eyes. "They left."

Himiko looked stunned and stammered, "Asian. That is not good, especially if they are evil, like you said, Gaea."

"C'mon. Let's get out of here." Marc urged. "I don't want to run into them if they choose to come back. I'll feel safer up in Bill and Bob's room."

They quickly finished gathering their belongings and went upstairs.

"Unfortunate." High Priest Sergev said after hearing the progress report from Archmage Argante. "Right under his very nose and let them slip away."

Isobel didn't tell him that she was lenient in her response to losing the Asian girl. She kept her reasons to herself, but she believed that Gunther couldn't be trusted completely. Since she met him at the meeting, she suspected he had ulterior motives. She couldn't quite figure him out, but her gut feeling was mistrust.

"Yes, very unfortunate. Perhaps another member of our coven will find the girl," she replied, and she meant it. The other members she trusted completely and knew they would follow through with their orders. As for this man, she wasn't so sure. Why hadn't he brought his daughter to the meeting? She was a member of the Obsidian Circle and had the right to attend. Was it intentional to keep the girl from understanding the full scope of the task? Maybe Gunther was only giving her some of the information he wanted her to have, and some of it could even be false or misleading. Still, since the girl was his daughter, Argante was willing to give him the benefit of the doubt, at least for now.

"Do we have any leads?"

Yes, my Lord. A small store called Crosby's Five and Dime appears to be the local Wiccan shop for the area. The Asian woman has been seen going into the store. The purpose is unknown to us.

"She may just be buying some herbs or candles," Sergev suggested. "What could that store possibly have to offer that would be of interest regarding the Grimoire? Bah. I don't believe a word of it. We'd better, however, have someone check on it regularly."

The order has already been issued. I have sent Sage Burpee to monitor the store. He is to alert me immediately if she returns. I didn't think it was necessary to assign a more capable or valuable member to such a simple task. He is also well-known in town and would not attract attention."

Sergev nodded and poured himself a cup of tea. "Keep me informed of any developments, no matter how menial they might be."

"Of course." Argante bowed and left the room.

"Ransacked?" Bill asked, alarmed. "I don't like that at all. We should pack up and get out of here."

"Hold your horses, Bill," Bob said, locking the door, not that it would do much good to keep whoever broke into the kid's room out of theirs. They would have to know which room to look in, however. "The meeting at Crosby's still needs to take place. That is our only lead in getting rid of the book."

"It's probably being watched," Himiko said, peeking out the window through a small opening in the curtains.

"True," Gaea was thinking about what she had seen downstairs. "Himiko? Did you write anything in your spell book?"

Besides notes on spells? She paused to think about the question. "I don't think so. Oh, I wrote my name inside. I bought the book to use as a fancy notebook for school but then decided to write down spells and other notes about magic in it. Why do you ask?"

One of the men was looking through your book. I was wondering if anything in it would lead to you. I think your name is compromising if they research you. Did it mention the school?

"Yes. I bought it at the school bookstore. They stamp The University of Maine, Orono, on everything they sell there. You know that."

"I do."

"This is not good," Bob said, glancing through the peephole in the door. Seeing nothing, he turned back to the group. "They can easily find information on you, Himiko, through the registrar, even though it is privileged and protected. There are ways to bypass and access that data. It will take some time to do so, and I plan to have us all out of here by then. They won't be able to track you to Bar Harbor, will they?"

"No one knows that I go there except for Gaea and Marc. They are my only two friends on campus. So, no, I don't think there is a way that they can."

"That's a relief." Bill had calmed down a bit. "We still need to talk to the woman at Crosby's."

"Marc can do that," Gaea said. "No one will suspect a single young man going into a store to buy a soda and a candy bar. He can arrange a new meeting spot. Tasha must know of a place away from here that would be safe."

Marc looked at his girlfriend. "I can do that."

"Just don't wear that sweatshirt." Himiko pointed at what he was wearing. Across the front of it in large print was "Property of UMO Athletics."

"Ah, no." He replied. "That would not be advisable. "What time should I go?"

"Now," Bob advised. "The sooner, the better; we need to arrange the new location and time. Luckily, the Grimoire isn't here, which is a plus. A place to hand over the book still needs to be decided."

"Marc, Himiko, and I have discussed doing that at Cinnamon Woodfire. The restaurant is not open yet, so we think it would be safe and unassuming."

"What will your sister think about that?" Her father asked.

"This entire mess started at her restaurant, and the three of us fell right into the situation. Somehow, it feels right to end it where the Grimoire was found." Himiko said.

"I will talk to my sister," Gaea said.

Marc had changed his sweatshirt to something gray and plain and covered it with his coat. "I'm going."

"I'm going along with you," Bob said, grabbing his coat. "Even more unassuming, just father and son out shopping."

"Ok, Dad," Marc joked.

"We will hold down the fort," Bill said, rechecking the peephole. "Call or text if you run into problems, and I'll come try to help, although I don't know how I would."

"I think the two of us will be fine. We'll be back soon."

After Bob and Marc left, Gaea sat down on a bed. "How did things get to this point? My entire family and friends are wrapped up in this mess, and I feel responsible."

Himiko sat down next to her and put her arm around her friend. "It's not your fault. It's no one's fault except for a dead man. If it weren't for Douglas, none of this would be happening."

"Speaking of that ghost, I wonder how he made out."

Bill let the two girls chat and kept vigil at the window.

High Priest Aoki could not believe what he was being told by the three Magi who had searched the room, which was suspected to be occupied by the two girls and the man he was looking for. "Are you certain of the name that was written in the spell book?"

"I am certain of it." One of the Magi said. "Himiko Aoki."

The High Priest rubbed his temple with his hand. "You may leave."

If this was trustworthy evidence, and he was sure it was, then his daughter might be involved with the Grimoire. But there was always the chance she was just here to celebrate the Winter Solstice and attend the concert with people from the University. Either way, he didn't like her being in Van Buren during the hunt for the Grimoire. She could get caught in a crossfire. If she really was involved with the book, then the situation had changed significantly and not for the good. He wondered why Belphegor hadn't warned him about her presence or possible involvement. He knew the answer before the question even crossed his mind. The demon was secretive with information, and what he did reveal was usually to his advantage. Who had his book didn't matter, nor did why they took it. The Defiler only cared about getting it back by any means. That had been the focus in all of Aoki's dealings with Belphegor. Now, he had to decide what to do next.

He could have had his men bring her to him once she was found, but he rejected the idea. If she was here to enjoy the festivals, then it would be pointless even to let her know he was here. It would raise too many questions he was not willing to answer. If she was involved, then decisions would need to be made as events unfolded. He had come to believe that the Grimoire was not in Van Buren but was nearby, perhaps somewhere in Maine. If his suspicions were correct, then bringing his daughter to him wouldn't be necessary. A watch-and-wait approach would be wiser.

Aoki slammed his fist into his palm in anger. More information was needed. Acting without it was foolish and dangerous, and gathering it took time. Time he didn't have. Once the Winter Solstice ended, everyone would leave, and those who knew would leave with that very information he desperately needed to find the Grimoire. If it were discovered that Himiko knew about the Grimoire and had any knowledge of it, she would need to be questioned. Not by him, but by one of the Magi, and done gently. He would not tolerate harm coming to her. He has plans for Himiko within the Coven—grand plans that would not be thwarted. No one would get in the way of those plans.

Aoki decided to increase his efforts to gather information by sending more of his Magi into the streets. They would search tirelessly until they found something—anything—that could give him the answers he wanted. If needed, he would go himself, though if he was spotted by his rival, the coven could ruin all of his plans before they even began. For now, he would sit and wait.

CHAPTER 20
Crosby's Five & Dime

Aerin was frustrated. No matter how hard he tried, he couldn't get a read on the Grimoire in the Pepper Mansion's root cellar. The protection spell that the ghost had placed on it might be shielding it from his abilities, preventing him from sensing it. He believed he should be able to detect its presence, but so far, he had seen nothing. If only he were there instead of in Cape Neddick, forced to study as a refresher before returning to school.

Logan had been enjoyable to be around, distracting him from the book with the games they played together. However, his father had taken him home, and he was now forced to study as well. The thought of the book lying in that cellar once again haunted his mind, and with nothing he could do, he felt frustrated; it was maddening.

He had tried to persuade his mother to let him visit the Peppers for a weekend, but she refused. She explained that his father and grandfather were away on a fishing trip, so there was no one there to visit. With that as his reason for going, the plan quickly fell apart like ice cream left in the sun. So, he was left to keep trying with his mind and skills, hoping for a breakthrough.

Opening himself up also caused another unexpected problem. He had to drop his Charismatic Shield to try to contact the book, and in doing so, exposed himself to the dead, who had come seeking him for help. He could only open himself briefly to use his abilities before blocking the dead when they appeared. He was used to dealing with them and their nagging, usually shutting them out.

However, in his efforts to achieve his goals with the Grimoire, they were making things harder. Psychic mediums attract those who have passed and are in limbo. His sister was better at this, and Gaea's instruction on dealing with it had been more than helpful; it was vital for his sanity.

If he could locate the book, it would prove that it was still in the root cellar and hadn't been taken by the ghost or someone else. Aerin could then call his sister to confirm that it was truly safe. He sensed that she was very worried about the Grimoire and the ghost's visit afterward.

It was a rainy morning, and Aerin's mother had gone into town, leaving him alone with the house staff. An idea had been nagging at him since he got up, involving entering an off-limits part of the Manor: the widow's watch, located at the very top of the house overlooking the Atlantic Ocean. It was Bill's private office where he wrote when he was home. As it was, the novelist was not home, so if Aerin planned carefully, he thought he could sneak up to the Dreamer's Hideaway, as his dad called it. His plan was quite simple. He would try to make contact with the resident ghost, Tracy Duchamp, who had been his mom's best friend. Tracy had met an untimely death, falling to her death on the rocks below the balcony. Aerin didn't know the whole story, as it had happened before he or Gaea were born. He had only caught bits and pieces of it when his parents or a visitor mentioned it. Neither his mom nor his dad was willing to talk about it openly to their children.

Aerin had sensed her presence more than once, but the ghost seemed to keep his distance and never approached her. He thought it was because of Gaea, who didn't want her bothering him, as other spirits constantly bombarded him.

He planned to go up to the widow's watch and try to contact her. If he succeeded, he might be able to persuade the ghost to check the Grimoire to see if it was safe. The whole process, Aerin thought, shouldn't take more than a few minutes. The entire plan depended on avoiding detection by Mrs. Douglas and finding and talking to Tracy. Aerin had promised his sister to watch over the book, and one way or another, he wouldn't let Gaea down.

He set out to execute his plan that afternoon as Cathy headed into Kennebunkport to visit the antique shop. Mrs.. Douglas was also heading to town to do the weekly grocery shopping, a bonus he had only just learned about. Getting past the housekeepers would be a breeze. He hoped the entire plan would take less than thirty minutes. For now, he just needed to bide his time and wait for the two women to leave the Manor.

Bob and Marc walked directly to Crosby's Five and Dime, not bothering to hide themselves. There was no reason. The two blended in with the crowd seamlessly and would garner no undue attention. Why should they? A father and son are out enjoying the festival together. Who would suspect an ulterior motive?

Most people were still at the Winter Solstice or the concert, so pedestrian traffic was relatively light on the main street of Van Buren. Light, since they didn't have to weave and push their way to get to the store. As the evening set in, people would begin returning from the solstice, so Bob and Marc intended to take care of their business and return to the hotel before the swell of the crowds.

Marc opened the door, and the bell hanging on it jingled as they arrived. They both let out a sigh of relief, seeing only one other person in the store, and she was in the process of checking out. Setting up the meeting should go quickly. He hoped.

The woman and the girl behind the counter exchanged pleasantries, and the woman pushed past them and left. Marc recognized the girl as the owner's daughter and approached her, Bob at his side.

"Hi," Marc said, smiling. "I don't know if you remember me…"

"I remember. How can I help you?"

"This is Bob, ah, my grandfather," he began. "We are here on behalf of Gaea and Himiko. They had decided to accept your mother's help regarding a certain book."

"You were supposed to come tomorrow morning?" The girl opened the countertop, letting the two men walk through. "Come with me, my mother is in the back."

Tasha was sitting at the table, looking over paperwork that was arranged in front of her. Bob immediately took in how beautiful she was and how prominent her red hair was.

"Sit down, please." The witch said, folding a ledger and setting it aside. "Where are Gaea and Himiko?"

"It was too dangerous for them to come," Bab answered. "Things have well, escalated."

"And you are?" Tasha asked.

"Bob Pepper. I am Gaea's grandfather." He didn't see the need to mention that he was not her biological relative. "We, her father and I, came to Van Buren to support Gaea, Marc, and Himiko. We know about the Grimoire and what it is, and we support their plan to get rid of it."

"I see. My name is Tasha," the witch replied. "I know of at least two Wiccan covens that are here searching for the book. They're not pleasant people to deal with. You were smart to come here alone and avoid them. What do you have in mind?"

"Another place to meet and plan on how to deliver the Grimoire to you. Somewhere safe." Marc said nervously, looking back over his shoulder.

"You are safe here, Marc. Please feel at ease."

"I'll try."

"There is another coven of witches that are sworn to guard the Grimoire, and their High Priestess is on her way here as we speak."

"Is she to be trusted?" Bob asked.

Tasha smiled. "She is my sister."

The widow's watch was as Aerin remembered it the last time his father had let him into it. A few changes of décor and new curtains for the French doors caught the boys' eye; other than that, it was the same.

He didn't waste time and sat on the floor facing the Atlantic Ocean. He opened his mind and focused.

"I seek the spirit of Tracy Duchamp. Are you here in the house?" Aerin thought he could feel a presence, but it wasn't clear what or who it was. He hoped it wasn't another random dead person.

"I seek only Tracy Duchamp; all others are not welcome." Aerin relied on his sister's teachings for precise spirit summoning, but it wasn't foolproof. The first ghost that responded to his call was a man in a trench coat who appeared to be partially decapitated. Aerin quickly dismissed him.

The man was followed by six more, all of whom he was able to send on their way without incident.

He was beginning to become frustrated when an apparition came through the bookcase opposite the French doors. It floated until it was in front of Aerin, then began to materialize. A woman in a green dress stood before him.

"Are you Tracy Duchamp?" He asked standing up.

"I am the spirit of who lived as Tracy Duchamp." The apparition answered. "You are Aerin, Gaea's brother."

"Cool," he said. "Yes, I am."

"Gaea has made it clear to me that you have abilities and that I should leave you alone."

"I am learning, and lots of dead people bother me all the time. This's why she said that."

"I see. Why do you summon me now?"

"I need a favor." Aerin was grinning.

"My sister should arrive tomorrow, and she will meet with us because she will assume custody of the Grimoire. Once she has it, the book will be safe from the black covens who are after it, as well as you and everyone involved. No one will pursue you anymore," Tasha explained, standing, gathering the paperwork, and placing it into a nearby closet. "Did you have a place in mind to meet?"

"No," Marc said. "The plan is to meet initially to build trust between you, Gaea, and us, and now with your sister. Once we've done that, a second meeting will be held to hand over the book."

"Two meetings are not necessary, but I see your caution, so I agree that we will proceed with this plan. The Grimoire is close by?"

"It's with the State of Maine," Bob said. "Where exactly will be revealed when the time is right. There are other lives on the line here, and I am not willing to risk those who are dear to me."

"A wise decision. I would do the same in your place." Tasha was beginning to like the older man. He was formidable, she could tell. "So, we need a place to meet tomorrow, and I think I know just the place. There is a church some thirty minutes' drive south of here in the town of North Lyndon. I know the pastor as he is a customer of mine."

Bob raised an eyebrow. "A pastor, a witch?"

"Don't be so surprised. Many are involved in organized religion, yet they also practice white magic. They believe in the betterment of humanity and achieve this through both Wicca and their religion. I do not do both. We can meet in the church's basement, which serves as a meeting hall. The church uses it for gatherings such as wedding receptions and bake sales. It will serve our purpose well."

"That sounds like a plan." Bob agreed. "You say it is south of here? Marc, we can pack up, go to the meeting, and then leave the dangers behind. Gaea will be able to tell if we are being followed."

"Maybe she will be able to, but I wouldn't rely on that completely. Magic spells can make a medium's abilities useless, hiding the witch or warlock from detection. Gaea is strong, though, and might be able to see through the protection spell."

Bob frowned. "Noted. We will have to be vigilant about our movements. Gaea and Himiko will stay where they are and not go out into the open until it is the right time. Marc, you will stay with the girls once we return to the hotel. Bill and I can get anything that is needed, such as food. We have come this far, and there is no need to do anything foolish that will expose us all."

Marc nodded his agreement. "What time tomorrow?"

"My sister will be here sometime in the morning. I suggest mid-afternoon. Those who look for Gaea and Himiko will more than likely be looking at the Winter Solstice festival or the concert, although Van Buren will be a focus of their attention as well. When you leave, disguise Himiko and Gaea well."

"Winter clothing should do the trick," Bob suggested. "Both girls have hoods on their winter coats."

"Perfect. Just one moment." Tasha said, standing and disappearing into the store.

Bob and Marc looked at each other questioningly. A few moments later, she returned with three ski masks, which she handed to Marc.

"I have been selling these like hot cakes, so they are being worn all over town. They work great to fend off the cold, especially when it's windy. Have them wear these; they will cover their faces entirely, and they also won't look out of place."

"Awesome," Marc said, holding one of them up.

"Do you think Himiko can cast a protective spell to help keep them from being detected by a psychic? I know for a fact that one of the covens has people with abilities within their ranks." Tasha asked.

"I know that Himiko used one on the Grimoire. Would that work on a person?" Marc asked, stuffing the masks into his pocket.

"It's possible, but I can't be sure, nor do I know which spell she used. Bring that up when you get back to them. If she knows such a spell, it will help keep them cloaked."

"There is another thing," Marc said. "We have another book that we have used already as a diversion."

"Oh? How so?" Tasha's interest was piqued.

"It's a grimoire and looks somewhat like the magic book, but it's not magical. Himiko cast a spell on it, bewitching it so that it cast an aura that made it seem like the real deal. We used it when we had to break the protection spell on the Grimoire for a brief time. If someone was looking for it at that moment, the thought was that they would get two impressions that would be confusing and allow us to escape. Could we do that again? Leave the enchanted book somewhere while we make for the church?"

"It wouldn't hurt," Tasha said. "I must say that was very clever of the person who came up with the idea. Magical auras are not always distinctive from one another. For example, a magical book and an enchanted stone may seem similar when discovered from a distance. Only searching for the object and finding it would satisfy what was giving out the aura. Leaving that book in a place, such as a library, for example, would buy you time to get out of town. Quite clever indeed."

"And there is a library just down the street," Bob added. Bill and I could take it there just before we leave town, so Gaea, Himiko, or even you, Marc, wouldn't be involved.

"Ok, so we agree," Tasha said as she finished the meeting. "We will meet at 3 pm tomorrow at the church. The town is small, and there is only one church on the main street, so it's easy to find. My sister and I, along with a few members of our coven, will be there, which is good. Protection for all of us."

"Perfect," Bob said, standing. "We will see you then. C'mon, Marc, let's go."

Aerin's plan proceeded smoothly. Tracy was more than happy to assist Cathy's daughter, and checking on a magic book was an easy task. Traveling to the Peppers' root cellar would take her no time, as time and distance held no meaning for a spirit. The physical laws of the living did not bind her.

No sooner than the spirit of Tracy Duchamp left the widow's watch than she reappeared.

"The book is as you said. Locked within an iron box in the darkness of the root cellar. It has not been disturbed." She said in no more than a whisper.

"Thank you very much," Aerin said.

"Is there anything else I can help you with? It is good to be useful again."

No, that's it for now."

"Very well."

"Oh, Tracy?"

"Yes, Aerin?"

"Feel free to come visit me anytime you want."

The apparition of Tracy smiled and vanished.

Aerin hurried out of the widow's watch, down the spiral staircase, and through the master bedroom into the hall. He made sure to close the door behind him. He headed to his bedroom as a telephone call to his sister was of the utmost importance.

CHAPTER 21
A Daughter's Deception

Gunther and his daughter, Seraphina, were having no luck with their search at either venue: the Winter Solstice or the concert. He was growing more discouraged and angry over the time wasted, and it was starting to show. Seraphina could tell that her father was on edge, and he tended to snap at her for no reason. It wasn't her fault they couldn't find the psychic or the weak witch. She was beginning to distrust some of his decisions, like making her stand alone and search the crowds while he ran off on some wild goose chase that went nowhere. She was starting to fear him.

That evening, when they came back from the concert and looked through the digital pictures he had taken—finding nothing—he blamed her and almost hit her, only to stop himself at the last moment before raising his hand to her face. It was then that she decided to leave him and planned to do so that very night. She would go back to the university, summon Belphegor, and complete the blood pact. Then she would find the Grimoire herself and take it for herself.

She had never trusted her father, and this trip to Van Buren only strengthened that distrust. She also planned to leave the Obsidian Circle. She didn't need them. After all, what had they done for her? Nothing, as far as she was concerned. She preferred to practice her magic in the shadows, alone, and with the Grimoire, she would have everything she needed to fulfill her goals and desires.

She even doubted the story he told her about her mother. As far as she knew, he had murdered her himself. Yes, her true feelings were surfacing. She hated him.

She plans to leave this very evening. It's simple because they keep their bags packed just in case they need to move quickly. She will hitchhike to the nearest town, buy a bus ticket to Orono, and leave him behind. After completing the blood pact with the demon, she will also leave the University of Orono and Maine entirely. Maybe a warmer climate like Florida or even California.

She inherited the money left to her by her mother, which she had never used except when attending school. It wasn't a lot, but it could pay for an apartment wherever she ended up. But first, she needed the Grimoire.

She slipped into bed and pulled up the covers. She would wait until he fell asleep.

Gaea received the news of the upcoming meeting with relief. She had some reservations about trusting Tasha; however, she was becoming more confident with everything she was learning from the witch. She was also growing tired from the entire ordeal, and the idea of going back to school seemed more realistic than it had a week ago. That week felt like an eternity in her mind. Now, if things went as she imagined, the Grimoire would be nothing more than a bad dream and out of their lives entirely. If.

Himiko confirmed she could cast a protection spell to shield them from psychics, and to prove it, she cast it on herself, daring Gaea to see through it. She could not.

Gaea also liked the idea of using the decoy grimoire to help them leave Van Buren unnoticed. The library seemed like the best place to hide a book. If placed correctly, it could take someone quite a while to find it. By then, they would be at the church and, hopefully, on their way back to Bar Harbor. Everything would need to fall into place and remain undetected before they execute their plan.

As she understood it, Himiko would cast the protection spell on everyone, including her father and grandfather, to prevent a psychic from discovering their plans by reading their minds. She would also enchant the grimoire, after which her dad and Bob would take it and hide it somewhere in the library. While they hid the book, she, Marc, and Himiko would load up and drive her Jeep out of Van Buren to meet the two men at the church in North Lyndon, where they would meet Tasha and the High Priestess of her coven. They would decide where the Grimoire would change hands. Everything seemed simple, so why was Gaea's stomach tied in knots? The threat of mortal danger was lurking like a thick fog over the water of Bar Harbor.

People who weren't friendly were searching for the Grimoire, and they suspected Gaea and Himiko had the book. She knew they would stop at nothing to get it. If the girls got in the way, they would be dealt with. Gaea knew this completely, and her instincts confirmed it. A mistake or misstep could cost her and her friends their lives. She couldn't even hand over the book if forced. The Grimoire was in a root cellar about 250 miles away, give or take a few miles. But that was close enough for her pursuers to reach the Pepper Mansion and seize it by force, risking Dottie and the estate staff. That was not an option. The plan they had made had to succeed.

It was going to be a long night until they started on their quest to rid themselves of the Grimoire.

"I am canceling it, Isobel," High Priest Sergev informed his Archmage. "The Black Sabbath is of no importance to us at this point. Time is running out, and we are still no closer to the Grimoire than we were at the start."

"It is frustrating, my Lord," Argante said. "The psychic and the witch are proving very elusive. But I remind you that there are many people in a small area to search."

"Yes, but not so much as a possible sighting. Perhaps we are going about this wrong?"

"How so? We are visually searching, and the three psychics that are here have been using their abilities to search the crowds as well. What can we do differently?"

"I don't know. And what of this news of another coven that may be here as well? What do we know of them?"

"Very little, except they seem to be made up entirely of Asian men."

Argante's words halted the High Priest suddenly. "Asian, you say? Have any names surfaced?"

"One, my Lord. A psychic has picked up the name Aoki, but that is all."

"Aoki." He repeated. "That is a name I have not heard for a very long time."

"An old friend?"

"Adversary, Isobel. An old adversary."

Aoki was equally frustrated with the lack of progress in finding the two girls, whom he believed knew the location of the Grimoire. None of his Magi were giving any clues about where they might be. As far as he knew, they had left town, which was definitely a possibility. After an exhaustive search turned up no sign of them, he had to believe they had come to do what they planned to do and then left. Aoki thought they meant to deliver the Grimoire to his enemy.

One of the Magi brought him a photograph of two girls, one of whom was Asian. The two were the right age; however, one had blonde hair and did not match the description of the person they were searching for. The Asian girl was also not his daughter, which was a relief. He found it strange that reports of many Asian girls of his daughter's age were coming from across town, the festival, and the concert. Unbeknownst to the High Priest, both the Universities of Maine in Presque Isle and Orono had a significant number of Asian students, some of whom were attending the town festivities during winter break. The High Priest was unaware that this made his task harder, as was the case for his rival Sergev.

He had ruled out his daughter, Himiko's, involvement in the Grimoire. It was absurd to think she could be involved. She was studying psychology at the University of Maine. She was a beginner witch and had no knowledge of the book. There was simply no reason for him to believe she had come into such knowledge. He would let his daughter enjoy herself with her friends. There was no reason to make his presence known to her.

Aoki could only reach one conclusion. If the Grimoire was in Van Buren as he believed, and the two girls were no longer in town or in possession of the Book of Belphegor, then it must have fallen into his enemy's hands.

It was time to visit Sergev.

"That's good to hear, Aerin. Don't let Mom find out you went up to the widow's watch." Gaea hung up the phone and shook Himiko awake.

"What time is it?" She groaned, rolling over to face her friend.

Early. 5:30 in the morning, to be exact. Aerin just called to tell us that the Grimoire is in the root cellar and safe.

"Why did he call so early?"

"He tried to call last night, but he had a dead battery."

"I thought he was in Cape Neddick?"

He had a plan, and it worked. He used his abilities to communicate with a ghost in our house, a friend of my mom's who died at Shaw Manor. She fell to her death. Anyway, Aerin asked her to check on it, and she did. Safe and sound according to the spirit.

"He did say he would keep an eye on it."

It seems he can't make contact with it. I guess the enchantment Douglas cast on it is working perfectly. No one can detect its aura.

That is great news. It means everyone is safe back in Bar Harbor, at least for now. We should inform your dad and Bob.

"We heard," Bob said, sitting up in bed. "You two aren't exactly whispering."

"What?" Bill said groggily.

"Nothing, Bill," Bob said. "Go back to sleep."

"I can't sleep anymore." Gaea climbed out of bed. "Where's Marc? I'm hungry."

"Right here." Marc walked out of the bathroom, drying his hair. "I couldn't sleep anymore either. I figured I'd get up, go down, and get some breakfast for the three of us to go. Your dad and Bob can go down and eat so they can keep an eye out while at the restaurant."

"Good idea, Marc," Bob said, standing and stretching. "C'mon, Bill, up and at 'em."

Bill sat up and yawned.

Himiko headed for the bathroom, sidestepping Marc. "I'll take a fruit salad and coffee."

"Make it two," Gaea added.

Bill shook his head. "Fruit. I want bacon, eggs, and a stack of pancakes. Oh, and extra-large, strong coffee. Let me get dressed, Bob, and we can go downstairs."

"You bet. You girls stay low. We'll be back soon," Bob said, peering out the window at the street lit only by the streetlights along one side. The sun had yet to rise.

"The restaurant opens at six, and that is in a few minutes," Marc said, opening the door. "I'll swing by the Jeep and grab the decoy while I'm out. There is no spell on it, is there?"

Gaea shook her head. "Of course not."

"Just checking." After a quick look down the hallway, he slipped out and shut the door.

"Good idea, and we'll be fine. We will pack while you're gone." Gaea promised.

Bob nodded, and he and Bill followed Marc out the door.

Gaea was definitely nervous. They had hours before they had to leave, and anything could happen in that time. Staying quiet and hiding in the room was their best option. Hopefully, the three men wouldn't be gone long.

High Priestess Riana and four of her most powerful witches and warlocks arrived at Bangor International Airport at the same time Aerin was making his phone call to Gaea. She was ecstatic about the news of the resurfacing of the Grimoire and the chance to return the book to its safe house in Vancouver. For too long, it had been missing, possibly in the hands of those who would use it for evil purposes. If her sister's information was accurate, then the Book of Belphegor was within her reach if she acted quickly.

The meeting was scheduled for 3 pm in the afternoon, so she had plenty of time to rent a car and drive the three hours north to the church chosen for the meeting. She hoped to get the Grimoire and return to Vancouver that same evening; however, whether the book was even in their possession was unknown to the witch. Riana was ready to stay as long as it took to complete her mission.

Learning about two possible covens of black magic in Van Buren searching for the Grimoire was disturbing, but her sister assured her they hadn't found it and were nowhere near discovering the three young people who possessed it. Her sister said one was a witch, another a psychic medium, and the third a boy. Maybe the witch was using magic to keep them hidden from the black magic users. As long as they stayed safe and hidden until 3 pm this afternoon, she hoped to get the Grimoire as planned.

An hour later, Riana looked out the window at the snowy landscape of northern Maine as she and her coven members rode in a large SUV toward the Canadian border.

Seraphina was picked up by the first car that approached her, a maroon Ford pickup truck that looked like it had seen most of its better years. Rust had created holes in many areas of the steel that was once the truck's usable bed. Now, it was mostly gone, and the farmer who drove it used it to tow the trailer hitched to it. She climbed into the cab, placing her duffle bag on the floor between her legs, then looked at the old man sitting next to her. He was in his seventies, with eyes that matched his gray hair. Hands, wrinkled from years of hard work, gripped the steering wheel, and his overalls were worn but clean.

"Where to?" He asked in a thick down-east accent.

"Does the next town have a bus station?" She asked. "I need to get back to school in Orono."

"That would be Presque Isle, and I just happen to be goin' there. You are more than welcome to ride along. I'll drop ya right at the station."

"That would be perfect. Thanks so much."

"No trouble at all." He said as he put the truck into gear. It lurched and headed off down the road.

Seraphina couldn't believe her luck in catching a ride so quickly. Hopefully, she could board an early bus. The farther away she could get from her father, the better. She hoped that he would not follow her. She doubted that he would. He was intent on the Grimoire and, unless he thought she had it, would stay in Van Buren.

She had not left him a note and now second-guessed not doing so. What if he thought she had the book? He would come after her if he did. She pushed the idea out of her mind. She had more urgent matters to address. Getting her trunk from his house was second only to picking up her truck from the university parking lot. The trunk held the items needed for her magic practice, sitting in her father's garage. Entering it was no problem since she still had the key he had given her during her brief stay.

Another problem was where to stay. Returning to the cathedral on campus was not an option. Gunther knew about it, and it would be the first place he would look for her. After considering it, Seraphina decided to go back to upper campus, even if only for a few days. The psychic and the weak witch were thought to be in Van Buren, and if that was true, she would be safe at her old lair. Safe to complete the blood pact with Belphegor and find the Grimoire. Then, she planned to leave Maine and start her life over.

The older man was not much of a talker, to her relief, so she sat back and tried to enjoy the ride. She should be back in Orono before dark.

CHAPTER 22
A Dangerous Decision & A Daring Plan

Sergev was beginning to think that the Order of Mazoku might have obtained the Grimoire. He wouldn't put it past his rival, High Priest Aoki, to have entered Van Buren, used his ruthlessness to find the girls, taken what he wanted, and gotten rid of them. Killing was in his nature, and he did it often and efficiently.

If Aoki did have the Grimoire, Sergev would be forced to move quickly to confront him before he was able to leave Van Buren. He knew from his coven members that Aoki was encamped on the outskirts of town with a dozen of his Magi—highly trained magic users who were also trained in the martial arts of the Ninja. Sergev would confront the High Priest one-on-one. He also knew that Aoki had a score to settle with him and would not shy away from that confrontation. He also knew that only one would survive the encounter.

He would invoke *'futari no mahōtsukai no tataka'*: a battle of two wizards. It was a formal challenge issued when a conflict existed between two people or parties. The request was formal, and refusing it would bring shame to oneself and one's coven. Aoki would not decline, Sergev was sure of that.

The question was how to contact Aoki and present him with the challenge. He also needed a viable reason to do so, which was simple enough: Revenge. Both men desired it, as they believed they had been wronged by the other. Invoking *futari no mahōtsukai no tataka* to settle the claims that they brought against each other. If Isobel happened to find out where the fight was to take place and happen to be in the area, so be it. If not, Sergev was confident in his ability to defeat the man. His magic was more potent.

He would write out the formal challenge and send Sage Burpee to deliver it. A Magi would find the boy well before he could find Aoki.

His mind made up, he sent for Archmage Argante. Isobel needed to know about his decision.

Gunther was furious when he woke up and discovered his daughter was gone. He confirmed it because all of her belongings were also missing. She had left no note or anything to explain her leaving. "Maybe she had found the Grimoire?" he wondered, then dismissed it. She had been by his side most of the time, and when he left her, it was only for a short while, and she was exactly where he had left her when he returned. No, she didn't have the book. There were other reasons at play, and he didn't have time to find out what they were. He needed to drive out to the farm and report to High Priest Sergev. He wasn't looking forward to admitting his failure in finding anything related to the grimoire.

He checked and found his car keys and wallet. She had not stolen from him, which was a relief. It would have been simple to take both and high-tail it out of town. But if he knew one thing about his daughter Seraphina, it was that she was honest to a fault. Sometimes, it didn't hurt to bend the truth a little. He sighed, heading off to shower and shave. He needed to be on the road within the hour.

"We will do battle here." Sergev pointed to a point on a map. Isobel leaned forward and read aloud.

"Forked Tongue. It looks to be a ravine a few kilometers from town. Are you certain you wish to engage in combat with Aoki, my Lord? There is still time to find the Grimoire."

I believe that Aoki already has it, Isobel. That being the case, the only way to get the Grimoire back is to finish something we started a long time ago but haven't yet completed.

"Futari no mahōtsukai no tataka," she said. "There will be only one winner, you understand that, Sergey? One must die."

"I am well aware of that fact, Archmage."

"When do you plan to do this?

"That is up to Aoki. I choose the location; he chooses the time."

"I see. Who will you send with the challenge?"

Sage Burpee. He poses no threat to Aoki or his Magi, and they won't harm him. They will simply use him to send the reply when it's time. I do, however, want you to follow him to keep him safe, but be careful not to get caught. The Magi won't be so merciful if you fall into their hands. Now leave me, as I need to prepare what's necessary.

"As you wish, my Lord," Isobel said and left him to write the challenge.

"There is no sign of anything out of the ordinary," Marc said, closing the door behind him. He was carrying two paper bags containing the breakfast he had purchased downstairs at the restaurant. Your dad and Bob are sitting at the table with a view of the front door. They will be able to see everyone who comes in and out. Right now, it's primarily people leaving. Heading out to the festival, I guess."

Gaea took the bags from him and handed one to Himiko.

"My food is in one of them." He said, sitting down on the bed. "They had the fruit salads, and I also got a couple of cinnamon rolls."

"Yum!" Gaea said, taking a bite of the roll.

Himiko was having trouble with the plastic top covering her salad, but she finally took it off. "Coffee?" she asked.

"Oh. Hold on a sec." He stood and retrieved another bag and a satchel that he had left in the hallway.

You should not have left the satchel out in the hall, Marc.

"Sorry. I had to open the door." He apologized. "So, Bill and Bob are talking about getting out of here early. They think it will be safer to kill time in North Lyndon than remaining here. I tend to agree."

"Ok," Gaea said, sipping her hot coffee. "The sooner we are out of Van Buren, the better as far as I am concerned. How about you, Himiko?"

"I am ready to leave now."

"I brought you these." He said, reaching into his coat pocket and pulling out the ski masks. "Tasha wants you to be disguised, and these will do the trick."

"Ski masks?" Himiko asked.

"Yeah. It's super cold out this morning, and lots of people are wearing them. I saw them when I was buying breakfast. It's good. We will blend in, and no one will be able to tell who we are. Plus, they will keep our faces warm."

"You have one too?" Gaea asked.

"Yeah, Tasha ended up giving us all a ski mask." Marc thought for a moment. "I was thinking, I should go get the Jeep when we are ready and pick you guys up here. Bob thinks that you, Gaea, and your dad should ride in the Jeep while Himiko goes in the pickup with Bob. Mix it up a little. They are looking for you and Himiko, so keeping you two separated seems like a good idea. At least until we get out of town."

"That sounds like a plan to me," Gaea said, digging into her salad.

"Ok with me, too."

As soon as Bob and Bill get done eating, they are going to take the decoy to the library, so you're going to have to do your thing to it, Himiko."

"No problem." She said, grabbing the satchel and pulling the book from it. "It only takes a minute to bewitch and put an aura on it. I will do it right before they leave for the library."

"Sounds like a plan," Marc said, smiling.

"It's damn cold this morning," Bill remarked as another person opened the door to leave the hotel lobby, letting a blast of cold air in. "Those masks will come in handy. We still have to go to the library after breakfast."

"I'm glad I brought my long underwear," Bob said, swallowing his last bit of pancake. "I think that your idea of leaving early is a smart one. We can get lost in the crowd, so to speak."

"I will be glad when this entire ordeal is over with. I still have a novel to finish writing."

"Yeah, I am anxious to get back to Dottie and home myself. We have to make sure the girls are safe and finish this first, Bill."

"I know that. A guy can bitch a little, can't he? Damn that stupid book."

"Well, library, here we come," Bob said, standing and dropping the cash for the tab onto the table.

Neither of the two noticed the man who was set to open the door when he caught the word book and paused. Then Gunther heard the word library, shrugged, and left. He was getting jumpy at the very mention of the word book. He needed to get a grip on himself.

"So, you want me to take this to the campground and give it to a man named Aoki?" Kenneth asked Sergev. "How will I find him?"

I believe he will find you, or at least one of his Magi will. They are from another coven and will recognize you as a magic user. They will confront you and ask what your business is. Tell them you carry a message from High Priest Sergev for High Priest Aoki and want to deliver it to him. They will take you to Aoki, and you should remain silent unless spoken to, waiting for him to give you a reply. Do not read the messages, do you understand?

"Yes, High Priest Sergev. I understand."

"Good," Sergev said, handing a brown envelope with a wax seal to him. "Go now and return as soon as possible."

Kenneth turned and left quickly. He did not see Isobel following him.

Kenneth climbed into his Buick and started the engine. The drive to the campground was twenty minutes at the most, and fortunately, he would not have to deal with festival traffic as it was located on the north end of town. He wouldn't have to enter Van Buren.

What was written in the envelope gnawed at him as he was curious by nature, but he dared not try to look at what was in it. The envelope was sealed with wax, so he couldn't look unless he broke the seal. He dared not even think to do such a thing and face the wrath of two High Priests. He would follow his orders to a tee.

The road was clear as he drove, and he turned on the radio. His favorite station, the University of Presque Isle student station, was playing oldies from the '60s and '70s, which he enjoyed. He tapped the steering wheel with his fingers to the beat of the music, oblivious to the sedan that followed behind him.

Isobel had taken the limo they used to drive up from the airport. It wasn't a stretch model but a simple black sedan with tinted windows, which served her well in tailing Kenneth. She would stay well behind him and observe from a distance once they arrived at the campground. She dared not drive in too far for fear of being discovered. She would park and then enter the office pretending to look for a campsite. She hoped to keep visual contact with Kenneth at least until the Magi confronted him.

Bob and Bill hurried toward the library, with Bill's satchel securely tucked under his arm. The street was quickly filling up as people headed to the Winter Solstice festival. Their plan was to enter the library, with Bob distracting the librarian while Bill found the door to the cellar. Bill meant to take the decoy down and hoped that, like most libraries, it stored shelves of books. He would find a place for the decoy and hide it among the other books. Then he would go back to Bob, and they would leave together. Hopefully, they could avoid anyone who might sense the aura Himiko had cast upon it.

The first part of the plan went smoothly, and Bob was able to get the librarian, an older woman, to pay attention and engage her in conversation. Bill wandered off looking for a way into the cellar. He found the door at the very back of the library, and to his dismay, it was locked with a padlock.

He needed a plan B and needed it quickly. Next to the locked door was a staircase that led upward. "If you can't go down…" He muttered. Quickly, he climbed the stairs, entering a large room that was full of shelves stuffed with books.

"Bingo," He whispered and found a spot in the corner. The shelf had encyclopedias from a long-forgotten year that were of the same size as his book. Carefully, he removed the decoy from the satchel and slid it between two of the volumes.

"Can I help you?" A man's voice said from behind him.

Bill turned and feigned a smile. "I was just admiring the old encyclopedias that you have. I don't imagine anyone has use for them anymore?"

"No, sir, they don't. This area is off limits to patrons."

"Oh?" Bill stammered.

"I guess you didn't see the sign at the bottom of the stairs?"

"No, I didn't. I am sorry for the mistake." Bill said, turning to leave.

The man grabbed his arm, stopping him. He took a glance into the satchel Bill was holding, then let go of his arm. "Please watch your step going back down."

"I will," Bill said, hurrying to the stairs and back down to find Bob, who was happily chatting about the festival with the woman. Bill cleared his throat.

"Did you find what you were looking for?" Bob asked.

"Yes. The gentleman upstairs was most helpful. We should be heading back to the kids."

"Ok. Well," Bob said to the woman, "it was nice to make your acquaintance." He turned and followed Bill out the door.

"Have a nice day." She called after them.

"I almost got caught hiding the book in a restricted section, but it's done. I tucked the book in with a bunch of old encyclopedias. Let's hurry and go get my pickup truck."

"Right behind you."

"Marc had gone to get the Jeep while Bob and Bill were running their errand to the library. He found a spot across from the hotel and parked. He locked it and ran across the street and up to the room to help with the luggage. Gaea and Himiko were all wrapped up in their winter coats, their faces hidden behind the ski masks.

"It's about time," Gaea said, pulling off her mask. These things are hot!"

"Let's go then," Mark said, shouldering his duffle bag. "Your Dad and Bob should be here shortly. Remember, Gaea, you're with me, and Himiko is going with Bob in the pickup. Masks on in the lobby, ok?"

"You're the boss," Himiko said.

As Bob and Bill pulled up, Bill jumped out from the passenger side and spotted Gaea's Jeep parked on the opposite side of the street. No one was in it.

Bob took advantage of a delivery van that was leaving and pulled the pickup into the vacant parking spot. He noticed there was a no-parking loading zone sign, but he didn't intend to be parked for long. Besides, he was loading passengers and luggage.

A few moments later, Marc exited the hotel, followed by Gaea and Himiko, the three wearing the ski masks. He was able to tell them apart by the colors and patterns of the masks. Himiko came directly to the pickup and climbed in. Bob put the truck in gear and drove off.

Bill had arrived at the Jeep before Marc and Gaea and opened the doors for them. Gaea climbed into the back, Marc put their bags in the back and then got into the passenger seat, and Bill became the designated driver, starting the Jeep and heading off in the same direction that Bob had gone.

Five minutes later, they were well clear of Van Buren, and there was no sign of anyone following them. In the Jeep, the three of them sighed in relief.

"I think we are clear," Bill said, picking up his phone and quickly dialing Bob.

"Yeah, we're clear of town," Bill spoke into the phone. "Good. Let's keep our distance from one another. We'll meet up in North Lyndon. We should be safe there. Great, you be safe as well." He hung up.

CHAPTER 23
An Agreement

Aoki was not impressed by Sergev's messenger; in fact, he felt insulted that someone so weak had been entrusted with a communiqué of such importance. The boy practically shook with fear as he handed the sealed envelope to Aoki.

Once he opened and read it, a smile crossed the wizard's face. It seemed that Sergev was invoking an old Japanese challenge that he had to accept. Refusing to accept would show cowardice, and his coven would turn against him. However, declining wasn't even a consideration as Aoki welcomed the duel with Sergev. Finally, revenge would be his.

He instructed the boy to go outside and wait for his reply to the message. Eager to comply, Kenneth hurried away. But why was Sergev insisting on a duel now? He was on the hunt for the Grimoire. Perhaps he had located it and now claimed the magical book. Aoki suspected that Sergev was aware that both he and the Order of Mazoku were also in Vam Buren in search of it. Aoki theorized that if Sergev possessed the Grimoire, he thought he wouldn't be able to leave with it, as the Magi of the Order of Mazoku would intervene, potentially igniting a minor war. To prevent a confrontation that would certainly reveal both covens, Sergev chose a private way to decide the Grimoire's fate. Aoki considered this a rather smart strategy. It would also resolve their longstanding conflict.

Logic told the High Priest that Sergev must possess the book, as no other explanation made sense. The duel would leave one coven with the Book of Belphegor and the other shattered beyond repair. The losing coven, now leaderless, would disband, and its members would vanish into the shadows. The solution was so perfect that Aoki was angry with himself for not thinking of it. Both men considered themselves superior to one another in both cunning and magical ability, and their egos reinforced this claim. Another stipulation of inciting *futari no mahōtsukai no tataka* was that no one else could be anywhere near the two when they battled. This ensured that the stronger magic user would emerge victorious without outside assistance or interference. One would live, and the other would not. The only thing Aoki had to do was choose the time of their meeting, as Sergev had already selected the location.

Aoki would give himself the rest of the morning to consider when he would destroy his adversary. Seeming to be hasty would not look good in the eyes of Sergev. Besides, letting the older man stew for a few hours seemed rather satisfying to the High Priest. He motioned one of his Magi to admit the boy. Kenneth walked meekly into the room.

"Leave and return at precisely 1 pm. I will have an envelope for you to bring to Sergev."

"But High Priest Sergev told me…"

"Silence!" Aoki said his voice rising with oncoming anger. "Do as you are told."

Kenneth didn't have to be told twice and almost ran out of the RV towards his car.

Isobel had been watching for Kenneth from the moment that he had entered the black RV, and when he suddenly appeared walking quickly toward his Buick, she moved to follow him. Had he gotten the answer from High Priest Aoki? She would find out soon enough. Kenneth had started his car and was driving off towards the farmhouse.

Gunther felt it was essential to inform Sergev about his daughter's abrupt departure from the search for the Grimoire, and he swore that she did not have it. He had no explanation for why she would turn tail and flee. He found that Sergev was not concerned about a girl he had never met, let alone a witch who lacked the powers to impress him. If he had mentioned her dealings with Belphegor to the High Priest, Sergev might have taken a different stance on the matter. As it stood, his command to Gunther was straightforward.

"Do not search for the Grimoire any longer, Mage. I believe that we know where it is and who it lies with." He told an exasperated warlock.

"But where? Who?" He pleaded with the High Priest to no avail. He was told, "It was none of his concern any longer, and to go find his daughter." Which wasn't exactly what he wanted to hear.

Gunther left the presence of High Priest Gunther, and as he walked toward his car, it became clear to him what he needed to do. First and foremost, he required information, a clue about what was happening with the book, and he believed he knew exactly who could provide it. That person was standing next to the barn: Kenneth.

The boy was a dolt; that was clear, but he did seem to possess knowledge about certain things. He lived in the farmhouse where Sergev was staying, and the High Priest had just promoted him to the position of Sage. Why, he had no idea. It was time to talk to Kenneth and find out what he did or didn't know.

"Sage Burpee!" Gunther chirped as he approached the Mage. "Congratulations on the promotion. You must be very proud. You know the Mage of the coven has direct contact with the High Priest whenever he likes. A fundamental right indeed. Don't you think?"

"Yeah. I guess so. I haven't talked to him a whole lot yet, but yeah, I guess it's a big deal."

"You bet it is." Gunther put his arm around Kenneth. "Did you know that the only other member of our coven who has the High Priest's ear is Archmage Argante?"

He shook his head.

"Well, that's the dead-on truth. Oh, by the way, have you heard any updates on the search for the Grimoire? I think I'm getting close myself, but I still need a little more time." Gunther lied.

"Nothing much. I delivered a message to this High Priest of another coven this morning. I have to go back to pick up the answer."

"Any idea what the message was about?"

"No. I was forbidden to even think about trying to read it."

"Probably for the best. No need to get involved in something that does not concern you."

"Oh, when I was waiting outside of High Priest Sergev's room, I heard he and Archmage Argante talking about Forked Tongue."

"What's Forked Tongue?"

"It's a ravine up the road from here, a couple of miles. There's not much there but a stream running through it."

"I wonder why they would be talking about a ravine?" Gunther said half to himself.

Kenneth shrugged, "Beats me. I'd better be going because I have to pick up the message at precisely 1 pm. I don't want to be late. That other High Priest is not a very nice person."

"Run along then and be careful."

"I will."

Gunther watched Kenneth drive off towards town, then walk to his car, questions filling his mind. Another coven? Who could they be? It seemed evident that they must be after the Grimoire as well for Sergev to be interested in them. Perhaps they had the book, and he was trying to make some deal. The ravine could be where that deal was going to go down.

He started his car and began driving toward Van Buren. With his daughter out of the way, he was free to pursue the Grimoire on his own terms. He was determined to reach that rendezvous point, even if it meant camping out there until whoever showed up. He would have to play it by ear then and hope the Grimoire would be there as well.

For the moment, he would follow Kenneth into town and see just where this coven was. There could be some helpful information from Kenneth or the other coven members if he got the chance to engage them in conversation. Only time would tell.

Kenneth parked where he had before, and before he could walk five feet, he was being escorted by two Magi, one on each side. Neither of them spoke, and Kenneth moved swiftly. It only took a few moments before he was being shuffled into the room and found himself face to face with the High Priest.

"Take this to Sergev," Aoki said, handing him an envelope similar to the one he had delivered. "Do not open it or your life will forfeit your foolish mistake."

Kenneth nodded and swallowed hard. He tucked the envelope into his coat pocket and was immediately escorted out of the RV and sent on his way.

Isobel had followed Kenneth back to town and felt satisfied with how the exchange had appeared to go. Kenneth was in one piece and was driving back to the farm, hopefully with Aoki's answer. She wasn't enthusiastic about Sergev invoking *futari no mahōtsukai no tatak,* but she was confident in Boris Sergev's abilities, especially in combat. She had, after all, been present at his last duel with another Archmage, which he had won decisively. She expected a similar outcome in this battle. Sergev was cunning, and his age was misleading. His physique resembled that of a man in his twenties, and he had the agility of a gymnast. Few, if any, could match him. He had bested Isobel numerous times in their mock duels, usually through clever deception. Few knew that Sergev was a master in the art of illusion.

Kenneth didn't even know that the Archmage had followed him as she entered Sergev's chambers immediately after he did. His audience with the High Priest lasted less than a minute, just long enough to deliver the envelope, and then he was dismissed. Isobel closed the door behind him as he left.

"Sit," Sergev said to her. Argante straddled a chair facing him,

He examined the seal on the envelope: wax and imprinted with a serpent. It had not been tampered with. Sergev picked up a dagger and cut through the seal, breaking it. He set the blade down and pulled out a piece of parchment from inside. He read it, then read it again before handing it to Argante, who read it in turn.

"He accepts the challenge," Isobel said. Tonight, at midnight."

"Appropriate, don't you think, Isobel? Two covens, each with a high priest who has unfinished business with another, meeting at the stroke of the bewitching hour to do mortal battle." Sergev smiled. "It sounds like something out of a modern horror movie."

Isobel handed him the parchment. "But this is no movie, my Lord. Your life hangs in the balance of what is to come. Is the Grimoire worth your life?"

"It is. The fate of the world may hang in the balance depending on who controls the Book of Belphegor. Aoki would seek to take down powerful governments to advance his agenda, Isobel. I know the man, and I know his demeanor. I would not be surprised if he has made a blood pact with the demon already."

"Then you will need to be exceptionally careful. The demon might intervene on Aoki's behalf. If that is the case, I should be there."

"Belphegor will not intervene on anyone's behalf. He had never come to the rescue and never will. If one is strong enough to win the Grimoire and possess it, the demon will wield its power through the one that has it, but only for its own purposes and ends. Belphegor answers to no one except the Master of Darkness himself, and such a book would not even interest him. No, the Grimoire was created by Belphegor for one purpose: to steal souls for his master by any means possible, even if it means a war between governments."

"How can such a beast be stopped?" Isobel asked.

"He cannot. The demon can only be banished through the act of an Archangel, such as Michael, or kept at bay by taking the Grimoire, guarding it, and not using it. It must be hidden where no man or woman can try to master what is written on its pages. To do so would result in a witch or warlock of immense power."

"And you believe Aoki has the Grimoire?"

"It does not matter. We do not have it, and whether Aoki does or not is of no consequence. If he does and I defeat him, the book will fall into our hands. If he doesn't, an ancient feud will be settled." Sergev thought for a moment as he looked out the window. "How old do you think that I am, Isobel?"

"I have never given it much thought, my Lord." She answered.

"Guess."

Isobel took a moment, then answered, "Sixty."

Sergev chuckled, then reached to take her wrist. I don't remember my exact age, as too many years have passed. I have lived when

Emperors ruled the Roman Empire and probably before, although I do not remember."

"How can this be?" Argante asked.

I am one of the very few in this world called Tithonians who know ancient magic that contains spells to extend life. Some of us grew tired of living and faded away, disappearing into history without mention. Others vanished. As far as I know, Aoki and I are two of those who are left and may be the only ones in existence. The Grimoire holds that very magic that he and I learned centuries ago. I refrain from using it and have forgotten much of the text. I suspect Aoki has as well. If either of us were to obtain the book again and chose to awaken those spells, the consequences would be unimaginable. I would not use such power, but I cannot say the same for my rival, especially if he has made a blood pact with Belphegor. So, you see why I must invoke the *futari no mahōtsukai no tataka*. Not doing so would mean that the Grimoire in Aoki's hands would mean my death, as he would not tolerate me being a potential rival and threat to his power.

Isobel absorbed everything he had told her without interruption. His logic, as always, was indisputable. She could not and would not argue with the High Priest, even if she thought there was a reason to do so. There was not.

"Do you need aid in preparation?"

He shook his head. "That I must do alone. I have been preparing for this encounter for some time, and I will be ready. It is your task to keep this secret. No member of the Coven may follow me or attempt to assist me. This matter is solely between me and Aoki. Understood?”

“Yes, my Lord.”

“Very well. Leave me.”

She stood and turned, preparing to depart from him.”

“Isobel?” He called after her.

She paused and looked back. “Yes?”

“You have been of great service to me. More than you will ever realize.”

She nodded and left.

CHAPTER 24
North Lyndon Church

Seraphina stood in front of the service station in North Lyndon, Maine, a small town. The pickup truck that had given her a lift to Presque Isle had broken down, leaving her with no choice but to either keep hitchhiking or wait for the repairs. With temperatures dropping below zero, it wasn't a hard decision to stay. Nearly four hours had passed since the truck's failure, but thankfully, the coffee shop next door was open. She decided to grab some lunch and a much-needed cup of hot coffee. She informed the old man, who was busy bothering the mechanic working on his truck, that she would be back shortly before walking to the diner. She would return if and when the old pickup was fixed.

As she sat at a table waiting for her food, she looked out over a portion of the town visible to her. It featured a few buildings that housed stores, along with residences on a couple of side streets branching off from the main road that split the town in two. Directly across from the diner stood a small white church topped with a steeple. She pondered how simple life must be living in such a quaint little village, removed from the troubles of the outside world. She had never experienced such a simplistic life, even as a little girl. Witchcraft had always been the center of her universe for as long as she could remember, and it would be for the rest of her life.

She was halfway through her breakfast and on her second cup of coffee when a Jeep pulled up and parked in front of the church. When the occupants of the vehicle exited, she nearly choked on a piece of bacon. She recognized the girl who stepped onto the sidewalk, and her psychic abilities confirmed her suspicion. It was the psychic medium she had been searching for—the one who possessed the Grimoire.

Seraphina quickly mumbled an incantation, concealing herself from the girl— a protection spell that should keep her hidden from the medium's psychic abilities should she choose to use them. Seraphina turned away from the window, pulling the scarf she wore up around her face, partially obscuring it. The girls, along with a man and a boy roughly her age, were heading toward the diner. She decided to remain where she was and try to eavesdrop on the trio.

The bell on the door jingled as the three entered the diner. The lone waitress on duty met them and escorted them to a table not far from where Seraphina was sitting, clearly within earshot.

"I'm starved," Marc said, pulling a chair out for Gaea to sit on before taking his own seat. The girl's back was to Seraphina, and the boy looked away. Only the man could see her, and only partially.

"You just had breakfast back at the hotel." Gaea scolded playfully.

"I know, but I'm still hungry."

"Eat then," Bill said, reading over the menu.

"They should be here any minute," Gaea said, motioning the waitress to pour a cup of coffee that she was offering. "They can't be that far behind us."

"How will they know where to find us when they do get here?" Marc asked, blowing on his cup.

"I'm sure they are smart enough to look over here. There aren't many places to go." Bill said. "I think I'll have a burger for lunch. How about you two?"

"Burger sounds great!" Marc said. "And fries."

"I'm not hungry yet. Maybe I'll have something when Himiko and Bob get here."

"Suit yourself." Her father answered.

Seraphina focused first on the girl but could read nothing from her. The boy, however, was another matter entirely. He knew about the Grimoire and its location. If only she could extract that piece of information from his mind. It wasn't proving easy. Someone had placed a protection spell on him. It was wearing off but still had an effect. She cursed under her breath. She was closer than ever to finding the Book of Belphegor, and a foolish spell was blocking her path. Patience, she told herself.

A few minutes passed, and a pickup truck pulled up and parked behind the Jeep. Again, Seraphina recognized the girl who climbed out of it. It was the Asian girl, the weak witch. Seraphina had hit the jackpot if only she could capitalize on it.

The witch and the medium embraced when they reached their table and pulled chairs from a nearby table, joining their friends. Seraphina sat down and pretended to eat, listening closely to their conversation.

"Any idea when Tasha is supposed to show up with her sister?" Bob accepted a cup of coffee.

"The meeting is at three over at the church, so I would say anytime in the next hour?" Gaea guessed. Whether she was traveling with her sister was unknown, but they would find out soon enough.

"When do we tell them about our plan to hand over the book?" Marc asked. His burger had arrived, and he was busy dressing it with every condiment on the table.

"When we determine that this High Priestess is trustworthy, as well as Tasha. We are taking a big risk in doing this." Himiko showed the waitress the fish sandwich she wanted to order.

"We are, but at this point, I don't think we have too much of a choice," Gaea said, finally ordering a fish sandwich for herself. "There are too many that are after us to get the Grimoire, and I for one want to be rid of it sooner rather than later."

Marc nodded in agreement.

Two tables away, Seraphina couldn't believe her luck. They were even calling the book by name. She silently thanked whoever it was, if it was someone who had helped disable the pickup so that she could be here to hear all of this. She was so close to knowing where the book was. If only they would discuss it.

"I'm worried about my Dottie back in Bar Harbor," Bob said sincerely. "I've never left her alone for this long. I think the last time was when I went to New York City to sell my business."

Bar Harbor! Seraphina felt like she was getting closer. She had gone to that chapel only to find the Grimoire had been removed. Could the book still be on that island?

"True," Bill said. "I'm starting to miss Cathy something fierce. I'm looking forward to getting back to Cape Neddick and my writing."

Another possible location, Seraphina was absorbing everything they were saying.

"Are we in agreement on the location? I mean, Gaea, have you talked with your sister about using her restaurant?" Himiko asked. "What if she refuses?"

"She won't refuse. That building started this whole mess, and it's where it's going to end. If that dang spirit Douglas hadn't brought the Grimoire to it in the first place, none of this mess would be happening. Whoever wants the book would be fighting over it somewhere other than at the Cinnamon Woodfire."

Bingo! Seraphina had the name of a location!

"Well, once it's done with in Bar Harbor, I can go home," Bill said, wiping his mouth with a napkin.

"Cinnamon Woodfire, a restaurant in Bar Harbor, was where they were meeting someone to give the book to. But where was it now?" Seraphina thought. If it wasn't with them here, it must be kept somewhere safe where her coven or even another wouldn't find it. She suspected powerful magic was at work to disguise the Grimoire.

"Anything to get the damn thing out of my root cellar," Bob said accepting a plate of biscuits from the waitress.

"Well, Mr. Pepper, soon it will be out of there," Bill said, clapping his friend on the back.

Seraphina sat stunned by the words. She finally knew where it was after so long searching. And she did it without the help of the demon Belphegor. It was in Bar Harbor, hidden in the root cellar of a man named Bob Pepper. Everything fit. The witch and the medium knew about Pepper and took it from the chapel to his place, where they concealed it. The weak witch might not be as weak as she initially thought. It was advanced magic to cast a spell so powerful that it would hide the book from even the most formidable warlocks and witches. It was best to get away from the witch before she was discovered.

She wiped her mouth with a napkin and picked up the bill the waitress had left. She counted the money and placed it on top of the bill. Pulling her hood over her head, she stood and left the diner. As she headed for the exit, she nearly bumped into one of the men. Mumbling an almost inaudible apology, she opened the door and stepped out into the frigid wind. She hoped that the old man's truck was fixed because she needed to get back to Orono quickly. As she left, she passed by the window that had a view of Gaea's party inside, moving past them unnoticed.

Tasha had been in contact with her sister, Riana, via cell phone intermittently. She had arranged for their arrival to be simultaneous, mainly as a safety precaution. Although she had no evidence or reason to believe that either of the black covens had discovered them, it was better to be safe than sorry. Additionally, she had no coven members with her, necessitating the protection offered by the warlocks of the Guardians of the Grimoire. Despite being a member of the coven, Tasha had no companions other than her daughter, whom she was unwilling to let become entangled in the events about to unfold, especially if things turned ugly. The 16-year-old was better off tending the store. Thus, she drove alone in her old, rusty truck toward North Lyndon and whatever awaited her.

"We have detected an Aura, my Lord Aoki." A Magi informed his master. "Do I have your permission to investigate it?"

"There is no need, my brother," the High Priest answered. "I have sensed this aura as well, and it is not the Grimoire. It is some other magical relic that I have no interest in."

"As you wish." The magi said, bowed, and started to leave.

"Wait," Aoki commanded. "Perhaps it would be wise to check on this. You go alone. Bring the object to me if it is of any interest."

The magi nodded and set out to complete the task.

There was a chance that it did have some interest, Aoki surmised. It could be related to the Grimoire in some manner. If so, it could yield valuable information.

About the same time Aoki detected the Aura, Sergev had as well and had dispatched Kenneth to investigate without delay. He, too, did not believe that it was the Book of Belphegor but a ruse to lead those who sought the authentic tomb astray. Perhaps to bide time. But to what end?

The entire ordeal was maddening to the High Priest. The Grimoire was well hidden, wherever it was, and the people who knew of its whereabouts were elusive as a winter fox. They had not one concrete lead, and then there was Aoki, whom he believed had the Book of Belphegor in his grasp. If so, then what was this new decoy that appeared out of nowhere?

It took an hour before the decoy was located. It was discovered by Kenneth, who claimed to be searching for an old medical journal that he knew was located upstairs. The woman in the library let him pass into the restricted section, and why not? He was a longstanding member of the community whom she had known since he was a young boy. Once upstairs, he cast a simple spell that revealed the object giving off the aura. Excited that it was a book and possibly the Grimoire itself, he hurried out of the library and sped back to the farmhouse.

A Magi was about to head to the library when he lost the item's aura. Unbeknownst to him, it had vanished due to a protection spell that Kenneth had placed on it. Empty-handed, he returned to Aoki with news that the High Priest already knew. He dismissed it as insignificant.

At the farmhouse, a proud Kenneth handed the book to Sergev, who dismissed the boy without so much as a thank you. Alone in the room, he began his examination of the book: it was bound in human skin and quite old. Not as old as the Grimoire, but certainly ancient in mortal terms and of considerable value. The book had nothing to do with magic, as a spell had been cast upon it to make it appear magical. Sergev's intuitions had proven correct—it was a decoy for the Book of Belphegor. It was even the same size and could easily be mistaken for the Grimoire from a distance. Someone had intentionally placed the book in the library. The purpose eluded him. Perhaps it was left to give those who had the Grimoire the time and opportunity to leave Van Buren unnoticed. Or maybe for another reason that had yet to be determined.

The upcoming duel with Aoki had just become complicated. It was possible that he did not actually possess the Grimoire after all. Still, the challenge had been issued and accepted. There might be time for discussion before they commence battle. Perhaps this time, Aoki would stop being an adversary and become an ally, even if just for a short while. If the two could work together, they would be unstoppable in their search for the Grimoire. He would have to wait until evening to make the attempt.

Sergev sat back and sent for Isobel.

The sisters showed up and parked in front of the church within one minute of each other, Gaea and company waiting patiently in their vehicles, out of the punishing cold.

"They are here," Gaea said, pointing toward the two vehicles pulling up from opposite directions and parking behind Gaea's Jeep and Bill's truck, respectively. As they all climbed out, a man dressed in pastoral robes emerged from the church to greet them. "He must be the warlock reverend," Marc said, opening his door.

As they all exited their vehicles, Tasha took the lead in introductions. The pastor stood quietly by, waiting for the pleasantries to end. He knew who Tasha was, but none of the others, and she did not offer to introduce him to them.

He led them up the stairs and into the church, where he directed Tasha to the stairs that led to the meeting hall. As they descended, he made himself scarce, retreating to his office to complete the Sunday sermon.

The meeting hall was not large but adequate for their needs. The pastor had set out napkins, glasses, and cups, along with water pitchers and an urn of hot coffee, for his guests. They took their seats, with Tasha and Riana on one side of the table and Gaea and her party on the other. The warlocks Riana had brought with her took up positions both inside the church and outside. No one was going to get into the church if they could help it.

"You have the Grimoire? The Book of Belphegor?" Riana directed her question to no one in particular.

Gaea took the lead and answered. "We do, and it is safe and hidden well."

The witch looked relieved. "That is good. For a time, we had feared it had fallen into the hands of a black coven, which would have been most unfortunate. The news from my sister Tasha was most relieving. I understand that you already know of our coven and the purpose for which we exist?"

"Somewhat," Gaea accepted a cup of coffee from her dad, who had appointed himself waiter for the duration of the meeting. "You are the Guardians of the Grimoire and keeper of it, preventing it from misuse by those that seek its power?"

"That is correct. We have done this for centuries until it was lost from us. It has been our mission to recover it and return it to its vault in the western mountains of Canada."

Gaea nodded in understanding. Himiko and the rest of her party also acknowledged their comprehension.

Riana continued. "Our coven has no desire or intention to use the evil book to try to better ourselves. We do not seek power, but we do seek peace. The book would unleash horrible atrocities upon the world if certain individuals were to possess it. Two of them are in Van Buren as we speak. These men are not warlocks, unlike my members, whom you see here. They are beings that possess ancient magic. Magic that came from the writings within the Grimoire. As the centuries have passed, much of the ancient magic has been lost to them. Thus, they seek the Grimoire to reclaim that magic to harness the power to control men. Do you understand?"

Marc swallowed hard and nodded in agreement with the others.

"What are these beings called?" Bob asked, folding his hands together on the table.

"They are called Tithonians," she answered. Once, there were many such wizards, but as the decades turned into centuries, many vanished from the face of the Earth. A few, such as Aoki and Sergev, remain, driven by the lure of the Grimoire and by the desire to possess it once again.

"But if there were many Tithonians and only one Grimoire, how did they share it? Was there a High Priest or Priestess?" Himiko was deeply intrigued by the tale.

"There was not. It was decided that the book would remain with one until all that could be learned from it had been. Then the Grimoire was passed to another and so on until it eventually came full circle, in which it would begin again."

"You are a Tithonian, aren't you?" Bob seemed to be able to read the witch quite easily.

Gaea looked at him as if to shush him.

He glanced back with an assuring smile.

"I am," Riana confirmed. "As is my sister. But unlike Aoki and Sergev, we have disavowed the magic the Grimoire offers and instead reject it for the evil that it is. We have taken it upon ourselves, as I have told you, to guard the book and keep it hidden. Once it is with us, the book will once again vanish from the face of the earth."

"Why is Tasha living in Van Buren alone with her daughter if she is part of your coven?" Marc was curious.

"When the Grimoire was stolen from its vault, we set out to find it, which proved difficult. It could be anywhere in the world. Our members were sent, or in my sister's case, volunteered, to travel the world or station themselves in various locations, taking up residence with the local people. From these positions, they would wait in case the Grimoire should appear. They would be able to act quickly if such an occurrence were to happen."

"Such as us coming to Van Buren," Gaea stated.

"Correct," Tasha chimed in. "In this case, you came looking for me as you also wished to rid yourself of the book. I couldn't believe my luck when you three came into my store, and I read from Marc's mind that you had the Grimoire."

"What do you think, Himiko?" Gaea asked of her friend.

"I think we have found the solution to our problem."

"Ok, let's talk about how to get the book to you." Gaea said. "Dad, can you pour me a cup of coffee?"

CHAPTER 25
Forked Tongue

Isobel helped Sergev dress in traditional battle chain armor and a robe emblazoned not with the mark of his coven but with that of the Tithonians. This battle was between two members of an old sect, not between the Obsidian Circle or the Order of Mazoku. While it was not required of Sergev to wear the dress, something told him that Aoki would do the same. It had been more than five millennia since two members of the Tithonian sect had engaged in such a contest, and those two men had been Aoki and himself. That contest had gone without a victor, as Aoki fell from a cliff and was presumed dead by Sergev. However, that assumption was proven later to be incorrect. Aoki had been injured, nearly mortally but had survived. Ever since Aoki's recovery, he swore that he would finish the battle that had been started. The reason for their quarrel? Possession of the Grimoire.

Members of the Tithonians were dying out, and as they began to vanish, people started to covet the Book of Belphegor, desiring it for themselves. Sharing was no longer the norm. Power became the goal among the witches and warlocks of the sect. Four had risen above the rest, apparently the only ones who vied for the Grimoire. Two of them, who happened to be sisters, disappeared, leaving only Aoki and Sergev to attempt to dominate the Grimoire entirely. What the two men didn't realize until after their ill-fought battle was that the women had made off with the book and would not use it for their own purposes. They had seen how consumed their people were becoming, and their desire for the Grimoire was spiraling out of control, bordering on insanity. The sisters conspired to take the Grimoire and hide it from the rest of the world, placing it somewhere it could not be found by either Sergev, Aoki, or anyone else. They would use the magic they had learned from the Grimoire against the book, denying its maker the chance to complete his plans for mankind. They would deny the demon himself, Belphegor the Defiler.

Sergev had thought the Grimoire was lost forever until he heard it had resurfaced in the United States. He used every available means to gather clues and information, some of which came at a monetary cost. Large sums of money changed hands for the information he sought. It paid off. It was confirmed that the Grimoire had indeed appeared in a museum and that it would be easy for him to arrange to snatch it from those who displayed it.

Before he could execute his plan, the book was stolen, and once again, he had no idea where it was until the thief was apprehended. However, the fool did not have the book in his possession. Sergev believed that someone had paid the petty thief to steal it for him. He also suspected that the person who hired the thief was a warlock or a witch. It was clear that a memory spell had been cast on the thief, as he had no recollection of stealing the book and claimed he had no idea what it was. Still, other items from the museum were found in his possession. It seemed more likely than not that he was the perpetrator who had taken the Grimoire. There, the trail ended, and the State of Maine was where he would continue his search.

Now he found himself in the small town of Van Buren with more questions than answers, although he knew the Grimoire was close. He had glimpsed its aura, which was unmistakable. If he could only get a solid fix on it, he was sure the book would lead him directly to itself.

Unfortunately, his search would be delayed, although the delay might prove fortuitous if he could convince Aoki to cooperate. If.

He had three hours before the strike of midnight. He would spend the time in meditation, trying to recall some of the black magic of the Grimoire that eluded him. He would need it if things came to a battle.

Twenty miles away in a black RV, High Priest Aoki wore chain armor and a robe identical to the one Sergev had donned. He was a Tithonian, and his pride ran deep. Once, he had been a powerful ruler in a long-forgotten empire that crushed adversaries at a mere whim. His armies were mighty, and because of them and his magic, he amassed great wealth and land, expanding his empire to cover most of what is now parts of China and Russia. This empire lasted until the dawn of modern times. Alas, it was not sustainable, as the Grimoire had disappeared, causing its magic to fade from his memory. Unable to use the black magic, Aoki was forced to retreat into centuries of solitude, where he spent his waking moments relentlessly searching for the Grimoire. Only with its power could he regain what he had once accumulated and ruled. Now, it was within his grasp. He was not sure he could accomplish the task alone, however. He had doubts about who possessed the Grimoire. If it were the Guardians of the

Grimoire, then obtaining it would be most difficult, if not impossible. It was guarded by two powerful Tithonians, sisters of great power, who had the Book of Belphegor. If they had decided to use the Grimoire's powerful magic, then his task would be futile. He did not possess the strength to defeat them. However, there was Sergev. Perhaps he could be convinced to join forces. Together, they had a chance to defeat the witches and claim the book. After that, they could decide how to share it or complete the battle. The winner would claim the Grimoire for himself. He would need to persuade his adversary to talk before their combat. Aoki would then be able to discern Sergev's intentions. For now, he had three hours to prepare.

Seraphina only had to wait half an hour before she could resume her journey to Presque Isle, where the bus station awaited her. Now, she knew where the Grimoire was located and presumed it was not guarded, just hidden. Once she was near it, she felt confident she would be able to detect its aura, find it, and take it for herself. First, she needed to get back to the University of Maine in Orono, where her pickup truck waited in the parking lot.

She wasn't sure how much time she would have. From the conversation she overheard in the diner, it seemed they were planning to give the book to someone or some people. That would probably happen soon, maybe as early as tomorrow or the day after. This left her with very little time to act. She would need to pick up her truck and drive straight to Bar Harbor. Any delay would mean losing the book for a second time.

Once she had it, she would return to the university for a short time to gather her things before leaving the state of Maine forever. To hell with her father. She didn't need him.

Sergev arrived at Forked Tongue before Aoki and took a position on the west side of the ravine. He placed a torch into a patch of soft earth he had found and lit it. Then he unsheathed the sword attached to his waist and stabbed it into the ground so that it stood upright, a symbol of his presence. There was no hiding or ambush in a *futari no mahōtsukai no tataka*. Everything was out in the open, as no deceit was allowed. The ancient rules were clear regarding such matters. The first to arrive would signal his presence by lighting a torch, while the opponent would then light a responding torch. The two combatants would approach and face each other. Simple acknowledgment was made, and a brief time was allowed for anything that needed to be said, although either could choose to forgo conversation, and the contest would commence, continuing until there was a single victor.

Sergev could be a patient man, but when it came to what he was about to do, he did not appreciate tardiness. Fortunately, Aoki was on time and stepped into the open to face his adversary. He bowed, lit his torch, drew his sword, and stabbed it into the ground.

"You wear the dress of the Tithonians," Aoki said flatly.

"As do you," Sergev replied.

"Do you accept my invitation to discuss a matter before we commence?" Aoki asked. "There are matters more important than our mutual hatred for one another."

"I accept. Where is the Grimoire, Aoki?"

"I do not possess it. Logic told me that you had it."

"I do not. It has been, shall I say, elusive."

"It is maddening. It should not be difficult to track down the children who have it."

"It is. My magi have not had any luck, and I fear they have left Van Buren."

"I tend to agree with your assessment, and I also believe that they are receiving help."

"Who do you speak of?" Aoki said, running his fingers along the hilt of his sword.

"Do not make threatening gestures, Aoki. "Sergev said, watching the Archmage fiddling with his weapon.

"It is not meant to be a threat, Sergev. It is by habit. Why did you invoke *futari no mahōtsukai no tatak* now? "

"Because it was the only way that I could meet with you alone. I knew you would not refuse the challenge."

"And you were correct. If it had been me who called the challenge, you would have done the same."

"I would have. Aoki, I believe that the Guardians of the Grimoire are involved and may be here as we speak."

"Tasha and Riana? Here?"

"I have reason to believe that they are." One of my members reported a witch at Crosby's Five and Dime that matches Tasha's description."

My magi reported no such witch."

"She is not always there as a young girl tends the shop in her absence."

"I see. Why would a member of the Guardians of the Grimoire, especially one with the power that Tasha possesses, choose to take up residence in such a remote place?"

I have word that the coven has spread across the world in search of the Grimoire. Some are nomadic, wandering randomly from place to place. Others, like Tasha, have chosen to remain in one location, keeping watch in case the Book of Belphegor appears nearby. Fate had it that the book would surface in Maine, an area under her watch. I believe that the two girls who possess the Grimoire came to the Winter Solstice seeking counsel on how to handle it. They do not know its true potential or the power that resides within its pages.

"It is a tale almost too far-fetched to believe, Sergev," Aoki's interest was piqued. The potential involvement of the two sisters seemed to confirm his suspicions that the Guardians of the Grimoire were indeed involved. If true, it was a dangerous development. Neither he nor Sergev could defeat them alone. They had possessed the Grimoire for much longer than either of the two High Priests. While the spells and incantations faded from Aoki's mind, Tasha and Riana would no doubt have the magic fresh in their memory to call upon. He would be destroyed before he could cast a spell. "Are you suggesting a cooperative effort, Sergev?"

"I am suggesting just that. I cannot defeat them alone, and neither can you. Together, we have a chance if we unite our covens, even if for a short time. Time enough to reclaim the Grimoire."

"And what then?" Aoki asked suspiciously. "Do we share the book as we did in days past? Or do we finish the *futari no mahōtsukai no tataka* to decide the Grimoires master."

"That would be decided once we have the Book of Belphegor. As it stands, if the Guardians of the Grimoire come into possession of it, the book will vanish again, and we will not be able to locate it, no matter how hard or for how long we try. The sisters will not let it escape them again."

"I fear you are right about the sisters and what would happen if they gained the Grimoire. And time, it seems, is something that we are very short on."

"That is another reason for calling the *futari no mahōtsukai no tataka.* You are here now, and we can agree to formalize our cooperation. The duel will he placed on hold."

"How do we trust one another?" Aoki was still not wholly convinced.

"A blood pact," Sergev said. "We draw blood with our swords, bind our hands together, and swear to uphold the agreement that we make here today.

"As it was in ancient times," Aoki pulled his sword from the ground and extended his palm, drawing the blade across his flesh. A thin line of blood appeared. Sergev did the same, and the two men grasped each other, sealing the blood pact.

"We are now sealed together in blood as is the way of the ancient Tithonians. It cannot be broken unless an act of treason is committed by one of us. I accept this union to aid in the recovery of the Grimoire."

"I also accept this blood pact," Sergev said, gripping the other man's hand tightly, their blood mixing, seeping out from between their fingers, and dripping onto the ground. "On my very blood, I shall not break this bond."

Aoki repeated what Sergev said and released the High Priest from his grasp. "It is done, and our differences are set aside. We need to plan immediately and take prompt action."

"We can meet at the farmhouse where I am staying. Bring your magi as we have much to tell them. We must have a plan by morning."

"Agreed. I will be there shortly." Aoki turned and walked into the thick brush, vanishing from sight.

Sergev stood for a moment, pondering whether he had made the correct decision. Deep down, he knew that he had, and their cooperation was necessary. How it would all turn out in the end remained to be seen. He turned and headed back to the road where Argante waited. In a way, Sergev felt relieved. There would be no blood spilled in anger at the Winter Solstice.

Seraphina was making her way back to the University of Maine, Orono. Gunther had been stopped and turned away by Argante when he attempted to approach Forked Tongue. A meeting was scheduled to take place at Cinnamon Woodfire two days after the meeting at the church in North Lyndon, as Riana claimed she needed time before receiving the Grimoire. In the meantime, Gaea, Marc, and Himiko would return with Bill and Bob to check on and prepare. It seemed that the ordeal with the Grimoire was nearly over.

In the damp darkness of the Pepper Mansions' root cellar, the Grimoire lay contained within an iron box, protected by a powerful spell to keep it hidden. This ancient tome of power rested, waiting for a new master to claim it. Although it had its true master, it required someone earthbound to fulfill the demon's wishes.

Belphegor observed the game play out in front of him. Although he lacked control over the outcome, he found great enjoyment in it, just as he always had throughout human history. Ultimately, it was his book, designed for one purpose: to gather the souls shattered by the Grimoire, whether directly or as a result of its influence.

The Book of Belphegor awaited.

...To Be Concluded.

A Few Off the Old Royal:

The Widow's Watch: A Haunting on Cape Neddick (1 of 3)

The Widow's Watch: Dreamer's Hideaway (2 of 3)

The Widow's Watch: Shaw Manor (3 of 3)

Tales of the Little Lagoon: Kiwa's Story

The Dream Catcher

Spirits and Tales

Gaea & The Night Witch (1 of 3)

One with Paper In:

Guardians of the Grimoire: The Defiler's Nemesis
(*The conclusion of the Night Witch Trilogy (Book 3)*)